Two Days After the Wedding

**Center Point
Large Print**

**This Large Print Book carries the
Seal of Approval of N.A.V.H.**

Two Days
After the Wedding

JOAN MEDLICOTT

CENTER POINT PUBLISHING
THORNDIKE, MAINE

This Center Point Large Print edition
is published in the year 2006 by arrangement with
Pocket Books, a division of Simon & Schuster, Inc.

The text of this Large Print edition is unabridged. In other
aspects, this book may vary from the original edition.
Printed in the United States of America.
Set in 16-point Times New Roman type.

ISBN 1-58547-783-4

Library of Congress Cataloging-in-Publication Data

Medlicott, Joan A. (Joan Avna)
    Two days after the wedding / Joan Medlicott.--Center Point large print ed.
        p. cm.
    ISBN 1-58547-783-4 (lib. bdg. : alk. paper)
    1. Older women--Fiction. 2. Female friendship--Fiction. 3. North Carolina--Fiction.
    4. Boardinghouses--Fiction. 5. Retired women--Fiction. 6. Large type books. I. Title.

PS3563.E246T88 2006b
813'.54--dc22
                                                        2006001849

To Maxine Phillippi, in appreciation for all the doors she has opened for me and for being a dedicated advocate of my work.

And to Ann Morrison and the Glendora, California, Ladies of Covington fan club; Bev Whitlock and the Bradenton/Sarasota, Florida, fan club; Kathleen Evans and the e-mail Midwest and Southwest fan club; and Lucy Medina and the book/fan club of The Villages, Florida.

1
THE ARGUMENT

Clouds wheeled across the March sky, shading hillocks and valleys and creating a patchwork of green on the land. From her car, Grace Singleton gazed over the verdant, rolling pastureland, the piebald cattle with their patches of black and white, the lustrous peacock-green, low-lying hills. She half-expected a flock of bleating sheep to trundle across a rise, herded by a shepherd boy with a crook in his hand. The anger and tension that had knotted her gut after her argument with Bob Richardson drained away, and she began to relax.

Their argument this afternoon had revolved around his grandchildren, Melissa and Tyler. Grace thought Bob had reprimanded Melissa too harshly for tearing up her older brother's report on the Battle of Gettysburg. Screaming at the top of her lungs, Melissa had been dispatched by her grandfather to her room. When Grace started after her, Bob grabbed her arm. "That child is to be left alone," he'd said. "She needs to be taught a lesson."

Grace had shrugged his hand off her arm. "Melissa's just a baby, not even three years old."

"And she already manipulates you and her parents," Bob replied. "She knows exactly what she's doing and she can't keep getting away with everything. She's a tyrant in this family." He pointed to the dining-room table. "Look what she's done to Tyler's report."

Grace walked to the table and picked up the jagged halves and quarters of pages and turned to the boy standing by the table. "I'm so sorry about this, Tyler."

"My report's due tomorrow, Granny Grace. Now, I'm going to have to stay up all night rewriting the darn thing." He stamped his foot. "I hate doing papers."

"Easy there, young man," his grandfather said.

"I could help you rewrite it," Grace said.

Melissa's shrill screams funneled down the stairs. Grace looked from Bob to the stairs.

"No." Bob barred her way. "Don't go up to her. Melissa must learn that there are consequences to her behavior." He turned to Tyler. "And you, young man, need to exhibit better judgment and not leave your papers where your little sister can get at them. You can rewrite that report yourself."

His lips quivering, Tyler looked away.

Bob's authoritarian tone had infuriated Grace. Had he treated his son, Russell, like a little soldier when he was a boy?

"You're not in the military any longer, have you forgotten? You sound like some general ordering troops into battle." Grace turned her back on Bob, put her arm around Tyler, and led him from the dining room. Upstairs, Melissa continued to scream.

"She's got a mighty powerful set of lungs," Tyler said.

"Your grandfather didn't mean to be so harsh with you," Grace said.

"Yes he did," Tyler replied. "And he was right. I

8

should know better than to leave my stuff around. He's right about Melissa, too. She does have Dad and Emily bamboozled."

Grace had covered her ears against the screams. "I have to get out of here, Tyler. If you need help rewriting the paper, get Emily to drive you over later." She kissed his cheek, left the house, and drove away, paying little attention to her destination as she crossed the French Broad River, climbed a hill that looped and twisted, took a left rather than a right fork somewhere near a large brick Baptist church, then turned onto this road, where the sheer beauty of the landscape had brought her exodus and her anger to a halt.

Calm now, Grace started her car, pulled onto the road, and headed home toward Covington.

Back at the ladies' farmhouse, Bob paced the living room, his arms tight across his chest. His heavy tread flattened the nap of the carpet. "Where's Grace, do you think?" he asked yet again.

"Do sit down, Bob," Amelia Declose said.

"Pacing isn't going to bring Grace any sooner," Hannah said. "When she gets upset, driving in the country calms her. What did you two fight about?"

"We argued over the kids—Melissa, primarily."

Amelia's eyebrows shot up. "Miss Untouchable."

"She got hold of Tyler's history report that's due tomorrow and ripped some of the pages, so he's got to redo them."

Hannah Parrish's short salt-and-pepper hair was

9

windblown from working in her garden. She had set aside her tools and come inside at Bob's request. "And you reprimanded Melissa?"

Bob nodded. "A bit too harshly for Grace's taste. I gave her a smack on her bottom and sent her to her room. You know how Melissa can scream, and she ran upstairs. Grace thought I was too severe with her."

Hands crossed in her lap, Hannah sat in her wing chair by the fireplace. "Not severe enough, I wager."

"I imagine Grace went rushing up the stairs after her," Amelia said.

"No. I stopped her."

"Good!" Amelia said. "Someone needs to discipline that child."

Hannah cocked her head. "How did you stop Grace?" Grace might be gentle and softhearted, but when pushed too far, she could certainly take a stand on her own behalf.

"I barred her way, held her arm."

"That must have infuriated her," Hannah said.

"You're right. It did." Bob frowned as he returned to the topic of his granddaughter. "Melissa's mother's always working, and Russell was never much of a disciplinarian. He and Amy were lucky that Tyler was such a good-natured child." Bob stopped pacing and dug his hands into his pant pockets. "But then, Amy was a stay-at-home mom." An edge crept into his voice. "Emily has her law practice."

"Little girls have a way with them," Amelia said. "My Thomas was putty in the hands of our Caroline. She'd probably have grown up a spoiled brat."

"You never know with kids," Hannah said. "No matter how hard you try or what kind of a parent you are, you never know how they'll turn out. One child will assimilate your values, like my Miranda, while Laura, bless her heart, always rebelled. That girl did a hundred-and-eighty-degree turn away from whatever I believed or valued."

Bob walked over to the fireplace and placed both hands on the mantel. "Grace said I sounded like some general ordering troops into battle. She was right." He dropped his head between his hands, then pushed away and resumed pacing.

"Grace doesn't hold grudges, you know that," Hannah said. "It's just that she wants things to be harmonious all the time. The slightest tremor in her emotional environment feels like a major earthquake. She'll be fine when she gets home."

"You're right, but I worry about her driving when she's so upset."

"She's a cautious driver," Hannah said. "By the way, Bob, your contractor called." She fished a piece of paper from her pocket. "He said the finishing crew will be here next week to put up crown molding in the living room and finish painting the cottage. Then the carpet goes in, and they'll be out of there by May fifteenth."

"Good thing," Bob replied. "My apartment's finally sold, and I'll have to move my furniture at about that time."

"After all these years, you'll finally be our neighbor." Amelia smiled.

"I can't tell you how much I appreciate your leasing me the land for the cottage."

"Turned out nice," Hannah said. "It looks like a miniature of this farmhouse."

"That was the idea," Bob said.

From outside came the sound of a horn blowing. Bob moved to a window and pulled back a curtain to peer outside. Across the street in front of Max's farmhouse stood a large square van. "What's Max doing over there?"

Amelia joined Bob at the window. "He's had the interior painted, and now he's having the exterior of the house pressure-cleaned." She pulled the curtains wide open, then blinked as the rays of the afternoon sun struck her full in the face. "Max is preparing for his and Hannah's wedding." She glanced over her shoulder at Hannah. "Though *she* hasn't even set a date yet. She'll probably come in one day and announce that they've been to the courthouse and gotten married."

Hannah's face flushed. "I wish everyone would leave me alone about this confounded wedding. Anna's driving me crazy about decorating Max's living room for a reception. I could care less about a reception. Ellie Lerner's after me to try on wedding gowns, and Lurina keeps asking me what kind of flowers I want to carry." Hannah slapped her hand against her thigh. "All of Cove Road is caught up in my marrying Max. When will you people get it? I don't *want* a fancy wedding, flowers, and a matron of honor."

Amelia raised an eyebrow. "We care about you, and you're exhibiting quite adolescent behavior, really."

Before Hannah could reply, Bob said, "There's Grace pulling into the drive. Excuse me, Hannah, Amelia." He walked briskly from the room.

Bob met Grace in the driveway. She stepped from the car, arms extended to hug him, and they ambled across the lawn toward Bob's cottage arm in arm, as if they had never had an argument, as if she'd never rushed off in a huff. Grace snuggled against him, loving the fresh aftershave smell of him and the strength of his arms and chest.

"The cottage is nearly done. I can move in sometime in May," Bob told her.

"That's wonderful. I'll come over and help you pack."

He smiled warmly down at her. "It's sure gonna be great living right down the road from you."

Grace smiled back. "It's sure going to be nice having you close by."

2
A VIEW FROM THE WINDOW

Hannah's bedroom window offered a clear view of Max's farmhouse. Each evening she stood to the side of her window and peeked at Max. She would have been embarrassed if Grace or Amelia knew that she spied on him, but she would die of humiliation if Max were aware of her behavior.

Her eyes skipped from window to window, following the short, round figure of Max's housekeeper, Anna, carrying a dinner tray from the kitchen, through the dining room, and across the foyer to the living room. Hannah imagined the rustle of Max's newspaper as he set it aside, and the thud of his old recliner as it came upright before he took the tray from Anna. He watched television while he ate, and flashes of light from the shifting scenes intermittently lit the room.

When Max had first asked her to marry him, he had made it clear that his motives were based on trust, respect, and economics. Zachary, his only child, had married an East Indian woman and he stated flat out that he wanted no part of his father's estate or Covington. "I hate cows. I never want to see a dairy farm again," he'd said. Hannah thought he'd been unnecessarily brutal in this rejection.

Several years ago, after his mother's death, Zachary had crammed a backpack with his belongings and left. When Max finally heard from him via a postcard, it was to say that Zachary was working his way around the world on a freighter. Months flowed into years, and the occasional postcards bore the stamps of Mozambique, Istanbul, Sydney, Jakarta, and Murmansk in Russia.

And then one day Zachary had reappeared at the door of the farmhouse with a slender young woman. Her long black hair, huge dark eyes, and the tiny red ink mark between her eyes indicated the status of a woman from India, and he had introduced her as his wife.

Max had received no notice of, or invitation to, their wedding. Why, Hannah speculated, would Zachary treat his father with such disrespect? Had Max tried to turn an artistic little boy into a farmer? Had he been overly strict? Had he been so busy working that he had ignored his only child? She felt the reason lay in the past, but Max never spoke of that, and she wasn't about to pry. After a brief stay, Zachary and his bride departed, and several weeks later Max had dumbfounded her with his proposal.

"I intend to make you the sole beneficiary of my estate." He had squared his shoulders, and their eyes met. "I'd like you to marry me. That way you won't have to pay inheritance taxes." His eyebrows shot up. "Don't get me wrong; I'm not asking you to move in with me. There would be no obligations of any kind."

It had been almost two years since Hannah and Max began working as a team at Bella's Park, the seven hundred acres at the end of Cove Road that he had bought and saved from commercial development. Together they had planned the historical living museum now under construction, and as director of gardens, Hannah shared with him her dreams for education and horticulture. But, unwittingly, Hannah had fallen in love with Max, and eventually she had accepted his strange and practical proposal of marriage.

But how did Max feel about her? She flopped into the rocking chair by her window. "Why did I ever agree to marry him? I have no idea what he really wants from me. No wonder I can't make plans for this wedding, and no wonder I spy on the man."

Amelia's voice floated upstairs, calling her name.

Hannah called down, "You need me, Amelia?"

"Pastor Johnson's here to see you."

Hannah hesitated. She hated the prospect of an argument with the old man, but she couldn't ignore him. Pastor Johnson had surely heard her respond to Amelia's call. She would go down, look him in the eye, and tell him unequivocally that she would not be married in his church or in any church.

"Be down in a minute," Hannah called back.

The day's light was fading. The lines of Snowman's Cap, the mountain peak behind Max's property, were dark against the gold-streaked sunset. Across the road, she could see that Max had finished his dinner, for his chair was shoved back and the newspaper hid his face from view. Hannah went into the bathroom, brushed her teeth, ran a comb through her hair, and went downstairs.

Pastor Johnson stood wringing his hands in a nervous manner. How different he had looked last summer, when he took the stage at their Cove Road block party and brought the audience to their feet with his banjo playing. Infused with a vitality that astounded them all, he had seemed years younger and stronger, then suddenly seemed to fail. That led to the arrival of his protégé, Pastor Denny Ledbetter, who had stayed on in Covington. Denny's coming had bolstered the old man's health temporarily, but he appeared to have slipped back.

"Hannah, my dear." Pastor Johnson walked unsteadily toward her and grasped both of her hands, as if needing them for support. Hannah felt his thin fingers trembling.

"You're well, I hope?" he asked.

"I am, thanks. And yourself?"

"As well as can be expected." He paused for a moment and drew a wheezing breath. "I'll come right to the point. I speak on behalf of our small community. All of the residents of Cove Road, including myself, think very highly of you and Maxwell. We appreciate the fine work you're doing at the old Anson property." He paused and looked about him as if seeing the room for the first time. "I'm an old man. It would honor me, and all of us on Cove Road, if you would reconsider and be married in our little church. It isn't fancy, I know, but the hearts of those who wish you well will brighten it with their admiration and affection."

His cold, trembling hands reminded Hannah of an autumn leaf clinging to its branch against the gathering winter. His head quivered slightly, and a rush of concern and pity swept over her. *He may not be with us much longer, and this means a lot to him. I'm being mulish and selfish. Does it really matter where we get married? It'll only take a couple of minutes, and it's done.*

"Won't you have a seat, Pastor Johnson?" Hannah led him to the couch.

He uttered a sigh and sank onto the sofa. As she sat beside him, his eyes drifted across the room to the fireplace mantel. "Are those lovely photographs Amelia's?"

"Why, yes, they are." *He's been in this room before. Hasn't he ever noticed them?* "All the photographs above the fireplace have won blue ribbons, first prizes. I favor the one of the little girl who's overturned her tricycle and toppled onto the sidewalk," Hannah said.

He leaned forward and squinted at the photograph. "Fine work. Someone told me she never took pictures till you all moved here. That so?"

"Yes. That's true. Amelia began taking lessons with Mike when we moved to Covington."

"This is a good place to live." Pastor Johnson straightened his shoulders. "It's a right cold and lonely business to stand up and be married in the chambers of a judge. I'd be honored to perform the service myself."

Hannah felt herself softening.

"All right, Pastor Johnson. Max and I will be married in your church." A date popped into her mind. "April twenty-sixth sounds like a good day, don't you think?"

His eyes grew bright. "April twenty-sixth? That's a fine day, a fine day. Bless your heart."

Hannah stood and offered him her hand to rise, but he shook his head. It took him a long minute to push up from the sofa and steady himself before taking a step. Hannah slipped her arm in his, and slowly they walked to the front door. "I'll talk to Max, and—"

She felt the tug on her arm as he stopped walking. His

eyes grew worried. "Maxwell won't be giving an objection now, will he?"

"Goodness, no. Max doesn't care where or when we do this. If one of his cows could marry us, he'd be happy." Hannah held the front door open.

"He does love those cows of his, bless his heart. But getting married is serious business," the pastor said.

Once outside, Hannah assisted him down the steps of the porch and along the gravel driveway to Cove Road. Pastor Johnson gathered strength then, and his stride quickened as if seeing his church reinvigorated him. She watched as he ambled slowly down the road and around the church to the small cottage he shared with Denny Ledbetter.

Hannah found Amelia and Grace at the kitchen table chopping vegetables. "Poor old fellow," Grace said, her knife poised above several celery stalks lying side by side on the table. "He looks so frail."

"I agreed to be married in Cove Road Church on April twenty-sixth," Hannah said.

Grace set her knife on the table. "I'm so happy you've made a decision."

"I wholeheartedly approve," Amelia said, waving a celery stalk at Hannah.

Hannah picked up a carrot and studied its circular markings and rough exterior. "What are you cooking?"

"Stew, for tomorrow," Grace said. "I tutor twin girls at Caster Elementary School tomorrow, and I'll be exhausted when I get home and won't feel like cooking.

Now, don't you go changing the subject, Hannah."

Amelia asked, "What made you change your mind about the church?"

"Something about Pastor Johnson. I remembered how alive he was the night of the block party, and then he got so ill, and we all thought we'd lose him. Without Denny seeing to his eating well and watching out for him, we would have lost him, I believe." Hannah's eyes clouded. "Frankly, he touched my heart."

Grace placed her hand on Hannah's arm. "You know, Hannah, you're very much a part of this community now, and it's important to everyone on Cove Road to be part of your marriage to Max."

Hannah picked up a potholder and fanned her face. "Why is it so hot in here? You have something in the oven, Grace?"

"Oh, Lord." Amelia hastened to the stove. "I do. I had a craving for good old-fashioned caramel custard. I found this recipe an aunt of mine gave to me. When I was little, she'd make custard just for me when I visited her." Amelia opened the oven door, bent over, and tested the custard with the tip of a small knife. "It's done." Carefully, she removed the tray of water that cradled the Pyrex cups and placed it on top of the stove. "I love custard. I can't wait for them to cool. Want one?"

Grace snapped off the greenery from the stalk of celery, then methodically lined up several more stalks on the chopping block. "Sure I do, but let them cool a little."

With a dishcloth, Amelia lifted each cup from its hot bath and placed it on a wire rack.

"You really think our neighbors have fully accepted us?" Hannah asked.

"Yes, ever since the fire. Remember at the block party last fall, how people sat anywhere with anyone and not isolated in families? And then we all worked shoulder to shoulder to make the five weddings last Christmas happen." Holding the celery under the fingers of one hand, Grace used a seesaw motion of the blade to chop, then shoved the small pile of chunks to one side.

In cleaning out the church attic, Grace and Pastor Denny Ledbetter had discovered yellowed papers that stated that five Covington couples, including the Herrills and the Craines of Cove Road, had been married years earlier by a minister who, it turned out, had never been ordained. For forty years these couples had unknowingly lived together, owned property, and raised children. North Carolina was not a common law state, so after the shock of that news wore off, remarrying became imperative. It then fell to newcomer Denny, with the help of the three ladies and the whole Covington community, to organize and bring to fruition five weddings on Christmas Eve.

"There's something magical about couples our age getting married." Amelia tapped the area over her heart with her fingers. "It touches people here. Takes them back to when they were young and in love. I'm glad you changed your mind about the church, Hannah. I would have hated going to some drafty courthouse for something as special as your wedding."

Hannah's palm struck the edge of the table. "Now, don't you start with me about what I'm supposed to wear, or anything else about this whole business. I don't want to hear that since it's a church wedding I have to wear white, or a long dress, or whatever appeals to your romantic imagination, Amelia."

"Oh, stop it, Hannah," Grace said. "Wear whatever you want." She touched the custard cup. "Amelia, I think your custard's cooled."

News of Hannah and Max's church wedding spread rapidly. By eight that night, Brenda Tate, the principal of the elementary school where Hannah and Grace volunteered, phoned. "Lord, Hannah, we're all pleased as punch to hear the news."

Hannah feigned ignorance. "What news?"

"About you and Max getting married in church, of course."

"Who told you?"

There was a long pause. "Well, let me think. My daughter Molly, maybe. Yes, it was Molly. She ran into Alma at the market about an hour ago. Everyone's so excited."

Hannah suddenly realized that she hadn't said a word about her decision to Max. She'd better run across the road and let him know before the gossips got to him. "Thanks for calling and for the well wishes. Got to go now, Brenda."

"Don't go. Ellie wants to say something." Brenda and

Ellie shared a house farther down Cove Road.

"Got something on the stove. I'll talk to her later."

Anna opened Max's door. "Señora Hannah, you look good. Come in. Señor Maxwell, he in living room with TV."

Last month, Max's living room had been painted a pale robin's-egg blue that she herself had chosen. Her eyes traveled to the floor. This old worn brown shag rug of ancient vintage must go.

"Hannah?" Max set down his paper and sat forward. The springs of the old recliner squealed in protest at being forced to assume an upright position. "Sit, sit. You look flushed. You feeling all right? Have you eaten? I'm sure Anna has some chicken and rice left from dinner tonight."

"I'm fine. I've eaten, but thanks." Hannah sat across from Max. She must get him a new reading lamp, something tall to stand behind his chair. How could he read his newspaper with only the light cast by that table lamp? "Pastor Johnson came by earlier today. I agreed that we'd be married in church, and the news is up and down Cove Road."

"I apologize for not consulting you first, but I'm glad I got here in time to tell you before someone else did."

Max's grin was that of a schoolboy caught in some mischievious act. "Well, actually . . ."

Hannah sighed. "Who told you?"

"Word arrived on winged feet via Anna, who got it from God knows whom. April twenty-sixth eh? That's a great day. Should be nice and warm by then, and the dogwoods in full bloom." Max reached for his coffee cup and drank. HEAD HONCHO was written in big black letters on the white cup, which Hannah had given to him.

"You're okay with the date, then?"

"Sure. It doesn't matter what date, Hannah. Whatever pleases you, pleases me."

"You do want a church wedding, don't you?"

Max smiled. "Whatever you want is fine with me."

Hannah studied Max's expression and his body language. He was by nature a quiet, rather taciturn man, especially in private matters. His reply was all that she was going to get from him right now, but his eyes were kind and caring. At work, she could read him by the shifts of emotion in his face and eyes, from the slump or upturn of his shoulders, the animation or tiredness in his voice, the briskness or torpidity of his walk. At home he was different somehow, less transparent, more guarded, though why this should be, she could not fathom.

Hannah settled back in her chair and crossed her legs. "It felt like the right thing to do. Pastor Johnson was so kind to us after the fire."

"He's a good man. No wife, no kids. No home but that cottage behind the church." A cloud passed briefly across Max's face. "And yet, what's family? Blood isn't always thicker than water, is it?"

"I agree," Hannah said. "Denny's like a son to him. You can't choose your relatives, but you can pick a surrogate family. Grace, Amelia, and I couldn't be more committed to one another if we were related by blood."

Max's eyes fell to his newspaper. He rarely spoke of Bella, his first wife; was he still grieving for her? It had been almost three years since her passing. For a moment, doubts about their impending marriage derailed Hannah's serenity.

Max's hands gripped the arms of the big chair, as if he were about to get up. "Want to sit outside a bit?"

Hannah stood. "Don't disturb yourself. I just wanted to tell you the news, but you've already heard it."

"I'm delighted we have a date and place." He squeezed the hand she extended to him. "Good night, now. See you tomorrow."

Later, when she spied from her window, the newspaper lay haphazardly on his lap and his head was thrown back on the headrest. She could almost hear his snores. He was seventy-six, a year older than she was, yet between the park and the dairy, sometimes he worked a fifty-hour week. *We're a fine pair. Neither of us know when, or even how, to slow down.*

3
TEA ON THE PORCH

March had arrived not with a bang, but with a promise of a warm, delightful summer. On Sunday afternoons the ladies gathered on their porch. Tea was poured, finger sandwiches served, and a time of quiet set in. With the weather a gentle seventy degrees, it was pleasant watching Molly Lund's boys and the grand-daughters of Alma Craine ride their bikes on Cove Road. They raced back and forth, popped wheelies, and filled the air with peals of laughter. Alma's daughter-in-law, Susan, kept a watchful eye on traffic entering or leaving Cove Road.

Susan's husband, Timmie, had lost his job a few months back, and the young family had moved in with his parents. The strain showed on Susan's face. Her mouth turned down, and she looked as if she would weep if you spoke to her. So the ladies waved to Susan but made no effort to detain her.

The sky grew increasingly cloudy, and Susan hustled her girls down the road and into the house just as a light rain began to fall.

"I love spring rain. You know that soon everything will be green and lush," Amelia said. "I've been waiting for spring to complete the series of landscapes I shot last fall. I need about half a dozen more for the exhibit Mike's arranged at the museum at Pack Place in Asheville. Then, much as I hate to fly, Mike's sched-uled a gallery opening in New York."

"Why go, then?" Hannah asked. "Seems to me, you worry yourself sick before getting on a plane, and it's worse since nine-eleven."

Before Amelia could reply, a slick new Volvo turned into their driveway, and Ellie Lerner got out. She waved at them, rummaged in the back seat of the car, then started up the driveway, plastic bags draped over her arms.

"What is that woman doing?" Hannah muttered.

"Looks like she's bringing wedding dresses from her shop for you to check out," Grace said.

"I guess she assumes since you're being married in church, you need a gown," Amelia said, an impish look on her face.

Ellie climbed the steps. "Hi, there. I'm glad I caught you all together." She looked about, but with no table to lay out the dresses on, she deposited the bags on the floor of the porch, as if it were common practice to sell wedding dresses in this manner. She smiled at them. "I heard the news, Hannah. It's so exciting! I thought you might want a gown, so I brought some for you to look at."

Had she recognized Ellie's car, Hannah would have fled the moment it turned into their driveway. "I consider it rather idiotic for a woman my age to wear a wedding gown."

"Miss Lurina wore one when she married Old Man, and she was far older than you are," Ellie said.

"To each his own." Hannah rose from her seat and marched into the house, letting the door slam behind her.

"You might as well take them away," Grace said. "Hannah's quite determined not to wear a wedding gown."

"They're not all long, and they're not all white," Ellie said. "I deliberately selected several cream-colored dresses to show Hannah." She pointed to the bags. The plastic of one bag was torn, and tiny pearl buttons could be seen descending neatly from the neckline of one of the gowns.

Amelia kneeled and pushed back the plastic hugging the bottom of a bag from which delicate lace emerged. "This is lovely. Makes me wish that I were getting married. I'd love to wear a gown like this."

"It's gorgeous. Here, let me show you." Ellie lifted the bag and slipped off the plastic. "It has fine Chantilly lace at the end of the sleeves, also, and around the top of the bodice."

"Beautiful." Amelia sat back on her haunches. "Hannah's more likely to wear something she drags from the inner reaches of her closet." A grimace formed at the corners of her mouth, and she shook her head. "An occasion like this, and Hannah doesn't care what she looks like."

"Hannah is Hannah," Grace said, "and best left to her own devices."

Amelia helped Ellie reinsert the dress into its plastic shield, then Ellie gathered up the dresses. "I'm sorry I upset her, but I still think she could find one she likes among these." She hesitated. "Shall I leave one or two?"

"It was kind of you to bring them, but better not," Grace said.

"It doesn't take much to upset Hannah these days. You'd think she was waiting to march to the guillotine," Amelia said.

Grace rose. "I'm going inside and see how she is."

Ellie and Amelia toted the plastic bags to her car, laid them across the back seat, and shut the door.

"I wanted to talk to you about something." Ellie leaned against her car. "Brenda and I've been thinking that it might be fun to start a chapter of the Red Hat Society, and we wondered if you, Grace, and Hannah would be part of it with us."

"I've seen ladies with red hats in restaurants. What's involved?" Amelia asked.

"The whole idea is to have fun, pamper and enjoy ourselves."

"That sounds hedonistic. No good works? No fund-raisers for this or that charity?"

"None," Ellie said. "We've all done plenty of that. The whole purpose of Red Hats is to pay attention to ourselves and to have a good time. Brenda and I thought maybe we could call our group 'the Covington Cookies.'"

"Or something slightly more sophisticated, perhaps?" Amelia asked. "Rural Rascals, or Sexy Covington Gals?"

Ellie opened her car door. "Ask the ladies if they're interested. Then we'll get together, the five of us, choose a name, and decide who else we'll ask to be part of our group."

"Will do," Amelia agreed.

Hannah sat in her chair by the fireplace in the living room staring at nothing. "That darn Ellie. I hate being pressured. I have enough to do. I've got to get out invitations, and there's hardly time to have them printed, addressed, and mailed."

"Why send out invitations? With so little time, we can make phone calls. Who would you like to ask?" Grace said.

"Just you, our neighbors, of course; the staff from Bella's Park, I guess; Amelia, Bob, Russell, Emily, Tyler. Melissa's almost three. Think she could behave for a short ceremony?"

Grace laughed. "I'm not sure she can be trusted not to run up and down the aisle. We could give her a basket with rose petals and let her walk in front of you and throw them. Emily could walk with her, and keep her in check."

Hannah buried her head in her hands. "Oh, Lord, now we're talking flower girl. What next?"

"Ring bearer?"

"Spare me."

Grace ticked them off on her fingers. "Maids of honor, matron of honor, a best man for Max, music, flowers, wedding photos."

Hannah pulled the small pillow from behind her and threw it at Grace. "Stop, or I'm going to run away."

Grace caught the pillow and grinned. "Hannah, my dear, dear friend, I wish you would relax. Whatever you do or don't do, or whomever you ask or don't ask, the wedding will be done and over with in no time." She grew serious, held the pillow to her chest, and leaned toward Hannah. "All this angst isn't just about the wedding, is it? It's about what comes after, whether you'll come home or stay at Max's house? Have you even discussed this with Max?"

From the driveway, Ellie's car door slammed, and

Amelia's footsteps sounded on the porch. The front door opened and closed.

"Later," Hannah said. "We'll talk about this later."

"They were pretty gowns," Amelia said as she entered the living room.

Suddenly Hannah began to laugh.

"What's so funny?" Amelia asked. "Are you laughing at me?"

"No. I'm laughing at the thought of me walking down the aisle with you and Grace on either side, giving me away."

"Us giving you away? Not your son-in-law, Hank?"

"No. You and Grace."

The phone rang. Hannah put her finger to her lips to shush the others, and picked up the receiver. "Yes, this is Hannah. Yes, Grace is here." Silence followed, and the laughter went out of Hannah's eyes.

Grace leaned forward. "What is it? Who is it?"

Hannah covered the mouthpiece with her hand. "It's Emily. A court date's been set for Ringo's trial." She turned her attention back to Emily. "I understand. I'll tell Grace. Thanks, Emily."

"Tell me what?"

"April fifth is the date they've set for the opening of Ringo's trial. Emily wants us to attend. They wanted to put Lucy on the stand, but she's convinced the judge to talk to the girl in his chambers the day before and she'd like you, Grace, to go with them."

Later that evening, Hannah slipped into Grace's bedroom. The room was dimly lit by the lamp on the bedside table. The white wicker rocking chair and table sat like oversized opals on the emerald-green carpet. Grace closed the book she was reading and set it facedown on her lap. She smoothed the sheet across her chest. A lightweight frame, with prongs to hold it steady shoved under the bottom of the mattress, lifted the sheet off her toes. The stinging, burning sensation her doctor said was symptomatic of diabetic neuropathy, a deadening of nerves in her toes, kept her awake if even the lightest sheet rested on top of them.

"That looks so funny . . ." Hannah touched the frame with her hand. "Anyone coming in here would think you had Bob hiding under the sheet."

"I'd rather have Bob than this thing, but peculiar looking as it is, I sleep much better since Bob ordered it for me. He got one for his bed, too. He says it's to keep the sheets from wrapping around his legs, but I think he got it so I'd be comfortable when I sleep over at his place."

"You've been lucky with Bob."

"You're lucky too, Hannah. Max is a good man and very considerate of you."

"Considerate, yes—but does he care for me? You know, *really* care?" Her eyes teared. "Otherwise, this wedding seems like a sham."

"You love him, don't you?"

Hannah's face reddened. "I think maybe I do."

"You want more from this marriage than the business deal he proposed, is that right?"

Hannah hesitated. "I'm not sure what I want, exactly. Some reassurance, perhaps. Max suggested that after the wedding, we go away to Virginia for a few days. Is that for show, or does he want to spend time with me someplace other than at work?" Hannah paused a moment. "He said we could take separate rooms."

"What did you say?"

"I was tongue-tied. I can never think what to say when I ought to have a quick reply."

"What would you have liked to say?" Grace asked.

Hannah's eyes grew dreamy. "I'd like to think I have a chance at love, even this late in life. But my mind can't go there—not since I got that diary and relived the past with Dan. And . . . I can't imagine going to bed with Max. It seems improper, somehow, at our ages. He held me once, in the office, and said he'd been wanting to for a long time. I felt the same and said so. Then someone knocked on the door, and that was that. Sometimes when we sit on his porch, we hold hands. But then he says we can go away after we're married and take separate rooms. What am I supposed to think or feel?"

The hurt in her friend's voice pained Grace. "Can you tell him you're upset?"

Hannah shook her head. "Absolutely not."

"I'm sorry."

Hannah lowered herself into the rocking chair. Through the open window, a soft breeze nudged the raised shade and elbowed the curtains. "The stream sounds wonderful from here. I understand why you enjoy it so much." She leaned forward, rested her hands on the windowsill, and, as the screen had been removed to be brushed and washed, poked her head outside. A soft breeze cooled her hot face. "If we had a swimming pool, I swear I'd jump right into it. It's a wonderful night; you'd never guess it's March. When it gets warm early like this, you begin to expect the dogwood trees to burst into bloom. If they did, of course, we'd have a freeze, and that would be the end of the flowers." She pulled her head back inside. "I should have had the builders add a south-facing window in my bedroom. My windows face Cove Road so I can't hear the stream at all."

"But you can see the sun go down behind Snowman's Cap." Grace smiled. "It's going to be all right, Hannah. Whatever feels right is what you'll do."

Hannah turned worried eyes to Grace. "Is it really that easy? Is that how it was for you with Bob?"

"Don't you remember how I worried about intimacy with Bob? And when it happened, it was the most natural thing in the world. If you feel that Max doesn't love you, Hannah, you won't want to share yourself with him."

Hannah nodded. "I remember how concerned you were and how you told us it was all so easy when it finally happened." She shoved up from the rocking chair. "I'll hold that thought. Whatever happens, happens."

"Good," Grace replied. "Relax and enjoy planning the wedding. It's not as if you have a year to worry about it; it's just a few weeks. Anything you need me to do, just ask."

Halfway to the door, Hannah spun about. "I'm going to ask Lurina to be my matron of honor."

"What a great idea. She'll love that."

"And I really would like you and Amelia to walk me down the aisle. You two are my closest family: family by choice."

"But your daughters?"

"Like I said, you and Amelia are my closest family." She blew Grace a kiss and departed.

While Grace and Hannah talked upstairs, Amelia lay on a blanket on the grass in their backyard. Endless stars stretched to eternity. The winding silken path of the Milky Way reminded her of something her father had told her: his Swedish grandfather called the Milky Way the "winter street" that led to heaven, and ancient Norsemen considered it to be the path of the ghosts.

She was sure that other cultures had different interpretations and tales about the Milky Way. Amelia offered a silent thank-you for the gift of its great beauty and wished that she could replicate it in her photography.

She had tried setting up a tripod and time-exposing the shots, but had only gotten a white undefined lane and points and clusters of lights. None of the grandeur that the "great white way" offered to the naked eye. Perhaps some things should not lend themselves to replication, she mused.

Amelia's visit to Maine last winter lingered in her memory. She saw Maine's rugged coastline, the small villages, the pristine night sky, and she smelled, again, the salty sea, and heard the swish and whoosh of the ocean. The solid quality of life in those harbor towns had resonated deep within her soul.

She remembered sitting at the end of a weather-beaten dock in Maine. Her legs dangled over the water as she listened to the lapping of the sea against the pilings that supported the dock and provided a perch for seagulls. And there were other sounds, soft sounds, which she did not recognize. Mermaids, she had told herself. I'm listening to the mermaids sing.

4
BUT DO YOU LOVE HER?

It came as a surprise and a sign to Amelia when, the next morning, she found a letter in the mailbox from Maggie Smelter, the owner of the B and B where she had stayed in Maine.

Dear Amelia,
March arrived with its usual blast this year, with lashing winds and beating rains. But summer, when it finally comes, will be glorious. These past few months, old man winter has beat hard against my door, and my good friends at Joe's Bar have helped me batten down. I enjoyed our lovely visit last year and our open, honest talks. I invite you, as my guest,

to return this spring, before the summer tourists fill my rooms and make it impossible for me to accommodate you or to spend time with you. Think mid-May, and do plan to come.

Your friend,
Maggie

The letter stirred a longing in Amelia's heart. "I'm going back to Maine," Amelia yelled as she entered the house.

But there was no response.

"*Mes amies.* Where is everyone?" she called.

No one replied. In the kitchen, her eyes fell on a white sheet of paper on the table.

"*Didn't want to wake you,*" it said. "*We went to ask Lurina to be matron of honor and then to shop for a dress for Hannah. Grace.*"

Just as well. Watching Hannah shop would bore her to death. Hannah's selections would be without style, and she would have to smile and say how nice Hannah looked. Thank goodness they hadn't asked her to go with them. Unfortunately, it meant there was no one with whom to share her news.

Amelia took the cookie tin from on top of the refrigerator, set it on the table, and pulled out a chair. She was reaching absentmindedly into the tin when she remembered that it was filled not with Grace's delicious sugar cookies, but with oat bran muffins, which she found dry and tasteless. These days, Grace was intent on cooking healthy food. *Why can't healthy food taste as sweet and delicious as sugar cookies?* Amelia covered the tin and returned it to its home on the refrigerator.

Then she remembered Hannah's daughter. She would tell Laura her news. She'd be at Bella's Park, at work. They had grown close during those months after Laura, all banged up from that horrible storm that sank their yacht and killed her companion, Captain Marvin, first came to live with them. That young woman had been a sorry sight and a psychological wreck.

It was she who had sat with Laura on the porch late into the night and listened patiently to her lamentations. In time, she had convinced the young woman to accompany her on photography jaunts, which helped wean Laura's mind from the past and encouraged her to face the future. Now Laura was Mrs. Hank Brinkley, and the mother of six-month-old Andy, whom Amelia loved as if he were her own grandson.

When she reached Bella's Park, Susan Ellis, the receptionist, informed Amelia that Laura and her assistant, Molly Lund, were off on a field trip. Their jobs included verifying the authenticity of furnishings, clothing, tools, and other elements that went into life in an 1800s homestead.

Disappointed, Amelia closed the front door behind her. Suddenly she heard her name being called, and Max came running toward her from around the building.

"Amelia, hold up." He took her arm. "Come on into my office and have a Coke or something, please. I'd like your advice on a personal matter."

Flattered by his words, she agreed.

They sat across from each other in leather chairs with bottles of Snapple iced tea. Max drank deeply, then smacked his lips. The lines of his craggy face seemed deeper and longer. Amelia had sensed Hannah's feelings for Max, and she wondered what it was about him that Hannah found attractive. He wasn't suave, urbane, or sophisticated, qualities she appreciated in a man.

Max said, "I want to buy something special for Hannah as a wedding gift. I thought with your sensitivity and eye for beauty, you could suggest something she'd like."

Amelia sat straighter. *Smart man, to recognize my sensitivity.* "Well, let me think. The kinds of things I'd like aren't necessarily what Hannah would like." She wrapped her hands about the Snapple bottle and tapped the rim with a finger. "Jewelry. Have you thought about a nice piece of jewelry?"

"Hannah doesn't wear jewelry. I doubt she'd even wear a wedding ring after the wedding, what with having her hands in the dirt so much."

"In the bookstore the other day, I stumbled on an absolutely gorgeous book about gardens—*Gardens of the World,* or some title like that," Amelia said.

Max shook his head. "Her bookcase is jammed with gardening and horticultural books. Something of a more personal nature, I think."

Amelia considered Hannah's appearance. She wasn't much of a dresser, wearing mainly slacks and shirts à la

L. L. Bean, and the occasional dressy slacks and long jacket for evening. So, not clothing. What, then? Amelia set the bottle of iced tea on the Formica end table near her chair, leaned forward with her elbow on her knee, and rubbed her chin. "Mmm. It must be just right: not overwhelming like diamonds, not stodgy or underwhelming like gardening tools or an album for photographs."

His eyes brightened. "That's right. That's exactly right, but what?"

Amelia sat up straight. "I'll throw out some ideas. Some of them may be nonsense, but you might find one of them helpful."

Max stood, walked to his desk for a pad and pen, and returned to his chair. "Shoot," he said.

She sat back and counted on her fingers, like a child reeling off her Christmas wish list to her parents. "A fur stole, a new car, an easy-to-manage wheelbarrow with huge wheels, fur-lined boots and gloves, a huge box of chocolates, a recliner for Hannah for your living room." Amelia paused. "I like that idea."

"It's good, and I'll do it, but it's not that special gift I want for her."

"Maybe you ought to tell me what kind of gift you had in mind. Something personal, an item of clothing, furniture? How about a dog? Or take Hannah to a fine antique shop and buy her whatever she wants," Amelia suggested.

He scribbled on the pad. "Another excellent idea. I knew I could count on you."

"But I haven't hit the perfect gift yet, have I?" She folded her hands in her lap.

"I'm sorry, Amelia, expecting you to pump out ideas. I ought to be able to come up with something special for a woman I respect and value as much as I do Hannah."

Respect and value? Amelia stared at Max, unable any longer to tolerate the uncertainty of Hannah and Max's relationship. "But do you love her?"

Silence. Max leaned back. His hand slid off and over the arm of his chair. The pad hit the floor. "Now, that's a rather personal question, don't you think?"

"No, I don't think so. I love Hannah. We have our differences, of course, but she's one of the finest, truest women I've ever known. She loves you, and I don't want to see her hurt." Amelia wagged her forefinger at him.

"I—I . . ."

"You what?" she asked gently.

Max's hands gripped the arms of his chair. "I care for Hannah very much."

Amelia raised her eyebrows.

He looked away for a moment. "Well—yes, Amelia, I do love her. But I've never been certain how she feels about me. The last thing in the world I want to do is impose myself on her." He looked back at Amelia, flushed, and finished, "Not in any way."

"You must love her very much, to want her to have everything you own."

Max nodded silently.

41

Amelia smiled. "Thank you, Max, for being honest. Now I know the best possible gift you can give Hannah."

He leaned forward. "What is it?"

"Your love. Tell her how you *really* feel, and do it before the wedding. I can't think of anything she'd treasure more." With that, Amelia rose and left the office.

For a long time, Max sat as if glued to his chair. He finished his iced tea, picked up the pad from the floor, and deposited the empty bottles in the trash basket. How long had he known that he loved Hannah? He had always liked her. He had admired her courage and persistence when she fought, single-handedly, against the commercial interests that had sought to purchase Jake Anson's seven hundred acres and turn Cove Road into a giant development. It had given him great pleasure to buy this land with the money from Bella's trust and then to ask Hannah to develop gardens in which visitors might relax, where interested people could learn about plants, and where children could be taught to grow flowers and vegetables. In every way, he had involved Hannah in the overall plans for Bella's Park: he'd sought her counsel, shared his problems and his vision. He loved working with her, being with her. She was a splendid woman, and he loved her.

Max rose and walked to the window to look out past Hannah's four completed gardens to the far hillside. He could see the roofs of the Covington Homesteads, circa 1883, with their barns, hog pens, corncribs, and smokehouses, all part of the only living history restoration in

Madison County. It was their creation, his and Hannah's, and he could not recall a day this last year when he did not begin the day without thoughts of her.

Later, when he went home for lunch, his housekeeper looked at him oddly, a twinkle in her eyes, and said, "You think about Señora Hannah, yes?"

"Why do you say that, Anna?"

"You wake up with smile, and you whistle *mucho* before you go to work. Also I see your eyes light up when you speak about her, and your face . . ." Anna's hands patted her cheeks. "It get red like sunburn when she comes. Now you got that dreamlike look on your face."

It was true, what Anna said. Yet he also felt guilty for thinking of Hannah so, for loving Hannah. He had loved Bella. But Bella was gone, and she had loved Hannah, too.

When Anna left the room, Max rested his forehead against the glass pane of the window. "Bella," he whispered. "I need a sign, like Dolly Levi in *Hello, Dolly!* Remember that musical? We saw it together at the Fox Theater in Atlanta." He pushed away from the window. "I'm behaving like an idiot. I loved you, but you're gone. I've grieved for you, and now I love Hannah. I know you'd want me to be happy. But how can I ask Hannah to live in your home, to share our bed?"

You've got four bedrooms. Change rooms and get a new bed, stupid. It was almost as if a voice had said it. Max looked around. Anna had returned to the kitchen and he was alone. But something had changed. He felt lighthearted. Anna was right, and so was Amelia. How ridiculous not to tell Hannah how he felt.

Max raised his eyes to the ceiling. "Thanks, Bella. I'm going to tell her, and I know I have your blessing."

5
CHANGES

Max went to bed determined to share his feelings with Hannah the very next day. But life has a way of turning us upside down. During the night, a pipe broke in the dairy barn, spewing thousands of gallons of water. At five A.M. a horrified Jose found the cows standing in water to their ankles.

Jose pounded on the kitchen door. "Señor Max, we got big *problema.*"

Dressed in a bathrobe and slippers, Max followed Jose to the barn, where he surveyed the damage. "We've got to get these cows out of here." His feet, his slippers, and robe and pajamas were wet to his ankles. "We've got to drain and dry this floor."

"I find the leak, señor." He pointed. "Back there, near the pump. It gotta be fix, or we no can take out the water."

They opened the stalls and shooed all the cows out of the barn. Mooing loudly, their tails switching, they ambled across the grass to their hillside pasture. Max wrapped tape around the broken pipe, then hastened back to the house to dress, while Jose fetched the equipment needed to pump out the barn.

• • •

Hannah awoke feeling unrested; she had not slept well. Yesterday's foray into the mall to shop for "the dress" had been tedious and frustrating. And then there had been Lurina and *her* dress.

"I'd be right honored, but I ain't got one single dress that's good enough for a bein' a matron of honor at yours and Max's wedding," Lurina had said. "I'll show you." She'd gone to the old mahogany armoire in which her "church clothes" were jammed. When she opened its doors, the odor of mothballs permeated the room. Coughing, the old lady stepped back.

"Mighty fine smell, don't you think? Keeps clothes fresh." Then she slammed the doors shut. "Grace, girlie, you gotta find me a right proper dress for Hannah's wedding."

Several years ago, when Lurina married Old Man, aka Joseph Elisha, Lurina had insisted that Grace choose a wedding dress for her. What a job that had been!

Grace pushed aside the memories of that time-consuming and frustrating assignment. "What color do you fancy?"

Lurina had professed no surprise when Hannah said she would not be wearing a wedding gown, or even a white dress. "What color you gonna wear, Hannah? Reckon we don't want to walk down the aisle in the same color." Lurina had laughed that girlish laugh that belied her eighty-four years, and they laughed with her.

"Grace and I are going to shop for my dress today.

How about if we try to find something for you at the same time?"

Lurina had tipped her head, and placed her hands on her hips. "That's a mighty fine plan." She raised her arms, then, and held them out at her sides. "Grace, you know where my tape is. We gotta measure me up."

Now, Hannah faced the unwelcome task of calling and inviting her neighbors to the wedding in Cove Road Church. They would snicker behind her back. She could imagine Alma Craine telling the women at Lily's Beauty Parlor how stubborn, she, Hannah was. "Head as hard as a stone, bless her heart. All that fuss, and Hannah's finally gonna be married at Cove Road Church."

Hannah sighed. *I've only myself to blame for my indecision and crankiness about the wedding.*

She flung off the covers. Stretching out her legs and arms, bending them in and out, and up and down, helped her get going in the morning. A few minutes later, she glanced out of her bedroom window. Layers of fog banded the hills behind Max's dairy barn. But what was that light coming from behind Max's house?

Hannah's hand went to her throat and she stifled a cry. A fire? Never in her life had she worried about fire, until two years ago when it destroyed their home and the homes of the Craines and Herrills. Lord, it seemed like yesterday!

Hannah went to the window, lifted the sash, and sniffed the air. It couldn't be fire—no shooting flames, no acrid smell of smoke. What, then, at this hour?

Against the morning chill, Hannah pulled on jeans and a flannel shirt. In her haste, and with trembling fingers, it took longer to work her feet into boots, tighten the laces, and tie them. Yanking on a jacket, she ran from the farmhouse, crossed Cove Road, and hurried around to the rear of Max's house.

The roar of a small motor drowned out Jose's voice as he gestured, pointed, and spoke so rapidly that he lapsed into Spanish, then back to English, and Spanish again. Then, the motor ceased. Looking exasperated, Jose turned to Max. "I fix it, Señor Max." Jose bent over the motor. For a brief moment it roared to life, then clunked to a halt again. Max turned and strode into the house.

Hannah hastened across the damp grass, up the steps to the mudroom, and into the kitchen, where Max stood at the sink measuring coffee into the coffeepot. The tails of his plaid shirt hung over his jeans. He was unshaven, his hair uncombed. Taking the spoon and the coffee can from him, Hannah finished the job. "I saw the light. What happened?"

Max sank into a kitchen chair and ran his fingers through his rumpled hair. "A big leak. Jose found it. The water in the barn was over a foot high. We got the cows into the pasture, now Jose's pumping the water out." He struck the table with his palm. "Damn. It's always something."

The coffee dripped steadily through the filter into the glass pot, and the smell of fresh-brewed coffee quickened the air in the kitchen. Hannah's stomach rumbled. Max liked his coffee strong. Hannah poured him a large mug, then poured another, added cream and four teaspoons of sugar, and took it out to Jose.

"Muchas gracias, señora," Jose said above the roar of the motor.

Hannah smiled, then returned to the kitchen where Max sat staring into space. She half-filled a cup for herself and added milk to the brim. "Won't the cows be fine in the pasture, once the sun comes out?"

"Their udders will be ready to burst. We milk them early in the morning. But we have to pump the water out of their stalls, round them up, and get them back into that barn before we can hook them up—and we haven't a clue if any of the equipment's been damaged." He slapped the side of his head with his palm. "I have a bulldozer coming to Bella's Park today to prepare the site for the general store over near the Covington Homestead."

"Can I help? Can I at least cancel the bulldozer?"

He looked both determined and helpless at the same time, at a loss where to begin. "Please do that. The number's by the phone over there, and reschedule it, will you? It'll be weeks until they can work us in again." He shrugged. "Well, this certainly isn't the worst thing that could happen. It's good of you to come over, Hannah." A spark flared in his eyes for a moment, as if he were going to give her good news about something, then he looked away.

Hannah pocketed the phone number. "I'll call them

from home. Not much I can do here. Grace and I have errands in Asheville."

"You go on. I'll talk to you later." Max stood and stuffed his shirttails into his jeans. Coffee mug in hand, he left the kitchen for the mudroom, where he yanked on his boots, and was gone just as the roar of Jose's pump motor ended once again.

Grace and Hannah were gone when Amelia went downstairs to the kitchen. They had not left a note, so she called Bella's Park to see if Laura was there. Laura was there, and said that she would be glad to see Amelia, but must leave for an appointment by noon.

"I was going to phone and ask you if you'd be home this afternoon, and could I drop off Andy?" Laura asked.

"I'll be over soon, and I'll bring him back with me," Amelia replied. "See you in a little while."

"Bless you, Amelia. Mother and Grace are still shopping for her dress. That could take them all day, or longer."

"And your mother's asked Lurina to be her matron of honor."

"She told me, and she wants you ladies to walk her down the aisle."

"Are you all right with that?" Amelia asked.

"Sure. I'd never argue about anything concerning this wedding."

Amelia understood. She, too, was relieved that a decision had been made. And she hoped that before the wedding, Max would indeed open his heart to Hannah.

In the department store, Hannah tried on and rejected dress after dress. "I look sick in this color," or "much too frilly," or "this neckline's too plunging," and on and on until Grace's feet ached and her patience wore thin.

"Describe your ideal dress," she suggested.

Hannah yanked the tenth dress over her head and handed it to Grace, who slipped it back on its hanger. "Something cream, I think. Simple, without fancy sleeves, or rows of silly little buttons down the front or on the sleeves, or bows, or low necklines."

The saleswoman's voice came from outside the dressing room. "I may have just the thing. It's not in the fancy dress category, but it may suit you. I'll be right back."

Moments later, a slight knock on the dressing-room door indicated that the saleswoman had returned. Grace took the dress and held it out to Hannah. "It's cream colored and regular dress length. What do you think, Hannah? Want to try it on?"

Hannah shrugged. "It probably won't fit, but what the heck."

This dress slipped easily over Hannah's head and fell in straight, smooth lines from her shoulders to below her knees. It wasn't couture by any means, but it bore the stamp of classic common sense. The fabric was soft, a wool-cotton blend, the saleswoman said.

"I like this front, styled like a double-breasted pea jacket with a V neck," Hannah said. The dress fell in straight, simple lines, and the color pleased her. "Now, this is a sensible dress, at last. I'll take it." She slipped it off and returned it to the saleslady, then turned to Grace. "One down. Now to Lurina's dress."

In the petite department, they found Lurina a simple ankle-length, pale lavender, silky dress with a lace collar. Without looking further, they took it. A cream-colored felt hat with a cluster of small flowers on the brim caught Grace's eye as they moved through the store. She stopped to try it on and tipped the hat to one side.

"Not for me," Hannah said, backing away.

"No. This will be perfect for Lurina."

"I'm worn out with this shopping business," Hannah muttered.

Grace deferred mentioning pretty underwear and a nice nightgown for the honeymoon trip. She and Amelia could take Hannah for lunch somewhere nice— or would Hannah have a fit if they gave her presents in a restaurant? Still, Grace would present her with lingerie, and Amelia, who loved silky nightgowns and robes, would probably do the same.

6
WEDDING PREPARATIONS

March 17, 2002

Dear Maggie,

Thank you so very much for inviting me to visit with you in May. I accept with pleasure. We can work out the dates later. My housemate Hannah is finally going to marry Max, our neighbor across the road, and we are all very excited. It will be a church wedding in late April. Must be off now, but again, thank you. I do so look forward to visiting with you. I remember Maine, and you, with such pleasure.

Amelia

After sending the letter, Amelia set aside all thoughts of the trip.

With Hannah's and Lurina's wedding dresses bought, Grace left to throw herself into helping Bob pack for his move to the cottage. The details of the wedding weighed heavily on Hannah, who walked about grumbling under her breath.

Max was unavailable most of the time, for the flood in the barn was compounded by the fact that several of the milking machines malfunctioned, and for several days the milking had to be done by hand. Animal husbandry and agriculture students from a neighboring community college, and several back-to-the-land hippie types, homesteading in the mountains close to the Tennessee border, saved the day.

Amelia offered to help Hannah with invitation calls or selecting flowers for the church, whatever Hannah needed, but Hannah shook her head. Then followed days of talking to answering machines, a most inappropriate way to invite anyone to a wedding, she thought. She finally handed the invitation list to Amelia and turned the whole matter of food for the reception over to Anna.

Crises, however, continued to be the order of the day, the week, and the month. Pastor Johnson arrived at the farmhouse to report that the church roof had sprung a leak.

He wrung his hands. "They can't guarantee they'll be done fixing it before the wedding."

"Let them throw a tarp over the roof, then," Grace suggested.

Amelia assured the pastor that it would not rain on the day of the wedding. Her intuition, she informed him, was completely reliable. For a time Amelia delighted in taking charge of things, of being the coolheaded, calm member of their household. But by the second week, the job palled. She had obligations after all, to her work and to Mike, whose van swung into their driveway at that moment.

He loped up the front steps, consternation plastered across his face. This was all Amelia needed now, an irate Mike.

"For goodness' sake, Amelia," he blurted as he entered the kitchen. "You're letting your work go. We have a show in May and a deadline for the New York gallery, have you forgotten?" He slapped his forehead. "I forgot to tell you, Jay Jeffers sold the gallery." He held up his hand. "But not to worry! The new owner, Michael Saunders, is excited about your show and wants to keep the arrangement Jay had with us." Mike pulled out a chair and sat.

Amelia placed her hands on his shoulders. "It's all right. I'll get the rest of the photos shot and ready in time. Let's go through the old negatives in the lab tonight. I'm sure we'll find several we can print and include in the batch we're sending up."

He shrugged her hands off. "If they were good enough, we'd have sent them before."

She sighed and turned from him, his petulance annoying her. "We're not going for several months, Mike. Why are you so anxious about this? You know I do my best work under pressure."

"And I like things done weeks early."

She hugged him. "We're opposites. Ultimately we come together and make things work. It'll be fine. We just have to get through this wedding. Help me, and I'll be done faster."

He began to pace. "Where's Hannah? It's her wedding, why is this all on your shoulders?"

"Mike, please, sit down. You're making me nervous."

"You're nervous? I'm a wreck!" He plopped back into the chair, and Amelia set a china cup of decaffeinated coffee in front of him. Mike never used a mug.

"It's going to be over soon, Mike. We're counting on you to take the wedding photos."

"Already this wedding has cost me money," he groused. "I bought a new suit."

"I bought a new dress, pale green silk."

Calmer now, he sipped his coffee. "You'll look gorgeous in green."

"I thought, if you'd help me, we could do the flowers for the church together."

His eyes lit up. "We'll use lilies, roses, and tiny trailing orchids. It'll be gorgeous."

"Pick any flowers you like," Amelia said. "Max is paying."

7
A WAKE-UP CALL

On a quiet Sunday evening ten days before the wedding, the ladies sat on the porch relaxing. Grace held out both hands in front of her and turned them over. "Did I get something on my hands and put them near my mouth? I must be allergic to something. My tongue's swelling."

"I don't recall you being in the yard or fooling with any plants this afternoon. Take an antihistamine," Hannah suggested.

Grace disappeared inside and returned with two capsules and a glass of water. "I hope this stops the swelling." She swallowed the capsules, but a short while later, she said. "It's not getting any better. My tongue's starting to fill my throat. I have to breathe with my mouth wide open. See?"

"I'll get my purse, and keys, and your purse, Grace. We're going to the emergency room." Hannah was in and out of the house in a minute. Taking Grace's arm, she propelled her from the chair. "Come on. Let's go."

Amelia rose. "I'll get my—"

"No, please stay here, Amelia, and call Bob. Tell him what's happened, and ask him to meet us at the emergency room at St. Joseph's Hospital."

"There are decided disadvantages to living this far from a hospital," Hannah said as she increased her speed to seventy miles an hour. "Is it any better, Grace?"

"No. If anything, it's getting harder to breathe." Grace's words slurred and she drew a deep, labored breath.

"Don't talk." Hannah pushed her speed to seventy-five. "If I attract a cop, so much the better. He can get us there faster."

What had she eaten or touched to cause such a reaction? Grace's heart thudded in her chest. Her tongue pushed against her palate. She felt sick and weak, as if she were going to faint. She opened her mouth wide and sucked in air, less than half what she was accustomed to. *This must be what asthmatics go through. It's terrifying.* Grace clasped her hands tight in her lap. She prayed. "Dear God, please. I'm not ready to die. Don't let me suffocate, please. Let us get there in time."

Hannah raced through a yellow light as it turned red. The hospital was just ahead. The light on that corner was red, but no cars were coming. Hannah turned left on red and left again into the area designated EMERGENCY ROOM. She parked the car at the curb and the two women headed for the entrance. Grace stopped to breathe and almost collapsed. Two men in hospital garb met them at the door, lifted Grace onto a gurney, and whisked her away. Hannah, holding Grace's purse, was directed to the check-in window.

"Mrs. Singleton?" the woman behind the glass pane asked.

"No, she's been taken to the back. How do you know her name?"

"Mr. Richardson called. We've been expecting you. You can check Mrs. Singleton in. Come around and have a seat," the woman said.

Hannah did.

"Mrs. Singleton is on Medicare, I assume?"

Hannah rummaged in Grace's purse and extracted a wallet. She slid a Medicare card and Grace's supplementary insurance card toward the woman, who then asked Grace's age, date of birth, and address, and made copies of the cards before returning them to Hannah.

Meanwhile, the gurney transporting Grace moved swiftly along a corridor past tall metal cabinets with glass doors, past a nurses' station, past curtained rooms. Finally, in a cubicle curtained with green drapes, a male nurse assessed the situation.

"Just nod. Don't try to talk," he said, readying a shot. "You take medication?" She nodded. "For your blood pressure?"

She nodded and managed to say, "Atenolol and Zestril, and for diabetes, Glucophage."

"Fine. Relax now. This shot will reduce the allergic reaction. In less than a minute you'll be breathing freely."

His words helped. Grace closed her eyes. She did not

wince when the shot hurt, but grew alarmed when the medication produced a wave of nausea. "I'm going to be sick," she wheezed. She wanted to lie back and die.

The nurse squeezed her hand gently. "It's going to be all right. The nausea will pass. I'll stay right here with you until you feel better."

Trying to relax, Grace counted slowly, one hundred and one, one hundred and two, anticipating that by the time she reached one hundred and thirty, she would be able to breathe more easily. The change came even sooner. She was still nauseous, but she could breathe. Relief swept over her. "Thanks," she said.

A doctor stepped in. "I believe that you've had an allergic reaction to one of your medications, probably the Zestril."

Grace frowned. "But I've been taking that pill every day for four years."

"No matter," he said. "I've seen this reaction to that drug in people who've been taking it for longer than you have. Don't take it again. We'll get this report right off to your doctor. I suggest you see him as soon as possible." Then he disappeared.

Grace wiggled her tongue. It was still thick, but it no longer filled her throat. From the other side of the curtain came the shuffle of feet, the clink of something metal, a low moan followed by a soothing voice. From what little she could hear, she guessed someone had been injured in a car accident.

The nurse's hand was on her pulse, then he took her blood pressure again.

"I still feel sick," Grace said. "If I stand up, I'll pass out."

He rose, stuck his head out of the curtains, and said something that Grace could not hear to someone she could not see. Moments later, a woman in a hospital smock arrived with a small paper cup of orange juice.

"Drink slowly." The nurse smiled at her and patted her hand. "You'll be fine. Just lie here and rest."

"How long? Where's my friend?"

"Not long, maybe a half hour. Your friend will be along in a minute." He parted the curtains and was gone.

When Bob and Hannah entered the cubicle, Grace's eyes were closed, but her chest rose and fell in a steady pattern. "She's so pale," she heard Bob say. Relief swept over her, knowing they were here, but the effort to open her eyes seemed overwhelming.

The next day, Grace sat with Bob in her doctor's examining room. To cope with her anxiety, her eyes traced and retraced the outline of a large puffy cloud drifting over a mountaintop in the mural covering one wall. Her doctor shook his head as he loosened the blood pressure cuff and slipped it from her arm.

"Allergic reaction to this medication is extremely rare. I'm sorry. It must have been frightening for you."

"It certainly was. How's my blood sugar?" Grace asked. Margaret, his nurse, had pricked her finger a few minutes before.

"The drug they gave you to stop the allergic reaction sent your blood pressure and blood sugar sky-high. They'll return to normal. Just rest for a couple of days, then drop in and Margaret will check you again."

Alarm registered on Grace's face. Her blood pressure had been well controlled with medication, and her sugar . . . Well, it rarely topped a hundred and eighty, and then only when she really cheated. "Everything will normalize by itself?" Grace asked.

"It will. You'll be fine. I'll change your medication. I want to see you in a month."

On the drive back to Covington, Grace sat without speaking.

"Talk to me, honey," Bob said.

She sighed. "I've been healthy all my life, and now it seems that everything's crashing down around me: high blood pressure, diabetes, my toes stinging and aching at night. What's next?"

"At our age, that's how it often is—one thing or another."

"But it doesn't have to be that way. My mother-in-law lived to be ninety-seven years old. She was never sick. She began to fade the last year of her life. Everything shut down then."

"She was lucky."

"Maybe, but she ate right and lived right. She never touched liquor. She never smoked. As a Seventh Day Adventist, she didn't eat meat, and she was active. She gardened, she traveled with her little dog. In her late eighties, that woman would get into her car and drive to

Buffalo to visit her sisters. She'd come to our house to visit and couldn't sit still. She'd work in the yard or clean closets."

Bob laughed. "Rather an amazing woman. She sounds like a whirlwind. She would have driven me crazy poking about in closets."

"Bertha didn't poke, what she did was an act of love. She couldn't stand being idle. I appreciated her help. We were friends, good friends."

They drove for miles without speaking.

Finally Grace said, "I miss Bertha Singleton very much. If she were still alive, she'd help me get a grip on this food business." Remembering Bertha took her mind off her own condition. When she was ill, helpless, and afraid, it was to Grace that Bertha had turned with her last request.

"I trust you, Grace," the older woman had pleaded. "Please move me from this nursing home back to Belham."

"I loved West Virginia, I was happy living there. Please, Grace, find me a small nursing-care home in Belham. I want to be buried in the graveyard of the church there."

Grace had made several calls to the Seventh Day Adventists in Belham and found Alice Bills, a Seventh Day Adventist and former nurse, who was licensed to care for two people in her home. When Grace called Alice and explained the situation, it seemed miraculous and preordained that a space had just opened. Alice would welcome Bertha.

Grace had summoned the courage to defy her sister-in-law. Once arrangements were made with Alice Bills, she had hired an ambulance and paid for it with money inherited from Ted. Then Grace had stepped into the rear of that ambulance to sit beside Bertha and hold her hand on the two-hour journey to Belham.

Again and again, Bertha said, "Bless you, Grace. Bless you."

"I love you, and I'm glad I could be here for you," Grace had replied. Satisfying her mother-in-law's last wish was the finest thing she had ever done.

When Grace settled into bed that night, she rolled her tongue freely in her mouth and said a silent prayer of thanks. It was almost better not to know all the ramifications and downsides of diabetes, especially as she hadn't taken good enough care of herself. Before now, when her blood sugar fell below one hundred, she indulged in a slice of chocolate cake. The result was an immediate rise in blood sugar. Grace reminded herself that diabetes was a progressive disease that took a toll on one's heart, liver, and kidneys, and its progression might be delayed by eating right, exercising, and maintaining a normal blood sugar. She vowed that she would do better from now on.

Unable to sleep, Grace snapped on the light on her bedside table and went to sit on the floor in front of the small bookcase under the window. The bottom shelf bulged with books on managing and coping with diabetes: books she had bought, stored neatly away, and never read. The top shelf brimmed with healthy eating cookbooks.

Armed with cookbooks, a notebook, and a pencil, Grace returned to bed, where, late into the night, she turned the pages of each and selected recipes until she had chosen a week of meals. Then she went through her selected recipes and made a list of foods: swordfish, chicken for making soup and sandwiches, whole wheat bread from the health food store, spices like cumin and tarragon, sugar-free Jell-O, puddings, and much more. She could, she *would* take charge of her health and her life. *Please help me, Mother Bertha,* she whispered, and turned out her light.

8
MAY WE GIVE THE GROOM AWAY?

Torrential downpours turned dirt roads into gushing gullies. Ladies' hairdos frizzed. Shoes got soaked going from cars to stores and back again. After years of drought, rain of any kind was welcome, and sales of umbrellas and plastic rain gear at the Elk Plaza Drugstore skyrocketed. As the weather warmed, people sorted through closets and exchanged flannel and fleece shirts and sweatpants for short-sleeved shirts and lightweight slacks. The time had come to wash or dry-clean the blankets and comforters to store them away.

The excessive rain turned Max's pastures to marsh-lands. Roof leaks appeared inside the house, and one evening Max found Anna placing buckets to catch the drips in two of the bedrooms. At Bella's Park a leak developed over the reception area, and repairs under way at the church were temporarily halted. In the week prior to the wedding, Max spent his days on roofs helping to spread and tack down tarps.

Having promised Amelia that he would tell Hannah his true feelings before the wedding, Max felt guilty. But the right moment seemed never to present itself, and the time galloped past with unrelenting speed.

For Hannah there was still much to do: flowers would be handled by Amelia and Mike but the church must be cleaned and the order of the ceremony decided upon. Grace and Amelia helped where they could, but the ultimate responsibility rested on Hannah.

When Tyler and Lucy Banks asked for a private meeting with her, Hannah agreed with a sense of apprehension. They sat at the kitchen table. "Grace made hot chocolate. Either of you want a cup?"

They shook their heads.

Under the table, she could feel the stir of air from four legs swinging. Lucy's pixie face and Tyler's freckled face were serious. *Whatever it is, this is a matter of great importance to them.* "Well, out with it," Hannah said.

Lucy looked at Tyler and nodded.

"Miss Hannah, Lucy and I feel real happy about your marrying Mr. Max." He stopped, and Lucy nudged his arm to continue.

"Lucy and I were wondering if there would be a place in the ceremony for us?"

Lucy took over. "We think the whole world of you and Mr. Max, Miss Hannah."

Tyler nodded gravely.

"We know you got Miss Lurina for your matron of honor, and Miss Grace and Miss Amelia are gonna walk you down the aisle. We were thinking maybe we could walk down the aisle with Mr. Max, seeing as he ain't, I mean doesn't, have any kinfolk around these parts."

Wasn't the groom already at the altar when the bride walked down the aisle? "Well . . ." Hannah began, then thought, *Why not?* It was their wedding, and they could do it any way they chose. "You want to be part of our wedding?" She looked at the young faces eagerly awaiting her reply, and tears slipped from behind her eyes.

"Miss Hannah," Lucy said. "We didn't mean to upset you, to make you cry."

Hannah rubbed the ball of her hand across her eyes. "They're good tears," she said. "I'm touched that you want to be a part of our wedding. It's not traditional, but I don't see why not."

Their two small faces glowed with pleasure. Lucy gave Tyler a triumphant look as if to say, See, I told you she'd say yes.

"Please, we need to know what color your dress is, and if Mr. Max is wearing a tuxedo or a suit, so we can dress proper," Lucy said.

"Max is wearing a dark blue suit." Anna had reported that fact. "You two come on upstairs with me, and I'll show you my dress. It isn't fancy." For a moment, Hannah worried about Lucy being able to afford a new dress. But she or Grace or Emily would see to it that the young people had the appropriate clothes. "I'll tell Mr. Max that he'll be escorted down the aisle by both of you. I think he'll like that very much."

Later, as she watched the youngsters race down the porch steps and down the driveway, the old apprehension swept over Hannah. How could she marry someone who didn't love her?

Don't start now, Hannah. You've made the decision. If Max doesn't feel as strongly about you as you do about him, so what? We won't be living as man and wife anyway. And as Grace would say, "It'll all work out just the way it's supposed to."

Then she remembered she was supposed to meet Grace and the others for lunch in Asheville for the first meeting of their new Red Hat chapter. If she didn't hurry, she was going to be late.

9

THE BRIDAL SHOWER

Hannah slipped her arms into the sleeves of her new purple blouse and tucked it into her black slacks. She'd had no purple anything in her closet until a week ago. Looking in her dresser mirror, she tipped her new red straw hat, the first red hat she'd seen on a stand at

Kmart. It could have been a knit beret or a fancy hat with a feather for all she cared. This hat was what they had; this was what she bought.

At the restaurant, she searched for a table of red hats. Seeing none, Hannah wondered if she had the day or place wrong, until a waitress approached and escorted her to a private dining room. There Grace, Amelia, Emily, Laura, Brenda, Molly, Ellie, and Lurina, all smiles in their purple clothes and red hats, rose to welcome her.

Why are they all getting up? Hannah wondered. Piled on a side table were boxes of varying sizes, wrapped in red or purple. Was she supposed to bring a gift? Were they exchanging gifts, and if so, what was the occasion? They were falling over one another to hug her, and everyone was talking at once. It took Hannah aback, and it was another moment before she realized that they were congratulating her on her upcoming wedding. Grace took her elbow and led her to the head of the table. It was then that Hannah realized that she'd been conned into attending her own bridal shower.

I'm so embarrassed. This is so silly at my age. It's the last thing I'd ever imagine. I wouldn't have come if I'd known. I guess they knew that. It feels so anticlimactic after all my worries about this wedding and Max. Hannah started to speak and choked on the words as tears filled her eyes.

Grace handed her a handkerchief. "I thought you might need this."

"Let's order and eat, so we can get to the presents,"

Laura said. "Boy, Mom, do we have some fun gifts for you."

Oh, oh, Hannah thought. *I hope I won't be even more embarrassed than I am now. I'm glad they reserved a private room for this shower.*

Throughout lunch there was much laughter and joke-telling. Nothing off-color, just silly jokes that for some reason seemed very funny, like the one Molly told.

"A little boy had learned in Sunday school that God made people from dust, and when they died, they returned to dust. One day, very agitated, he called his mother into his room. He was on his knees at the bed-side and urged her to get down there with him.

"Is it true, Mom, that we come from dust and unto dust we do return?"

His mother nodded.

"Well, you better look under my bed, then," he said. "'Cause it looks like someone's either coming or going."

They laughed and held their sides and could not stop laughing. It was as if they'd been infected with a laughter bug.

Finally lunch was over, and the table had been cleared of all but coffee and teacups. Hannah braced herself for what was coming, and opened the first gift.

When the old *Playgirl* magazines tumbled from their wrappings of white and lavender, Lurina broke into a paroxysm of giggles. Hannah couldn't help but laugh. The magazines were well worn and she couldn't imagine where they had gotten them.

She opened another box, and Laura grabbed its contents and held up a baby blue satin negligee. She draped it about her mother's neck. "The color's great on you, Mother. Max will think so, too, I'm sure."

Hannah blushed, as much from the implications of the negligee as her uncertainty that Max would ever see it—even if she did wear it, which was highly unlikely. Purple bedroom slippers, embellished with lavender fake fur, came next. Amelia, whose gift they were, insisted that Hannah remove her shoes and try them on for size. When Hannah did, they urged her to walk about in them, to make sure that they fit. They fit all right, but Hannah knew that once they left this room, she'd never, ever, be seen in them.

Several unmentionable items from Victoria's Secret followed, and Hannah's face grew red. "I never expected . . ." Hannah said.

"Of course not," Brenda said, "Ellie and I figured you'd never buy anything like these, so we got them for you."

They laughed so hard, they cried.

"We're making too much noise," Hannah said, trying to shush them. "The whole restaurant can hear us."

"Oh, Mother, relax and have fun," Laura said. "How could anyone be anything but happy to hear us laughing and enjoying ourselves?"

A soft knock brought the waitress asking if there was anything else they wanted. They did not. Molly looked at her watch. "Goodness, we've played hooky from work all afternoon. It's three o'clock."

They paid their bill, packed up the gifts, and moved past empty tables toward the door. They waved at the bartender and maître d', helped themselves to mints in a round glass bowl near the door, and left the restaurant. The ladies followed Hannah to her car in the parking lot, piled the shower gifts inside, and hugged and kissed one another.

"Amelia and I drove with Brenda and Ellie. Lurina came with Laura and Molly. Would you like me to ride home with you?" Grace asked.

"I would love that."

More hugs and good-byes followed, and finally Grace slipped into Hannah's car and they were off. "That's one Red Hat meeting I won't forget," Grace said.

"Neither will I. In a million years, I would never have guessed that you ladies were going to do such a thing. And I have to admit, it was a lot of fun. I don't know when I've laughed so hard or for so long."

"We don't laugh enough. It was a treat. I loved every minute of it," Grace said. "And you now have all the ingredients for a very sexy honeymoon."

"Sure," Hannah said doubtfully.

10
THE WEDDING

On the morning of her wedding day, it seemed to Hannah that her wedding dress emitted a fusty odor. She should have removed it from the closet and stripped away its plastic wrappings days ago. They should have turned on the heat, or maybe even the air-conditioning to counter the dampness that had accompanied days of rain.

Grace, who loved to read about ancient Egypt, had once told her and Amelia that when men back then arrived at a dinner party, they were offered garlands of scented flowers to overcome their smell. And Amelia had read somewhere that the tradition of marrying in June stemmed from the fact that yearly baths were taken in May, so the couples were still, by the standards of the time, fairly clean in June. They had all laughed and kidded about the stinky "good old days."

But this was no laughing matter. Hannah laid her wedding dress on the bed, went into the bathroom, and returned with a bottle of rose water. Hannah spritzed the atomizer above the dress, and fine spray descended on the cream-colored fabric. Then she lifted the dress and waltzed it around her bedroom, waving it before the open windows, letting the sweet, cool breezes waft through it. A knock on the door stopped her in mid-twirl.

"Mother?"

"Miranda." Hannah laid the dress on the bed and embraced her daughter. "Come in. I'm so glad you made it in time. I would have hated getting married without you being here."

"A storm grounded the planes in Philadelphia last night and we were stuck until way past midnight. But here we are! How are you? Are you nervous?" She held

Hannah by the shoulders. "You look marvelous. I'm so happy for you and Max. Who would have imagined you getting married?"

Hannah considered telling Miranda that this was merely a business arrangement, but she smiled instead and hugged her daughter. Then she lifted the dress from the bed. "How does this dress smell to you? I've been airing it. It's new, but it's been in plastic for a long time."

Miranda brought the dress to her face. "Smells fine to me, like roses. It's a lovely dress. I didn't figure you for the white, flowing gown type; this is just right."

Satisfied, Hannah hung the dress on the closet door. "Go on down and chat with Amelia while I finish getting ready. Have you seen Laura yet?"

"Not yet, we're meeting at the church. I'll go ahead now so Laura and I can chat a bit before the ceremony starts. It's raining, but not too heavily. I have a car here and a huge umbrella."

With Miranda gone, Hannah scrutinized herself in the mirror. *If I were only shorter and not so square shouldered. If only I were delicate, more feminine, like Laura or Amelia.* With the palms of her hands she pulled the skin of her cheeks taut. Her wrinkles vanished. She removed her hands and they reappeared. Amelia had offered to camouflage those wrinkles with makeup, but Hannah had declined.

Why was I so stubborn? Maybe I didn't really believe this wedding would take place, or that Pastor Johnson would be up to the task. I like Denny, but I want Pastor

Johnson to perform the ceremony. Lord, I am fretting. I worry that I'll start down the aisle wrong foot first, and be out of step with Amelia and Grace, or they'll start before the wedding march, before I begin to move, or Melissa will freeze with fright, and I'll fall over her. Will people giggle when I walk in with Amelia and Grace on either side of me rather than Bob, or Hank, or even Grace's son, Roger? Stop already! You'll make yourself crazy.

Hannah tipped her head to one side. *If I get much grayer, I'll be white-haired. A hat would cover that, but I refused to wear a hat.* Frustrated with herself, Hannah turned away from the mirror. Oh, where was Grace? She needed her support and help to get ready.

Rain pelted the roof of the farmhouse like thousands of tiny pebbles. Water streamed along both sides of Cove Road.

"I'm so nervous, Grace. Do you think this rain is a bad omen?" Hannah asked, as Grace adjusted the lapels of her wedding dress.

"Goodness, no. Weather is weather, always unpredictable. So don't start working yourself up about ill omens. You're going to get to the church and walk down that aisle, and everything is going to be absolutely perfect."

Hannah turned worried eyes to Grace. "Don't say perfect. Nothing is perfect."

"All right, everything's going to be fine. Is that better?"

Hannah nodded.

"Hannah, you look lovely."

"You really think I look okay, Grace? You wouldn't lie to me, would you? I feel like an idiot."

"You look regal, like a queen. Just stop wringing that handkerchief into a knot." Grace checked the time. "We have to go now, Hannah."

Hannah peered from her window. "It's pouring! We can't go anywhere. We'll get soaking wet."

"No we won't. Wait until you see what the men have set up for you." Grace tugged at her arm.

From the steps of the porch to the open door of the waiting limousine, Mike and Bob, Russell, Roger, her son-in-law Paul, and both grandsons, Sammy and Philip, formed two lines. Above their heads they supported a thick, waterproof tarp. Hannah wanted to stop to hug her grandsons and their father, but Grace prodded her on. "There'll be time for hugging later."

Arm in arm, Grace guided Hannah through the dry tunnel and they slid into the limousine. Grace nodded to the driver, and the vehicle moved down the gravel drive and onto Cove Road. It stopped in front of the church, where a long white marquee had been erected, reaching to the road. Pastor Denny came out and opened the limousine door, then Hannah and Grace stepped out and, dry as sagebrush in the desert, proceeded to the church.

As she moved with Grace into the vestibule of the church, Hannah could hear soft music issuing from behind the closed doors of the sanctuary.

Dressed in pale green organza and standing quietly before her mother, Melissa held a basket filled with pink rose petals. Emily also held a basket brimming with petals. Her eyes bright as fireflies on a dark night, Melissa smiled up at Hannah, and Hannah knew there would be no misbehaving.

Amelia advanced toward them with Lurina wearing her lavender dress with her new hat tipped to one side in a jaunty fashion. For an instant, Hannah panicked. She should have bought a hat! Then Lurina smiled at her and patted her hand, and Lurina's touch and the tenderness in her eyes rendered Hannah less anxious, less eager to turn and run.

Then Amelia reached up and placed a crown of fresh flowers on Hannah's head. Standing on tiptoe, she kissed Hannah's cheek. "You look beautiful."

Hannah's heart filled with affection for her.

Mike handed her a bouquet of lilies and roses. "Break a leg, Hannah, darling."

Hannah clutched the flowers, her hands shaking. Then a rush of cold air heralded the opening of the front door. Max, elegant in his dark blue suit, entered with Tyler and Lucy, who were dressed perfectly for the occasion: Tyler in a light blue suit; Lucy in a pale blue, ankle-length dress with a bow at the waist.

Tears blurred Hannah's eyes. *He looks wonderful, so handsome. Is this really happening to me, after all these years?*

With a flourish, the heavy oak doors leading into the sanctuary swung open, and Pachelbel's Canon flooded the vestibule. Max and the two young people stepped into the aisle, then solemnly paced toward the front where best man, Bob, and Pastor Johnson waited.

Propelled by her mother, Melissa followed Max, sprinkling pink rose petals.

Next Lurina will start, and then I'll have to leave the safety of this vestibule. Everybody came—the church is totally full. Good God, help me get through this. Why did I agree to this? It's silly, walking down an aisle like a girl of twenty.

But it was all happening. Amelia positioned Lurina in the doorway. Max had reached the pastor. Lucy and Tyler joined Russell, Laura, and Hank in the front pew. Melissa and Emily were halfway down the aisle. Amelia nudged Lurina. Holding her head high, the old woman stepped into the aisle and moved forward. The music trembled and stopped, and the wedding march began.

Suddenly Hannah stood in the open doorway of the sanctuary. Grace and Amelia offered their arms, and Hannah slipped hers into theirs. Together, they walked gracefully down the aisle in perfect sync with the music, and as they did, Hannah's anxieties melted away. She simply walked toward Max, unaware of the filled pews, of neighbors and friends, of her grandsons, her daughters and their husbands, of her foreman, Tom, and Anna and Jose, and all the others whose bright eyes and happy faces were turned expectantly toward her.

Hannah saw only Max. His eyes were fixed on hers, drawing her to him. She forgot their ages, forgot how silly she thought this was. It wasn't silly at all. It was glorious! Her heart was the heart of a young woman, her joy the joy of a young woman, her love was the love of a young woman for a young man.

Later, Hannah could not recall the pastor's words, or even when they said, "I do." She did remember feeling proud and happy, and the feel of Max's strong arm as he led her back down the aisle. She would never forget the bright smiling faces looking at them, wishing them well. She had walked on a sea of rose petals, and thought one word: "Perfect."

The reception, planned by Amelia, Mike, and Anna, was everything anyone could wish it to be: soft music in the background rather than a band blaring, friends and family present, and delicious food set out buffet style on long tables in the dining room of the ladies' home. The rain had ceased and the front door was held open so that the guests could sit at tables hastily set up on the front porch, as well as in the living room.

Anna had outdone herself, cooking Southern foods like fried chicken, creamed corn, and mashed potatoes, as well as the more spicy Mexican dishes—enchiladas and burritos and more—for which she was famous. Grace had baked twoVienna cakes in several layers in decreasing sizes, so that they rose like miniature towers of Pisa without the slant.

Bright-colored balloons swayed in clusters about the rooms and on the porch, and Hannah found herself enjoying the party and the people, especially her family.

She hugged her grandsons again and again, thrilled to see what fine young men they had become. Her daughters looked beautiful, their husbands handsome, and Hannah realized that this was the first time she could recall them all being together celebrating a happy occasion. She felt important and attractive, and proud that Max was her husband. Whatever was to come when the last guest said good-bye, and she and Max left on their honeymoon, didn't matter. Whatever happened, happened.

"Cut the cake," Mike called.

Max led her to the main table. Hannah lifted the long knife, and Max rested his hand on hers. Together they cut one of the cakes, as everyone cheered and lifted their glasses in a toast.

"To the bride and groom!" Charlie Herrill said.

"To the bride and groom," a chorus of voices repeated.

The toasts went on and on, wishing them happiness and a good life together. The young people sat on the front porch, and one of Alma's older granddaughters played a banjo and sang mountain songs in a sweet voice.

In the house, someone wished Max and Hannah many children, and everyone laughed and toasted them again, wishing them many happy years together.

Yes, Hannah thought, may we have many happy days and years together. She turned to her husband. "A long, happy life, darling."

Max drew her to him and kissed her for a long time,

and Hannah didn't even care that everyone clapped and whistled.

It was late when all the guests and family departed for their homes and motels. Amelia yawned, said good night, and went upstairs to bed.

Hannah stood at their living-room window and watched Max cross the road to his home. "I wonder who else is watching Max go home alone?" she said.

"You can still go over to his place, or call him and he'll come walk you over," Grace said.

"How could I do that? He didn't ask me to stay with him tonight. It's humiliating being married and spending the night here with you and Amelia. I'm uncomfortable about leaving tomorrow on a honeymoon with a man who, as far as I know, is doing all of this for appearance's sake. I feel like canceling our so-called honeymoon."

"I wish you had gotten this out in the open with Max before the wedding."

"I didn't know how to broach the subject. How could I blurt out, 'Do you love me?' What if he had said no? I'd never have been able to go through with the wedding." Her face softened. "It was a lovely wedding, wasn't it, Grace?"

"It was a beautiful wedding and a lovely reception, and you looked like a couple in love. You're tired, and I'm worn out. Let's just go on up to bed."

"You go. I'll turn out the lights." Hannah watched Grace climb the stairs. Then, once more, she went to the window. The lights in Max's downstairs had been turned off; those in his bedroom were on, but the shades were down. *What is he thinking now? Is he relieved to have the wedding over? Is he anticipating resuming separate lives?*

Hannah sighed. Slowly, she moved about the living room, turning off lights, then she, too, climbed the stairs. Her packed suitcase stood near the dresser. Fool that she was, she had actually included that negligee. Hannah kneeled beside the suitcase, opened it, and removed the negligee. She buried her face in it, considered leaving it at home, then laid it back inside and slammed the suitcase shut.

She undressed, slipped into comfortable pajamas and got into bed, then lay awake, wondering and worrying. They would spend tomorrow driving to Virginia. What would they say to each other during all those hours? Max had booked separate rooms at the inn; how would she hide her embarrassment from the innkeeper?

The days after her wedding suddenly seemed very uncertain.

11
THE HONEYMOON

Max drove his new van along Interstate 81, heading east.

"There were so many people at the wedding," Hannah said. "I was so happy that Miranda, Paul, and the boys made it. Laura and Miranda seemed to enjoy being together. It wasn't always that way."

"Time and age change things. They do seem to like each other. And your grandsons are fine young men. I met them at your birthday party last year, but didn't really have a chance to talk with either of them. There'll be plenty of time for getting to know them all later, wouldn't you say?"

Hannah nodded.

"I chatted about the party-planning business with Philip, while we were waiting for you at the church. He seems to love it," Max said.

"Yes, Philip started working weekends at the shop when he was in high school and he took to it immediately. It seems to come to him naturally, the organization, and the way he handles people."

They were silent for a time. Then Hannah said, "Anna did a marvelous job with the food."

"Jose worked right along with her. Those two could open a catering business. Lucky for me, Jose says it's too much work, and they like things as they are. He prefers cows to cooking, he says."

"You like cows, too," Hannah said, "or you'd have closed the dairy long ago."

He laughed. "Very true. There's something about those creatures that warms my heart."

The rolling countryside was pleasant, and Hannah deferred thinking about their sleeping arrangements at the inn in the Shenandoah Valley.

Max said, "It was a beautiful wedding, don't you think? And you planned it all in such a short time." For a moment his hand covered hers, then returned to the steering wheel. "You're an incredible woman, Hannah."

"I never could have done it without Grace and Amelia. And Mike did the flowers. They were all marvelous."

"You were a beautiful bride," he said.

Choked with emotion, Hannah could not reply. Interstate 81 turned and descended into the Shenandoah Valley.

"You're probably nervous. I am, too," Max said. "It's been a long time for me."

What had? She couldn't ask, for her mouth was dry as beach sand on a hot, summer day.

It was evening when they arrived at the colonial-style inn that sat on a rise overlooking a river. True to his word, Max had requested separate adjoining rooms and her suitcase had been deposited in one. There was no time to unpack, let alone to deal with her feelings of rejection before Max knocked on Hannah's door.

"Ready for dinner?" he asked.

Hannah glanced at her untouched suitcase sitting on the edge of the bed. She had intended to unpack, to shower and dress, to unwind. She brushed away the sadness. If he was ready for dinner, well, so was she.

"I'm famished," Max said as they descended the wide oak staircase.

In the paneled dining room, with its wing-backed dining chairs and carpeted floor, a fire blazed in the massive limestone fireplace. There were two younger couples, each at their own table, at dinner. A wide berth between tables allowed for privacy and quiet conversation.

"What a lovely room," Hannah said, once they were seated. For the first time since they had known each other, their relationship felt awkward. She didn't know what to do with her hands. Put them in her lap, rest them casually on the table? She wanted to scratch an itch on the side of her cheek and refrained.

"For an old man, Pastor Johnson carried it off beautifully," Max said. "I know he enjoyed marrying us. He must have told me so fifteen times at the reception."

"Yes, he did a fine job." Oh, no—she hadn't meant to refer to their wedding ceremony as a job.

"Lurina was beaming, wasn't she?" Max buttered a roll. "You ladies have certainly perked up life for her. Before you came and Grace brought her into all our lives, she was a bitter, cranky old woman sitting on her porch with a rusty old double-barreled shotgun on her lap."

"Lurina is a gem. We all love her. And Melissa behaved well. I didn't know what to expect from her." Why was their conversation so stifled, limited to banalities?

Creamed celery soup arrived, and a small salad, and after a time the waitress brought their dinners: crisp-skinned duck dribbled with a rich plum sauce. "This is exceptionally good." Max dabbed his lips with his napkin.

Only then did Hannah remember her napkin, still sitting alongside her plate. She opened it and spread it in her lap, feeling a perfect fool.

Seated at the other end of the room, one of the couples held hands across their table. The longing and love in their eyes caused an ache in Hannah's heart. *What a shame that Max and I don't feel like that, behave like that.*

Dinner was over, and the waitress stood at their table handing them dessert menus. Max perused his for what seemed to Hannah an overly long time. Then he closed it and ordered bread pudding.

Hannah requested a cup of tea. *Perhaps it will relax me.*

From his jacket pocket, Max pulled several brochures and laid them on the table. "It's supposed to be in the high sixties tomorrow. What would you like to do? We could go into town and browse antique shops, or we could visit one of the Civil War battlefields, or tour a winery."

"Can we decide tomorrow?"

"Certainly. It's been a long day. You must be tired."

Hannah laid her napkin on the table and faked a yawn. "I'm exhausted."

Steam filled the shower, clouded the mirror, and rose to the ceiling of the small bathroom. Hannah turned, letting water run down all the curves of her body. It was just as well they wouldn't be sleeping together; she had sags and lumps everywhere. Afterward, with a large towel wrapped about her, she stood over the suitcase and considered the negligee Grace and Amelia had given her, but chose instead her comfortable, old flowered pajamas. Her hair lay in damp strands about her face, and she placed a dry towel over the pillow to absorb the moisture. Then she slipped under the covers. *This sham of a honeymoon is ridiculous. I regret letting Max talk me into it. When we get home, we'll pick up our lives and go on as usual. Not so bad, really. I like my life with Amelia and Grace.*

The knock at her door startled Hannah. It was a soft knock, much like Grace's knock, and for an instant Hannah anticipated Grace's entrance. The knock came again. Throwing back the covers, she clambered from the high four-poster bed. At the door, she asked, "Who is it?"

"Me. Max," came the whispered reply.

Why? She unlocked the door, scrambled back to bed, and yanked the covers high over her shoulders. "What's the matter?" she asked as he approached.

"Nothing's the matter."

His slippers flip-flopped across the shiny pine floor. Below his blue terrycloth bathrobe, she noted blue and gold striped pajamas. He had shaved and showered, and his hair, like hers, was still damp.

"I came to say good night." Without an invitation, Max sat on the side of the bed and took Hannah's hand.

Shivers exploded through her body. *Good heavens, at my age?*

"You've been a trouper, a great sport." He shook his

head. "Why is this so hard? Nothing I say comes out right."

"What is it you want to say?" She held her breath.

"That I want you to know I care very deeply about you." He shook his head so vigorously, it shook the bed. "No. That's not what I want to say."

Her heart plunged.

"I'm glad you consented to marry me, Hannah."

Well, why wouldn't he be glad? It was what he wanted. What *she* wanted was much, much more. Tears prickled her eyes.

Max took her hands in his. They were cool and clammy, like hers, and they trembled, like hers did. He leaned foward and for a moment hesitated as if wanting to say or do more, much more—but instead he kissed her forehead, and rose. "I'll see you tomorrow, Mrs. Maxwell." He smiled and she saw tenderness in his eyes. "I'll come and get you for breakfast. Is nine-thirty too early?"

"That's fine," Hannah said. *Go,* she thought, *go fast before I cry and make a fool of myself.* She squeezed Max's hand.

The innkeeper had told them that guests mostly came to enjoy the out-of-doors. There was a swinging bridge across the river and trails through the woods, and also canoeing.

Max and Hannah strolled hand in hand to the river and the swinging bridge. Although its floor was con-structed of wood, the bridge hung in a saddle of rope:

rope sides, rope railing, ropes suspended from tall tree limbs. As they crossed, Hannah stopped, dizzy for a moment, in the middle of the bridge.

Max was right behind her, his hand on her waist. "Don't look down, Hannah. Focus on a tree or something on the other side and just keep moving. I'm right here."

Made safe by his presence, so close that she could feel his breath on her neck, she took another step, and then another, and to her relief she reached the other side and stepped onto solid ground.

"I don't like that feeling of having nothing under me," Hannah said.

"That's how I feel on a ski lift," Max replied. "But there's less of a drop from that little bridge."

"That water looked awfully cold, though, and there were probably lots of sharp rocks down in that river."

Max shifted the picnic basket to his other hand, placed his free hand on her arm to guide her, and they headed into the woods on a wide, leaf-covered trail. Unbeknownst to them, they had entered the domain of the squirrels. Squirrels scurried into the underbrush and scampered up tree trunks. Chattering their complaints, they skimmed the branches high above and leaped from tree to tree. Rearing on his hind legs, supported by his wide furry tail, a stouthearted squirrel held his ground and glared at them with bright coffeebean eyes.

The leaves were slippery beneath their feet, and small twigs crackled beneath their shoes. Deeper into the woods it grew cooler, and Hannah untied the sweater about her waist and put it on. Through gently sloping land, they walked for what seemed a long while before reaching a clearing.

A large flat boulder off to one side provided a picnic table and seating. Their picnic basket, packed by the inn, yielded a checkered tablecloth, a variety of sandwiches, a pasta salad, and clusters of green, seedless grapes, as well as drinks. Warmed by the sunshine, they ate slowly and relaxed. It surprised Hannah when Max pulled a small book of poems from his pocket and began to read aloud from Percy Bysshe Shelley's sonnet "Ozymandias."

My name is Ozymandias, king of kings:
Look on my works, ye Mighty, and despair!"
Nothing beside remains. Round the decay
Of that colossal wreck, boundless and bare
The lone and level sands stretch far away.

He set aside the slim volume. "Do you think that, like Ozymandias, we crave immortality?"

"I don't know," Hannah replied. "It's quite arrogant to do so, really." She was silent a moment. "When I think of immortality I think of something that will last through time, and then I ask, what length of time? A person can achieve immortality when they do great evil, like when Booth murdered President Lincoln. Who knows how many generations will remember Booth—or listen to the music of a Beethoven? How long can anything or anyone count on being remembered?"

"The ancient Greek writers and artists, their buildings and statues, are still remembered. Yet how many people remember cultures once considered invincible, like the ancient Sumerians?" Max asked. "Christianity eliminated a pantheon of gods and goddesses who had been recognized and worshiped for generations. Christianity even wiped out the memory of ancient Greeks and their culture for centuries, until the Arabs translated manuscripts and books from Greece, and brought that knowledge to the west via North Africa and Spain."

"I guess the best most of us can hope for is a bit of immortality through being remembered by our children and grandchildren," Hannah said.

"Do you know anything about your family five generations back?" Max asked.

"No. But some people trace their ancestry back to England or wherever they came from. I bet the English and French can trace ancestry back for centuries, but then, as you say, it stops. So tell me." She poked his arm playfully. "A few generations from now, who will care about a carefully collected genealogy that an ancestor placed so lovingly in some old trunk? Most of the names will mean nothing." She tipped her head, put her hands on her hips, and asked, "Why are we talking about this, Max?"

He smiled and shrugged. "For the heck of it. I always liked that sonnet, used to try to imagine what old Ozymandias looked like. Did he have a beard, do you think? Was he tall or a little fellow? Was he a wise king or a son of a gun?"

Max turned the pages of the thin volume. "Now I'll get to the good part, the poem I really wanted to read to you. This is what I've meant to say to you, Hannah. These are my sentiments exactly." He began to read, and the soft tenderness of his voice touched her.

How do I love thee? Let me count the ways.
I love thee to the depth and breadth and height
My soul can reach . . .

Max set the book down beside him on the boulder and took Hannah's hands in his. "I'm not good at expressing myself about such things. Forgive me for letting Ms. Barrett Browning say it for me." He released her hands, and began to read again.

I love thee freely, as men strive for Right;
I love thee purely, as men turn from praise.
I love thee with the passion put to use
In my old griefs, and with my childhood's faith.

His eyes moved down the page.

I love thee with the breath
Smiles, tears, of all my life!—and, if God choose,
I shall but love thee better after death.

"This is what I've been wanting to say. I love you,

Hannah," Max said.

Tears rolled down Hannah's cheeks. Her face was radiant as she looked at him. *It is two days after the wedding, and I am hearing those words for the first time,* she thought. "I love *you,*" she said. "That I should love again is a miracle to me. I keep thinking this is a dream, and I must wake up. It's not a dream, is it, Max?"

"Not a dream, my dearest Hannah. Not a dream at all."

Their shoulders touching, they sat for a long while in comfortable silence.

Finally, Hannah said, "It's so still here. Amelia would call this a sacred place. She comes across them during her photo trips."

"How does she know if a place is sacred?" Max balled up the foil in which their sandwiches had been wrapped and dropped it into the picnic basket.

"She feels it, she says. She'll step into a glen, or round a corner, or come to a spot along a river, and something seizes hold of her."

"Do you feel that way here?"

"I do. This is a very special place. I'll remember you and it for the rest of my life." She smiled at him and brushed a strand of hair from his forehead. "For me, this moment is immortal."

Max lifted her hand to his lips and kissed it. "You look like a young girl, so happy."

She leaned into him. "I am happy. Very happy."

He kissed her gently.

Then Max stood and offered Hannah his hand. "We ought to start back. It's getting chilly, and we want to say good-bye to the squirrels before they tuck themselves into their cozy little dens."

When she rose, he grabbed her close to hug and kiss her, again.

If I died right this minute, Hannah thought, *I'd die happy.*

Later, in her room, Max held Hannah close. As his lips softly touched her forehead, cheeks, and lips, her shoulders sank into the pillows. Her body lost its stiffness and became liquid and warm. Her eyes closed, Hannah slipped her arms about Max's neck and pulled him closer.

Sunshine filled the room, illuminating the flowered wallpaper. Had Max really been in her bed all night? Had they made love so very gently at first, and then with increasing passion? Amazing! Wonderful! Max's pajamas and robe lay on the floor on her side of the bed along with slippers. Hannah smiled. Turned on his side, he slept facing away from her. She watched the rise and fall of his back and ribs. What a glorious man, so well muscled, like a younger man—and he loved her! Just as she loved him. Sheer joy pressed against her ribs, and Hannah laughed aloud. Reaching over, she tickled Max. Rolling over, he pulled her to him.

They spent the next two days exploring the charming

town that rose from the river and stepped in pretty, brightly painted houses up the hillside. In an antique shop, Max bought Hannah a brooch with Victorian filigree surrounding a delicate painting on ivory, a pastoral scene complete with shepherd and shepherdess.

"It's beautiful," Hannah said. "This I'll wear with pleasure." She pinned the brooch to her shirt and kissed Max full on the lips. "Thank you, my love."

The clerk seemed to eye them with amusement and curiosity.

She must never have seen older folks in love, and didn't think they could be as silly as young people, Hannah thought. *We're as silly, foolish, and romantic as twenty-year-olds, and it's marvelous.*

The following day, after a lazy morning and a late breakfast, they visited a winery. Max bought six bottles of red and white wine. "A bottle of each for Bob," he said, "and for Pastor Johnson. He wouldn't take a penny for marrying us. I insisted, but he was adamant."

"We'll find a way to pay him back," Hannah said.

"He says he's rich in friends," Max replied, "and that that's the best kind of wealth."

They roamed the back streets and visited a quilt museum, which was small and tucked away on a cobblestone side street. In the museum gift shop, Hannah purchased a Starry Night quilt in a deep, rich blue with yellow stars for Grace, and a Maple Leaf quilt in bright spring greens and gold for Amelia. "Quilts give a room such a cozy feeling," she said, and asked the salesperson to wrap them as gifts. For her daughters, she bought lovely handcrafted silver earrings.

On their last day at the inn, they discovered the swing and hammocks beneath a porch, and spent the afternoon enjoying the sounds of the river and birdsong. The sunshine had warmed the dogwoods into bloom, which delighted Max. He picked a blossom and handed it to Hannah, who told him she'd press it into a book to enjoy the memory of the day for years to come.

12
LIFE GOES ON

After leaving the Shenandoah Valley, they headed west toward Johnson City in Tennessee, from where they would drive up and over Sam's Gap into North Carolina.

"This is the route we took at forty miles an hour when we made our first trip to Covington," Hannah said. "I don't know what made Amelia and me more nervous: Grace's driving, or what we'd find when we got to Covington. That farmhouse needed so much work, we about cried when we saw it."

Max nodded in sympathy. "Bella and I'd sit on the porch and shake our heads at the way the farmhouse deteriorated year after year. We knew that old Arthur wasn't able to maintain it any longer, and we offered to buy it. He refused, said it held too many happy memories. He had a married lady love, and for many years they met at that farmhouse."

"How romantic. We never knew that."

Max nodded. "She died shortly after we moved to Covington. After that Arthur rarely returned, and the place went downhill. The last time I saw him, he said he was into genealogy, trying to find an heir. That's how he found Amelia."

They were leaving sunshine behind; menacing gray clouds loomed ahead.

"Think we can make it home before we're deluged?" Max asked.

"If it starts raining we can always pull off, have a bit to eat and wait it out." Hannah was in no hurry to get home. "Tell me about your childhood. Where were you born and raised?"

"Well, I was a city boy. Atlanta has these great suburban green belts close in to the city. That's where we lived, a hop, skip, and jump from downtown. My mother thrived on city life. She was president of the opera guild and an incredible fund-raiser. There were parties and more parties! Dad, a workaholic, traveled. Being an only child, I was left pretty much to myself.

"But my grandparents, bless them, lived in the country west of Atlanta. It was there that I fell in love with the land. When I majored in animal husbandry, my parents, especially my father, pitched a hissy fit. I remember thinking, he's got no clue who I am or what I like.

"Actually, both my parents were upset. They expected their only child to exceed them, as they had done. But instead of being a lawyer or a diplomat, I was just a peon at the Department of Agriculture. Worse yet,

I left the department and took a job on a diary farm in the foothills north of Atlanta."

They had driven past Johnson City and were starting up the mountain when the rain started. Max slowed the van and continued.

"By then, I was in love with dairy cows. For a couple of years I worked with kids and animals as coordinator of 4H clubs. Then, on a vacation, I drove up to North Carolina, wandered off the beaten path and stumbled on Covington. It felt as if I'd come home." He looked across at her. "Ever had that feeling about a place?"

She shook her head. She never had.

"In those days land went for a hundred dollars an acre, so I bought the land," he said.

They were crawling along behind a truck, and with the rain coming down, Hannah was glad for the truck's rear lights.

"I'd come up from Atlanta weekends and climb the hill behind where the house is now," Max said. "I planned, dreamed, and saved my money. I invested what little I had in the stock market, got lucky, pulled it out, and built the farmhouse and barns. Then my grandfather died and left me some money, and I bought cows and milking equipment. When I married Bella, for a while I thought I'd have to move back to the city. She was an artist and a city girl born and bred. She'd take off for Atlanta every couple of weeks. I missed her." He turned his head and smiled at Hannah. "But after a time, the country got under her skin, too."

"I really liked your Bella," Hannah said.

"It's a shame you two didn't meet before she got so sick."

"Even for that short time, knowing her meant a lot to me."

Max reached over and placed his hand on Hannah's knee. "Bella'd be real pleased about us."

"Anna says she would."

"Anna claims Bella visits her in her dreams," Max said. "Anna's not a whit older than I am, maybe even a bit younger, but she thinks she's my mother. Watch out for her. She'll mother you, too."

"That might be very nice. My parents were reserved and humorless. No hugs and compliments from them. Stiff upper lip, that sort of thing. I appreciate Anna's warmth, the way she laughs easily and goes about singing."

"Your turn, now," Max said, "Tell me more about your life."

She squeezed his hand. "I had an uneventful, repressed childhood. Lots of churchgoing. Lots of complaining about Dad's bad luck and the lack of money. Bill, when I met him, seemed the opposite—he was funny and laughed a lot. He was a car salesman and threw the cash around. I was impressed.

"At first he was a good provider, but that changed after the girls were born. He wanted sons, I guess, not daughters. He was as ignorant as Henry the Eighth was about the fact that his chromosome determined the sex of his children. And when I didn't get pregnant again, he fancied it was some kind of conspiracy I'd concocted with my doctor to deprive him of a son. He always drank some, but it really escalated, and the abuse started."

Hannah told Max about the dreadful winter night she had fled with the girls from their home in Canada, and how Bill caught up with them at a gas station in Michigan and shot the radiator of her car. She told him how hard it had been trying to support the girls by cleaning peoples' homes in the day and going to secretarial school at night.

"I'm going to see to it that you have the most comfortable and well cared-for old age," Max said.

She laughed and poked his arm. "And when, pray tell, does old age start?"

"Right today, as far as comfort and care goes. Otherwise it's about ninety minimum."

"As long as we're in good health," Hannah said, "I hope we live a long, long time."

13
GRACE AND AMELIA

While Hannah and Max were away Bob received his occupancy permit, and with great excitement Amelia and Grace helped him move into the cottage next door. Packing boxes of plates and pots, linens, clothing, and other small items had taken two days. Ignoring Grace's pleas that he wait for them to get there and help him, Bob had indiscriminately dumped clothes and goodness knows what else into boxes and labeled nothing. When the movers deposited the stacks of boxes in the living room and bedroom, the women helped him unpack and set up his kitchen. Then he had shooed them out, assuring them that he preferred to take his time and unpack everything else in his own good time.

Grace returned later to find Bob moving the new couch that had just been delivered from this position to that in the living room. They finally decided it looked best facing the fireplace. They also decided his army locker worked best not as the coffee table Bob first suggested, but in his bedroom for storing blankets. The locker, a small rolltop desk that had been his mother's, and the chair that went with it, were all that Bob had kept of his furniture. Everything else was new, most of it still to be delivered.

Having exhausted themselves shoving the couch about, Grace made them large glasses of iced tea, which they took out onto the front porch. Feeling as comfortable as an old married couple at the end of a busy day, they rocked and waved at passing cars.

Grace turned to Bob. "When we were young, time couldn't go fast enough, remember?"

"I sure do. I had to wait until I was eighteen to join the army, and those couple of months after graduating from high school seemed endless." He reached for her hand. "As they say, youth is wasted on the young. Gracie, my girl, days like this one, sitting here with you, could go on forever."

"If only we had forever."

They were silent for a time, then Grace said, "Having

diabetes makes me value each day that I feel healthy, each day I have with you. I'm worried about my weight, Bob. I'm going nuts trying to figure out what I can eat and what I can't eat. All the stuff about diets in books and on TV confuses me. Should I count carbs? Watch calories, or what?"

"I'd stick with the old-fashioned way," Bob said.

"And what might that be?"

"Well, Weight Watchers has been around a long time and people have a lot of success with that program. And eating a bit of everything is sensible," he said. "I don't believe it's good to just eat protein, or only vegetables, or to cut out all carbohydrates."

"You're probably right," Grace said. "I believe dieting begins in the mind. I have to be ready, really ready."

From the living room, the phone could be heard. Bob went inside and returned with the portable in hand. "It's Emily for you."

Emily's voice was terse. "I've had the strangest phone call. It rang two times and no one was there, but the third time a weird voice, probably disguised, said that if I valued my law practice and my good health, I'd drop the case against Francine Randall and the Department of Education."

"Have you reported the threat to the police?"

"I have," Emily said. "And we've gotten an unlisted number. I want you to have it, but please don't give it to anyone other than the ladies."

"I assure you, I won't."

A pause, then Emily asked, "By the way, did Lucy tell you about the recurrent nightmare she's been having?"

Grace's voice tightened. "No, she hasn't."

"She was here with Tyler yesterday and mentioned it. We've all been so caught up with Hannah's wedding. I'm sure when Lucy sees you, she'll tell you."

"I'm sure she will."

The day after Hannah and Max's return, Grace and Amelia sat in their kitchen having breakfast. Hannah had spent the night with Max.

"Well, what happened on the honeymoon? Did Hannah tell you?" Amelia asked.

"Very little, actually," Grace replied. "She called to say they were back and that she was staying over there. I think she's embarrassed at the idea that people will find out he lives there and she lives here."

"Hannah, embarrassed about what people think? That's a joke," Amelia said.

"She seems very sensitive about this situation with Max."

"That's probably why she stayed with him last night." Amelia stood with her hands on her hips. "I can't imagine Hannah sleeping with Maxwell, can you?"

"I don't see why not."

"Hannah and sex, they seem so, so . . ." Amelia struggled for the right word. "Incompatible."

"I don't agree with you. She's in love with Max. If he loves her, and you've told me he does, why shouldn't sex follow?"

Amelia shook her head. "Because it's Hannah, and she's just not, well—'sexy' may not be the right word."

Grace crossed her arms. "People are many things. Hannah is as complex as any of us." She raised her eyebrows. "You're the most sophisticated of the three of us, wouldn't you say?"

Amelia looked pleased and nodded.

"Yet you showed incredibly poor judgment with Lance. How do you account for that? And you didn't sleep with him. I thought you would have." Grace grew angry as she spoke. "And I'm plump, to put it nicely, yet Bob thinks I'm sexy. How do you account for that? Maybe back when we first moved here, and we had that little incident with Bob, you considered me too fat to be desirable?"

Amelia lifted both hands. "Okay, Grace. Don't let's go there, all right? It's years ago, and I was unbelievably stupid about many things. But you're right, I'm taking a narrow view. So Hannah sleeps with Max and likes it."

"And if she does, then let's be happy for her."

Amelia rose, poured herself another cup of decaf, and returned to the table. "I regret to admit I'm a wee bit jealous of her." She looked down at her hands, examined a fingernail, then looked at Grace, tears in her eyes. "Sometimes I'm jealous of you and Bob, too."

"I'm sorry. More than anything, I wish you would find someone wonderful to love."

"That would be nice, wouldn't it?" Amelia said. "But it would have to be the right man. A kind, good man, not another Lance. Most of the time, though, I feel quite satisfied and happy with my life as it is."

She had been a lonely little girl, a lonely teenager, a lonely wife. Months of therapy after the death of her husband, Thomas, had brought understanding of the long-term effects of childhood, whether it be scarred or blessed, driven by fear or love, and how longings and myths can color one's reality. As it had with Lance, who had been so deceptively charming, yet egocentric and cunning. Therapy had brought home to Amelia the reality of her dependence on others for feelings of self-worth. Her success with photography and being accepted, even fawned over, by "the people" in New York had helped to bolster her self-esteem. Increasingly, she felt a part of the community in Covington.

Grace's voice cut into her musing. "Hannah will probably be home sometime today."

"I hope so. I hate it when things change."

Grace shoved back her chair, rounded the table, and hugged Amelia. "Unfortunately, that's life. We think we've got it all figured out and things are rolling along smoothly, and bingo—things change."

"If Hannah doesn't come back tonight, may I come into your room and talk?" Amelia asked.

"Certainly. I'd be happy if you did."

Pushed to the wall, Grace would admit to being more attached to Hannah than to Amelia. Some people were just easier to be with. Bob was easy to be with, but he was not the centerpiece of her life. Bob had a full life of his own. His days and some nights bristled with activity: teaching at the Center for Creative Retirement, golfing with Martin—who, since his wife's departure, leaned more heavily on Bob for companionship.

After dinner, when it seemed clear that Hannah would not be coming home, Grace propped herself up in bed to read the adventure novel she had picked up at Accent on Books, her favorite bookstore in North Asheville. Something about the title or the cover had caught her interest. By the second chapter the story grabbed her, and by page 60 she knew she would be turning pages into the wee hours of the morning. She'd be a rag tomorrow. When Amelia knocked on her door, though, Grace set the book aside and called, "Come on in, Amelia."

"Reading something good?" Amelia asked. "I won't stay but a minute."

Grace folded her hands in her lap. "Sit. Be comfortable. What's up?"

Grace never stopped marveling at the sapphire-blue intensity of Amelia's eyes. The fine lines about them were pronounced, true, but she was still a beautiful woman. So, why, with her good looks and charm, didn't she have a man if that was what she wanted?

Amelia sank into Grace's rocking chair by the window. "Some days there are photographs everywhere waiting to be taken. Other days nothing, the light's at the wrong angle, or there's a vehicle, or power lines in the way; one thing or another."

"Any special focus to your work now?"

"Yes. A book based on the life of a family in an isolated holler, living the way their grandparents did. Sort of an 'out of time' book."

"And you've found such a family around here?"

"Yes, their name is Inman. They live on Old Bunkie Creek, way back in the hills."

"I've never heard of it."

"Hardly anyone has." Amelia stretched her legs out and rested her head on the high back of the wicker rocker. "You know, Grace, having your photographs exhibited in a New York gallery is not all it's cracked up to be. The gallery owner is demanding. He acts as if he owns me. Now he wants Mike and me to come to New York. I don't want to fly. I can't abide what they put you through at airports these days. Why can't the gallery accept the prints by mail and leave me alone?"

She raised her head to look at Grace. "But they insist on having a reception, at which I am to smile and shake hands and say polite things to strangers I'll never see again. So what if they're the so-called crème de la crème of the New York art world? I'm too old to be impressed with myself or them."

"What does Mike think?"

"Why should that matter?" Amelia's voice sounded weary. "They're my photos, not his."

"Yes, but he's very involved in your work. He's the one who placed your photos in that gallery."

"Yes, he did, and we were both thrilled at the time." She sighed. "Of course his opinion matters. It's just that

Mike's more ambitious for me than I am for myself. Mentors can be very possessive of their protégés. Mike wants the best for me, but sometimes the best, as he sees it, isn't what I want."

"He's pressing you to go, I take it?"

Amelia nodded and pulled her legs up to her chest.

"What do *you* want?" Grace asked. She had no idea that Amelia was under this kind of pressure. How could she live under the same roof and not have a sense of what was going on with Amelia?

"I've been struggling with this. I don't think I want fame. It's an intrusion into my life. Maybe if I were forty I'd feel differently—but at my age I'm happy just to do photography. Not that it isn't pleasant to be recognized. And I'm proud that I've published a book that still sells in local stores. I'd like to do another, but I don't want to travel, and I don't want to be at a gallery's beck and call."

She lowered her voice to mimic a man's voice. " 'We need another ten new photos pronto, Amelia.' I prefer to work at my own pace, not theirs. I want to shoot when I want to shoot. If I get up feeling yucky, I want to hang around the house in a bathrobe without feeling guilty."

"I certainly understand that. Seems to me you've earned the right to do what feels best for you, Amelia."

"I wish I knew exactly what that was," Amelia replied wistfully.

"I've found that writing down my feelings can help me sort things out. Have you ever tried that?"

Amelia looked skeptical. "I never have. Maybe I will.

I'd certainly sleep better if I had a clearer idea of where I want to go with my life and my work." She shrugged and rose from the chair. "Anyway, talking about this has helped me to see that we are committed to New York this time, so I'll just stop fussing about it and upsetting Mike. I'll go and do what's required." She was halfway to the door when she turned back to look at Grace. "But this is going to be my last trip to New York City. Thanks for letting me talk, helping me sort it out."

"You're more than welcome. Sleep well, now."

"I think I will." Amelia closed the door softly behind her.

14
COWARD VERSUS SUPERHERO

The Banks's small gray bungalow looked smaller and dingier than Grace remembered. When Grace blew her horn, the front door banged open and Lucy, trailed by two of her younger sisters, raced from the house. Aggie, about twelve now, was thin as a string bean, and nearly as tall as Lucy. The younger child's name escaped Grace.

As Lucy got into the car, Grace smiled at the younger child, then turned her attention to Aggie. "How are you? You've grown so much since I last saw you."

"Ma says she's sproutin' up like a weed," the youngest girl said, coming up to the open car window. "And Randy's a-comin' home!"

"Yep," Aggie continued. "He's got leave for two weeks, and then he's got orders to head for someplace called Afgan something or other."

"I wanted to tell it!" The younger girl stamped her feet. "Darn. I never gets to do nothin'."

"What's your name, honey?" Grace asked.

"Teresa Marie Banks," the child said. Her deep brown eyes were round as a full moon. Her dark thick braid was wrapped on her head like a crown.

"Her name's not Teresa, it's Audra," Aggie said.

Grace looked at the child. "Don't you like the name Audra? It's a very pretty name."

Audra shook her head. "I hate it. I like Teresa Marie. That's my name now."

"Oh, shut up, Audra," Aggie said.

The child looked crestfallen. Aggie's condescending attitude annoyed Grace.

"If you want me to call you Teresa Marie, I will." Grace smiled down at her.

The little girl's eyes danced.

"Do you miss your big brother, Teresa Marie?" Grace asked. There was something about the child that touched her. *Don't let this little one wrap herself around your heart. You've got enough people to worry about. It's enough that you help her family financially. Or is it?*

Grace touched the girl's glossy braid and the child smiled.

"Sure, I miss Randy a lot. He used to read to me when I went to bed."

"He's a fine young man." After his father died, Grace

had pressed Randy to finish high school. If she had not involved her friends and relatives in setting up a fund to help the Banks family, Randy would have had to quit school to help his mother support the younger children. "Please tell him that if he has time, Mrs. Grace would love to see him."

Lucy yanked at her seat belt and shuffled her feet. "I'll tell him. Back off the car, Audra . . . ah . . . Teresa. We gotta go."

Disappointment filled the child's face as Grace started the car, and they drove away. In the rearview mirror, Grace saw the little hand waving and the down-turned mouth. The sight tugged at her heart.

"You been feelin' good, Mrs. Grace?" Lucy asked.

"I'm fine, how about you? I haven't seen much of you lately."

"Been busy. I work over at the gardens on Saturdays and some days after school. It helps me buy school clothes, things like that. We've been gettin' the gardens ready to plant."

"Where would you like to have lunch?" Grace asked.

Lucy shrugged. "Ain't no matter to me. I like eatin' lunch with you anywhere."

Grace was pleased. "How about the IHOP in Asheville? I'd enjoy a nice stack of pancakes." She had been craving pancakes. Would it make a difference if she gave up white foods—rice, potatoes, flour, sugar, and pasta—and ate more protein? Would her craving for sweets go away?

"I love pancakes," Lucy said.

On the drive to town, Lucy chatted about school and work and seemed happy. So why was she having night-mares?

They were halfway through their stacks of pancakes when Lucy laid down her utensils and looked over the table at Grace.

"Something wrong?" Grace asked.

"I'm thinking you got a sixth sense about things. I been meaning to come to the house and talk to you, pri-vate like."

"You know you're welcome any time. Anything par-ticular on your mind?"

"Well . . . I been having really bad dreams."

"Bad dreams?"

"About Ringo, Mrs. Grace. They scares me so much, I wake up shiverin'," Lucy said.

"Take your time and tell me about them."

"It's the same thing every time. I'm sittin' in the cour-thouse. They bring in Ringo, and he's got chains on his wrists and ankles. Suddenly he breaks the chains, like he was the Hulk or a bionic man, and he comes after me."

"It would be impossible for him to break out of hand-cuffs and ankle chains."

"That's what I tell myself," Lucy said. "But in my heart, I feel so scared just to see him ever again."

"You don't have to go to the courthouse. There's absolutely no reason why you should."

"But Miss Emily says maybe the judge will want to talk with me."

"Maybe. And if he does, we'll bring you to his private office behind the courtroom, and you won't see Ringo."

"You'll be with me, Mrs. Grace? Please, if I gotta go, please be with me."

"I promise to take you there if you have to go, and I'll stay with you the entire time. What did Ringo do that night when the police came to the motel?"

"He grabbed a hold of me and shoved me in front of him."

"Not much of a Hulk, then. He's just a coward."

A big sigh escaped Lucy. "That's true. Thanks, Mrs. Grace. You've helped me a lot. You always do. He's nothin' but a rotten coward and liar." She lowered her eyes. "I wanna thank you for all you done for me and my family. I says a prayer for you every night." Lucy's hand slid across the table and rested on Grace's hand. "I'm truly obliged, Mrs. Grace. I don't see much of you lately, and I miss you. I could tell Mrs. Hannah I can't work on Saturdays, so I can spend more time with you."

"I love you, Lucy, and no, I wouldn't want you to do that. What you're learning and doing with Hannah is very important. I'm here whenever you need me."

An intergenerational party of eight crowded the aisle, waiting for a table to be cleared. One of the children, a boy of about four, tugged at his father's hand while he jumped about and screamed. The father ignored him.

"Let's finish and get out of here," Grace said.

"If I ever marry and have kids," Lucy said, "they won't behave like that."

Several days later, Lucy phoned Grace to say that the dreams had stopped. "I don't feel scared anymore, Mrs. Grace. Talking about it with you helped a whole heap."

15
THE INMAN FAMILY
AND THE OLD WAYS

Runoff from heavy rains wreaked havoc in the narrow gorges of Madison County. Swollen creeks surged, destroying the underpinnings of bridges, which collapsed, separating homes from roads. Bottomland flooded, destroying homes and barns, while the animals that survived wandered aimlessly in a sea of mud. Several days after the flood, the sun finally warmed and dried the earth.

Perched on high ground, Amelia watched a television crew shoot a bridge that had collapsed into Old Bunkie Creek. Then they packed up their gear, waved, and drove away—leaving the Inman family, whose cabin had been dislodged from its foundation and upended, standing silent in a state of shock. Thank God, for the blessed power of shock to insulate us in times of tragedy, Amelia thought.

For several weeks before the flood, Amelia had been photographing the Inmans, recording the day-to-day events of their lives: Leeanne Inman scrubbing clothes on rocks in the usually benign creek; her barefoot daughter in a too-long, too-wide hand-me-down dress sitting at her grandmother's feet playing with a well worn teddy bear; Alden Inman, the father, chopping wood on an old tree stump.

Amelia photographed Alden as he strode into the woods, his gun slung over his shoulder, and again when he emerged with rabbits dangling from a pole. She captured the light in the children's eyes when they saw the rabbits, and photographed the oldest boy, Billie, whittling on the front porch steps when he wasn't milking their cow or fishing in the creek with a homemade pole. She had photographed ten-year-old Frankie helping his father form softened strips of wood into a chair. Now their simple handwrought benches and chairs were pitched one upon the other in a corner of the tumbledown porch.

Today, the slump of their shoulders and the downcast eyes of the family, huddled together near the creek, bespoke their bewilderment, helplessness, and sense of desolation. Suddenly four-year-old Luanne dashed from her mother's side to a doll, which lay half-buried in the gooey mud, and threw herself upon it. The weight of her body buried the doll even farther. Her hands dripping brown goo up to her elbows, her face splattered with it, the little girl flapped her arms like a duck and screamed.

Billie ran to his sister and scooped her into his arms. Their mother, her eyes blank, folded like a beach chair and collapsed. Reaching for the child, she gathered her to her bosom and rocked back and forth, back and forth. Even as she ached, remembering her own losses, Amelia adjusted the long lens on her camera and continued photographing their shattered lives.

Mike leaned over the developing bath and studied each sheet as it gave up its image. "These are fantastic photographs, Amelia." Using metal tongs, he lifted each photograph and passed it to Amelia, who attached the wet images to a line strung across a section of the darkroom.

Amelia stared at the pictures, then covered her face with her hands and shook her head. "I can't do this book."

"Why not? What do you mean?"

"I can't take this family's anguish and display it in a book. When they agreed to my photographing them, they didn't anticipate a tragedy."

The idea for the book had presented itself to her in a dream, and seeking a family who lived isolated and pretty much as their ancestors had a hundred years ago, she had turned to Laura and Molly for help.

"The Inman family's the closest thing to what you're looking for," Molly had said. "They live up a holler across Old Bunkie Creek."

"Where's Old Bunkie Creek?"

"It's west and north, in a remote part of the county. They probably have no electricity or indoor plumbing, and grow their own food, fish, and hunt. It used to be a good three-mile walk from where you'd have to park a car, but last year the government cut a single-lane dirt road fairly close to where their cabin is. You could probably take a car as far as the bridge over the creek."

Following Molly's directions, Amelia had located the rutted dirt road, which led to the bridge on Old Bunkie Creek and the worn and weather-beaten cabin on the other side. After hours of chatting, Alden Inman had agreed that for a fee, she could photograph his family as they went about their daily routine, and he had placed his *X* on a contract.

Mike joined Amelia at the line of drying prints. "But think about it, Amelia. You could do 'before and after' shots."

Amelia turned pained eyes to Mike and shook her head. "You didn't see the look on that mother's face. That's how I must have looked when Caroline died in my arms on that airplane. We were taking her back to England for medical treatment. None of this woman's children died in that flood, but the family lost every-thing they needed to survive: every tool, their loom, the father's gun, his plow, their cow and chickens. I recog-nized in her face and eyes the hopelessness and despair I felt that day on the plane."

"Okay, well forget about this for now. We've got the 'Seasons in the Mountains' show in Asheville in May, and our New York trip's coming up. Maybe you'll revisit the family after we get back and see how they're doing. After all, they didn't shoo you away the day you took these shots after the flood."

"They were in shock, Mike." She shrugged his hand off her shoulder. "It's one thing to read about a flood or see a thirty-second piece on television, and quite another to witness and record a family's anguish. You didn't see their old wood-burning cook stove buried in mud, or the metal bedstead mangled and covered with debris in the riverbed. All their meager tools and furnishings were either destroyed or had simply vanished. The empty look in the father's eyes when little Frankie held up a broken homemade flute tore at my heart. They already had so little, and now they have nothing." Her shoulders slumping, Amelia walked from the room.

The faces of Alden, Leeanne, her mother Blanche, and the children stayed with Amelia. They haunted her waking and sleeping hours, and as the days passed she decided she could not wait to return from New York, but must find out where the family was and see if she could help.

On one of her visits to the various agencies, who claimed never to have heard of the Inmans or of Old Bunkie Creek, Amelia stumbled onto a reporter from the television station. He suggested that she try Laurel Creek Community Center.

"They've taken in quite a few families the flood wiped out," he said.

It was a huge relief for Amelia to hear that a woman at the community center had seen and processed the family. "The children are being looked after by several families in the area, and far as I know, the father is working down in Hendersonville clearing brush for a developer. The mother refused help. She and her mother are camped out at Old Bunkie Creek."

The following day started out at a chilly fifty degrees,

but by one in the afternoon had warmed to seventy-two degrees. Amelia packed a basket with cornmeal, potatoes, powdered milk, rice, sausage, coffee, sugar, salt, oatmeal, and canned beans and soups. She folded several blankets and stashed everything in the car, then left for Old Bunkie Creek.

The deeply rutted road was nearly impassible in places. Amelia stopped twice to remove fallen branches from her path, and she almost plowed into a tree when a heavily leafed limb whacked her windshield, blinding her for a moment. Several times she considered turning around, but then the road would become smoother, and bits of blue sky showed through the branches. Amelia clutched the steering wheel, and ploughed ahead.

At Old Bunkie Creek, Amelia pulled on high rubber boots, lifted and positioned her basket firmly on her head, then stepped into the swirling water. Blanche noticed her first and waved. The woman was tall and wiry, with dark, lively blackberry eyes. Years spent in the hot summer sun scrubbing clothes at the river and eking a garden from the rock-hard soil had leathered her skin and tooled it into deep grooves. Yet she remained an optimist, seeing the cup as half-full.

Blanche reached Amelia as she stepped from the creek and took the basket from her. "Sure 'nough, you ain't need to bring nothin'."

"I didn't know what you had out here. There are blankets in the car."

"Well, ain't you kind," Blanche said. "It's right chilly come night."

They had erected a tent near the foundation of the old cabin and had gathered what remained—miscellaneous wood, piteously few foundation rocks, and some window frames—close about the tent. A circle of stones surrounded a small fire. On a platform of rocks, steam rose from a battered tin coffeepot.

"We been findin' some of our stuff downcreek, Lord be praised," Blanche said.

"All beat up and broke," Leeanne said. She stood in front of the tent holding in her hands what might have been a skirt. "Wondered if we'd be a-seein' you agin."

Her mother eyed her sternly.

"Bein' as the road's washed out and all," Leeanne said.

"It took some time for me to find out where you were," Amelia said.

"Times like this, we gotta keep the best view of things." Blanche poked at the fire.

"How are you? How are the kids? I heard Alden's working down in Hendersonville," Amelia said.

"Kids ain't happy. They're staying with folks they don't know and goin' to regular school. They're too old for the grades they put 'em in. We'd been teachin' 'em to read and write at home, and they ain't used to all the people," Leeanne said. "Heard there's a man a-comin' round these parts to give us folks money to help us along. We gotta be here to catch him."

"Maybe you should be staying closer to the Laurel Community Center, so you know when he comes. Then you could bring him out here."

Blanche shook her head. "I done told her that, but Leeanne is stubborn as a mule."

Leeanne shook her head. "Where we gonna stay when we get there?"

"There are government agencies that will help you find a place to live," Amelia said. "I'd be glad to drive you back."

Leeanne shook her head again. "Can't trust no government agency."

Amelia stifled her frustration. *The FEMA man they're waiting for is from a government agency.*

Blanche walked over to her daughter and grasped her arm. "Come on now, Leeanne. How you think the kids feel, with the two of us out here where we can't see 'em? Something happen to one of 'em, who you think's gonna come lookin' fer us out these parts? What if Alden needs to call you up on one of them phones they got up in Laurel? I'm goin' back with Miss Amelia. You set on stayin' out here, you can just do it alone, missy." Blanche rubbed her arms. She looked as if she hadn't slept in days.

"You're cold. I have blankets in the car. Let me get them for you. You can throw them over your shoulders."

"I done prayed for a sign, and the good Lord sent Miss Amelia," Blanche said.

Amelia turned back to the creek. As she stepped into the water, words Thomas used to quote from some philosopher came to mind: It is not possible to step twice into the same river. Nor would this family be able to step completely back into their old way of life.

Leeanne grunted. "I ain't got a choice now, do I? A woman can't be stayin' out here alone." She doused the fire with the coffee from the pot, dipped the pot in the river to cool it, wrapped it in the tattered skirt she had been holding, and disappeared into the tent. She emerged moments later with several thin blankets, a small cloth bag, and a mesh bag holding what looked like cooking utensils.

Leeanne gave her mother a disgruntled look. "Okay, let's get a-goin'."

16
THREATS

When the phone rang, Emily answered it. Russell saw that her whole body tensed. "I'll be right over," she said.

"What's the matter?" her husband asked.

"Someone's left a dead squirrel on the front steps of my office." Her arms were already in her coat. "Whoever did it left a note that said, 'This is a warning. You'll get more than a squirrel next time.' Who would—?"

"My God." Russell reached for his jacket. "I'm going with you. This time, Emily, we're going to the police."

"Okay, but don't tell Grace we didn't report it the first time. I said we did. Promise?"

"I won't say a word about that to Grace, but this is serious business."

The policeman at the desk listened as they explained

that the lawsuit against Francine Randall and the middle school had to do with the fact that no one had been monitoring a study hall when a student hacked into a computer. Lucy Banks had gotten on a chat room that had caused her to be in grave danger from a sicko named Jerry McCorkle, alias "Ringo."

He nodded and made notes. "Probably some prankster, maybe even kids. But just in case, we'll have an unmarked car drive past your office several times a day."

"You think whoever did it did so in the daytime, when people could see him or her?" Russell asked.

The policeman shook his head. "Maybe. Maybe not."

"So we're supposed to sit and wait for someone to harm my wife, or one of our kids?" Russell felt like a time bomb waiting to explode. "Most likely it's coming from the Randall family. I bet they've done this as a scare tactic." Russell leaned both hands on the desk and glared at the policeman. Emily placed her hand on his arm, and he relaxed a bit and sank back into a chair.

"Best we can do is check the place couple of times a day," the cop said. "We can't be arresting someone without cause."

"We understand, Sergeant Holmes, and thank you." Emily stood. "Come on, Russell, let's go." Outside, in the bright sunshine, she said, "Calm yourself. At this point, it's harassment from we don't know who."

"I don't understand this kind of sick behavior."

"There are crazies out there," Emily said.

"I'm going to hire a detective."

When Russell left home with Tyler the following day, the sun had vanished, swallowed by a heavy bank of clouds. "When will this darn rain stop? The farmers must be going nuts," he said to Tyler on their way to school.

"Yeah." Opening his textbook, Tyler bent his head to read.

Teenagers, Russell thought. *They wish their parents would just shut up and go away. But look at him, he's growing into such a tall, good-looking young man. Amy would be so proud.*

Thinking of Amy triggered memories of a December day long ago, of rain unexpectedly turning to snow, of black ice, of the total sense of helplessness when his van had skidded off the road, barely missing a car already on its side in the ditch. Sitting unbuckled in the back seat, Tyler had pitched against the door and to the floor. At the hospital where they set Tyler's broken arm, Amy had never blamed him. Russell had blamed himself for not watching the road more carefully, for not driving more carefully, and for not buckling Tyler in.

At the school entrance, Tyler stuffed the textbook into his pack and hastened to join his friends, leaving Russell alone to drift back into painful memories of that horrific February day, a few months after his accident with Tyler, when a lousy, rotten drunk driver had plowed into his wife's car. In the snap of a finger, Amy was dead. Sadness weighed his spirit. Would it always be this way when he thought of Amy? He turned the car and headed for Bella's Park and Max's office.

• • •

Max welcomed Russell into his office and waved him to one of the leather chairs across from his desk, which was cluttered with architectural sketches, folders, and stacks of paper. "Coffee?"

Russell shook his head. "Just had breakfast. How are things going?"

Max smiled and sank into his leather chair. "Real good. Hannah and I should have gotten married a long time ago."

"Glad to hear it's turned out so well." Russell didn't want to talk about someone else's happy marriage.

Max waved toward the window. "Looks like we're in for another bout of lousy weather. It's holding up construction of the homesteads and other buildings, and Hannah's garden's taking a beating with all this rain."

"It's darn depressing. It's May already, for heaven's sake."

"Happens like that sometimes," Max said. "They're predicting that the rain will continue all night and fog, too. A dangerous combination." They were silent for a moment. "What can I do you for, Russell?"

Russell cleared his throat, then he told Max about the threats they had received. "In your experience, is this the way people do things around here?"

"I've never known anyone who had threats made against them. What Emily's up against, seems to me, is a powerful family with a lot of connections, and they're trying to scare her off. A lawsuit and court case is the last thing they want. And they want to distance themselves from that whole McCorkle clan. That bum Jerry McCorkle's locked up, and it looks like the law's finally gonna get him for murdering old Hilda years ago. Hopefully they'll throw the book at him. The Randalls don't want their name mixed up with Jerry's. Emily must know that. Why's she so hell-bent on going after Francine anyway?"

"Moral indignation, I think. When Emily gets her teeth into something, she won't let go—even now, when her family's threatened. She just gets madder and more determined on staying her course."

"That might not serve her well in the long run," Max said. "Especially now that she's got a family."

Emily was a study in contrasts. It had been a shock to Russell when Emily ignored holidays. She disliked them, in fact, and even the children's birthdays would pass unnoticed unless he planned for them.

Her father, Martin, had tried to explain. "Emily's mother, Ginger, hated holidays. She always forgot Emily's and my birthdays, and we celebrated Christmas and Thanksgiving dinner in a restaurant. But I'm to blame, as well. I never stepped in and made holidays for Emily, except for Halloween, when I got candy and she and I distributed it to kids at the door. Ginger would arrange to be out playing Scrabble. But the major holidays? Well, Emily never learned how to enjoy them. Maybe you can teach her."

Russell forced his mind away from his wife and his conversation with her father, and back to Max, who said, "Sometimes it's easier to bend than break. Who knows where this will end up, who will get hurt?" He shook his head.

"Are you suggesting that I try to persuade her to drop the case?" Russell asked.

"I wouldn't presume to suggest that," Max replied. "I don't have an answer for you, Russell. I wish I did."

When Emily walked in the door later that evening, the kids had eaten and Russell had tucked them in their beds. She shook her head at the pizza Russell had picked up on his way home and offered to reheat for her. "Just a cup of coffee, please. I've got a lot of work to do tonight."

Russell's mind raced. *Damn, she hasn't even asked about the kids, how they are, what their day was like, or mine. She could take a minute and run upstairs to check on Melissa, or ask about my day, hug me, even a kiss, perhaps.* He poured the coffee and handed her the mug.

Emily gave him a tired smile. "I have so much work, I can't think straight. I'm going to have to hire a legal assistant as soon as I can afford it."

"Hire someone now. I'll cover the cost," Russell said.

"You're a dear, Russell. I'll take you up on that." She kissed his cheek and hugged him, leaning into him for a long moment. Then she pulled away. "I'm so tired, but I've got a lot of work to catch up on. I'm so sorry, Russell." She walked to the den, turned and blew him a kiss, then she closed the door behind her.

Russell suppressed his loneliness. *Lord, but this is a far cry from what I anticipated when we married. After she hires help, it'll be better. She'll have more time for us.*

From upstairs came the thin wail of Melissa, awakened from sleep. Russell waited a moment, but Emily did not appear. *Maybe she can't hear Melissa.* Russell sighed as he climbed the stairs.

Russell switched on a light in Melissa's pink and violet bedroom. With outstretched arms, the child leaped into her father's arms, and they settled into the rocker near the window. Between hiccups, Melissa said, "I'm scared. A big cat was in my room, Daddy. I saw it." She burrowed her head into his chest.

"How big?" he asked, holding her close.

Her arms went wide. "This big, bigger than you, bigger than this house. It had claws, big claws like this." The little girl curled her fingers and pawed the air.

"Like this?" He copied her gestures. "It's gone now, honey."

"You chased it away, Daddy." She clung to him. "Stay with me."

"Sure."

"Stay a long, long time."

"A whole lot of time." He glanced at the window. "Look, honey, the clouds are gone. See the moon?"

They pressed their noses to the glass. Their breath clouded the panes. "Can we go out and see it better?" Melissa asked.

"It's late, honey. Too late."

"But Daddy, I wanna go out now. Now!" She pounded a fist on the windowsill.

The child was an angel and a vixen rolled into one. "Sorry, Melissa. Not tonight." He scooped her up, spun her around, and settled back in the rocker. "We'll sit and rock for a while, and I'll tell you a story."

Melissa's thumb slipped into her mouth. Her brown curls fell across her father's chest, and his chin rested lightly on the top of her head. Russell began to spin a tale.

Far, far away, in a castle way above the clouds, there lived an old man called George the snowflake maker. It was his job to shape each tiny snowflake. The old snowflake maker was very proud of the fact that no two snowflakes were alike. Not ever, not in all the years he had been making them, were any two snowflakes alike. George would hold each one up to the light, snip a bit here, tuck a bit there, until the flake was just right. And when he was done, he gave each snowflake a name: Calvin, Tommy, Lucy, Marili. He especially liked Marili, the way her points sparkled.

After a group of snowflakes were shaped and named, George sent them on to snowflake school. Old Jack Frost was their teacher and his son, Young Jack Frost, the assistant teacher. They taught the snowflakes important things like how to jump from the edge of a cloud, how to ride the wind, how to slow their drift to earth, and how to cluster together in silence as they reached the earth.

"Your job, little snowflakes," Old Jack Frost said, "is to bring peace into the hearts of men, women, and children on earth." He'd shake his frosty old head. "They

lead such busy lives, always running here and rushing there—hurry, hurry, hurry. That's why it's so important that you slide to earth slowly and in silence, for then you can fill the world with the most beautiful quiet and calm. This is a very important job. Remember that."

At last the day arrived when Merili's group of snowflakes lined up in a row at the edge of the cloud.

"Jump," said Old Jack Frost.

The snowflakes jumped over the edge of the cloud. Down, down, down they floated, holding out their little arms and banking into the wind to slow their descent.

"Where's Calvin?" Merili called. "I didn't see him jump. I don't see him anywhere."

"He must have jumped. He wouldn't just stand there." This came from a fat snowflake named Flinn, who liked to think of himself as a snowflake boss.

"Do you see him?" Merili asked.

She did not hear Flinn's reply, for the wind snatched her and whirled her around and around. She watched her friends drift down toward the earth while she was pulled up, up, up away from them. "Help me! Where are you, Flinn? Blanca? Clair?" she cried.

But no one answered.

The wind lifted Merili and tossed her high. All around and below her, snowflakes she did not know passed by her as they began their descent to earth. Some of them looked confused, some looked frightened, while others appeared to be as serene as angels.

Suddenly Merili noticed that the sky above her was deep blue. She was above the snow clouds. Struggling to reverse direction, she tipped her head and shoulders forward and spread out her arms to slow her ascent. But the wind was powerful and pulled her away from the other snowflakes and up, up, up.

What had Old Jack Frost taught them about being caught in a strong wind? Merili tried to remember.

"Don't be frightened. Be brave," he had said. "Don't waste your strength fighting Grandfather Wind. In time, he'll tire of playing with you. He'll go off to make mischief elsewhere, then you'll sink to earth. When you get there, your friends will be waiting."

Merili relaxed and let the wind transport her wherever he would.

Suddenly from below her came a voice she knew.

"Merili!" It was Calvin.

"Calvin, where are you?"

From behind, someone grabbed her hand, and there was Calvin. "Hold tight," he said.

Merili was no longer frightened, not even a little, for Calvin was a big snowflake and very smart. She grasped his hand and held tight, and together they let the wind carry them along.

"I wonder where Grandfather Wind is taking us?" Calvin asked.

"It doesn't seem that he's taking us anywhere," Merili said. "Just around and around, and higher and higher."

"That may not be so bad," said Calvin, who could turn the gloomiest situation into a happy adventure. "The higher we go, the colder it gets, and the stronger *we will become. We'll last longer once we do get to earth."*

Melissa's eyes had closed, and Russell tucked her into bed, then returned to the chair by the window. The pale moon slid behind dark clouds. Once again, Russell surrendered to memories of his life with Amy and Tyler.

He could have rocked Tyler and told him stories that sent him off to sleep, but he'd let Amy meet their son's every need, the way she'd met his needs. Tears welled in his eyes. Lord, but he missed Amy. He had fallen in love with her at first sight in their college cafeteria and never stopped loving her. When she died, he wanted to die. It was the strong firm presence of his father, who came up from Florida and stayed on in Covington, that had been his salvation.

"Pull yourself together," Bob had said. "You owe it to Amy to raise this boy of yours and to do it well."

"I owe it to Amy" had become Russell's mantra those first months as he dragged himself out of bed, prepared slipshod meals, washed the accumulated piles of laundry, and worked.

He shook himself now, forcing his mind back to the present. He had loved Emily when they married, but without the pure, clear passion he had felt for Amy, his first love. Did Emily sense that? Had he cheated her? Was that why she buried herself in work?

She had given up a lucrative law practice in Florida to marry him. Had it been worth it, from her point of view? There were times, too often perhaps, like tonight, when he was bitterly lonely in this marriage. Was she lonely, too? Could he have been more loving, more attentive? Would it have made any difference? Could a workaholic change, or was it an addiction like drinking or overeating?

Russell didn't have the answers to any of his questions, and went to bed feeling frustrated and unhappy.

While Russell sat with Melissa, Hannah lay in the crook of Max's arm in the big four-poster bed, and Max related Russell's visit. "He's very worried what might happen."

"I don't blame him. Emily's bullheaded. Who would have guessed? She seemed so sweet, so eager to marry and make a home for Russell and Tyler. It takes time to get to know a person. Thank heaven you're so good-natured." She tickled him and they laughed. "I am so lucky that you came into my life. I thank God often."

Hannah sat up. "Max, do you realize that for two people who planned to live in their own houses, we're together an awful lot? I sleep over here four, sometimes five nights a week."

He smiled. "Want to make it seven?"

"I'd like to talk about this, if you don't mind," Hannah said.

Max pushed himself up and settled back against the headboard. "What's on your mind? Out with it, woman."

"When Grace, Amelia, and I came here we felt as if we were alone in the world, and we clung to one another for friendship, comfort, and support. Grace could have moved in with Bob, she could have married him. We all know how he's nagged her to do so. Most women of our generation want to be married. Most of them wouldn't understand the arrangement Grace and Bob have. Bob had a difficult time for a long while, because Grace has insisted that she live at home with Amelia and me."

"You're feeling guilty being over here so much, aren't you?"

"I expected that we'd go on working together, visiting now and then, but that essentially I'd be home at night with my friends. I'm conflicted. I never in my wildest imaginings . . ."

Max stroked her arm again. "And what would those wild imaginings be?"

"I'm serious, Max."

He withdrew his hand. "Of course you are. I'm sorry."

"Don't be sorry. I love you to touch me. When you do, I feel seventeen and utterly alive. But I . . . miss Grace and Amelia." She laughed. "I remind myself of a little girl who goes to spend the night with friends or even her beloved grandma, and in the middle of the night she wants to go home."

Hannah also felt jealous of the increasing intimacy developing between Amelia and Grace. She felt left out and missed her special alone times with Grace.

Outside, the wind rose and the old windowpanes rattled. Hannah snuggled close to Max. Before their honeymoon, he had purchased a large new bed and moved from the room he had shared with Bella to another of the rooms facing Cove Road.

"Would you mind if sometimes I went home after we . . . you know?"

"Sweetheart, you do whatever you'd like. You and your girlfriends are a bunch of odd ducks. In some ways, you're all quite traditional with your appreciation of family, the holidays, things like that. Then there's this loyalty and attachment you have for each other that's quite rare and precious. I wouldn't want to see anything damage that. I'm here. You're just across the street. It's okay."

"You really mean that, you horny old man?" She leaned against him and turned her face to his.

He kissed her. "I really mean it, my love. To be an obstacle to your friendships would be like trying to drive a wedge between a mother and her child. It would bode no good."

Hannah snuggled against him. "You and Bob hooked up with a strange bunch of broads. I think you're both terrific."

Later that night, Max awakened thinking about Russell and Emily. Perhaps he ought to talk to Emily, explain how things were in these mountains, and remind her that Jerry McCorkle would undoubtedly be going to prison or be executed, regardless of whether she pursued this matter with Francine. How important could "getting" Francine Randall, the school principal, be? Lord only knew what could happen to her family if she persisted with this case.

17
RECONNECTING

After his longtime partner Charles died, Roger, Grace's son, bought land and began to build a house in Salem, South Carolina. During those months, Grace had had few opportunities to visit. Now, he was spending a few days with her.

"Come sit awhile with me," she said the evening after his arrival, after Bob had gone home and Amelia retired to her room. "I'd like to hear more about your house and what you're doing in Salem." Grace led him into the living room. "Here." She pushed the hassock in front of the armchair by the fireplace. "Put your feet up and be comfortable."

Roger removed his shoes, sank into the chair, and lifted his feet onto the hassock. "Dinner was great, as usual," he said. "Thanks for going to the trouble."

"It was no trouble at all. Now, tell me about your new life. Have you been to Clemson University yet? Do they have the courses you wanted to take?"

"As a matter of fact, I have, and yes, they have astronomy, but I decided on horticulture instead. If I'm going to grow my own food, I need to know what I'm doing."

"That's a splendid idea. Is it a long drive to Clemson?"

"About thirty-five or forty minutes. I take the back route along Lake Keowee for part of the drive, which is always pleasant. By the way, I had the bank of the river cleared and plans drawn for that deck you wanted."

"Oh, Roger. How nice. You'll enjoy it, I know you will."

"You know, Mother, this is the first time I've lived alone since I left home at eighteen to go to the university. I had roommates there, and then I met Charles, one of my professors at the university. When he died, along with the pain of losing him, I felt the fear of living alone, of eating alone, and waking up in an empty house. I'm sure that's why I plunged into a relationship with Mike. I'm sorry about that—sorry that I hurt him. It was selfish of me."

Grace agreed with him. He had been selfish, and there was plenty she'd have liked to say about his lack of consideration for her over the years, but she held her peace. Instead she said, "You'll explain to Mike one day. And you know you're welcome here anytime. You don't have to live alone on your land in an RV while the house is being built."

"I may take you up on your offer. I'd like to spend some time with you. I'd like to get to know Max and Bob better, and yes, apologize to Mike. In a couple of weeks I've got to make a shopping trip to select kitchen and bathroom fixtures. I'll come here rather than go to Greenville, if that's okay with you."

"Of course it's all right. We have the guest room, and I'd love to have you."

Roger yawned and stretched his long arms above his head. "It's been a great evening. Terrific food. Good company. Thanks for asking me up for a visit. I'd better go to bed now, or I'll fall asleep in this chair."

Grace felt disappointed. But what was it that she wanted to say to him, or hear from him? After years of no communication, they couldn't catch up on each other's lives, ideas, or goals in one short evening. "I'm ready for bed, too," she said.

Spring nights in the mountains were deliciously cool, and Grace pulled her soft fleece blanket, a gift from Bob, up to her chin. Her body relaxed into the comfort of her bed. The last few days had been sunny and relaxed, and dinner had gone well tonight. The growing friendship between Roger and Bob pleased her. Roger amazed her. She'd never imagined that he had ever been lonely or afraid. He'd always appeared so confident. Charles had clearly been his rock and his anchor.

So why had he chosen a small rural area like Salem, South Carolina? And if he must live in that area, why had he not bought a house in Walhalla, where there were people around and lights at night? *Nothing's ever fixed in stone. One can buy or build a house, change one's mind about the house or the area, and sell it or rent it. All I want is that Roger be happy.* "Oh, God," she whispered into the darkness. "Please help my son find contentment."

18

THE ICE STORM

"This shouldn't be happening folks. A snowstorm in early May." The weatherman sounded shocked as he pointed to the mass of gray hunkering over Tennessee and heading their way. "We're in for a big one—it could dump a foot of snow on us before it's over. Some of us could lose power if the lines come down under the weight of snow or ice."

Lurina Masterson snapped off her small TV. Going to the window of her living room, she shaded her eyes from the glare of snow, already several inches thick on her field, the road, her shrubs and trees and the bird-feeder. This was no winter wonderland to her. With a storm like this the electricity would surely go off, and the gas fireplace Grace had insisted that she install in this room wouldn't be sufficient to keep her warm.

Grace, bless her heart, had begged her to stay with them, had offered to drive over and bring her to the ladies' farmhouse. "They're calling for heavy snow, Lurina, can you believe that? Maybe even ice."

"Happens like this once in a while," Lurina had replied. "Happened one time when I was about twenty-two, no, twenty-four years old. Ma was sick and old Doc James couldn't get through. The roads were dirt then, and we hadn't got no snowplow. We just stayed put and waited for it to melt off some. Pa and me took turns sitting with Ma all night, putting cool cloths on her head to try to break her fever. And all the time, the snow just kept a-coming. The electric pole came down, and we was in the dark and cold. We dragged quilts from trunks and piled them atop of Ma. Finally we climbed into bed with her so's we could all three of us stay warm." She shuddered, remembering. "Haven't given that a thought in years."

"The roads will freeze, everything will. Trees could come down, and the lights could go off," Grace said. "I'll come get you."

Lurina had hesitated. "I got me a fireplace."

"True. But there's no way to close off your living room, and the hot air will go right up the stairs. Over here, we can shut doors and keep at least one room nice and warm. And you won't be alone," Grace had replied.

"I'll be a-callin' you if I change my mind," Lurina said. "How bad can it be this time of year?"

She had made a mistake. On the television, the weatherman grew increasingly serious. "Its coming down heavy; gonna ice over. It's worse the farther north you are: there's more snow in North Buncombe County and Madison County than in Henderson County." He shook his head and waved his hand over patches of pink and white that indicated the heaviest snowfall on the map. "It's a regular winter storm. If you don't have an emergency, stay off the roads." Then he went on about jet streams, and a Canadian clipper coming south to dump snow on places that never got snow this time of year, and Lurina had turned him off.

When the snow started at three in the afternoon, it

tumbled with precipitous haste from ominous, thickly compacted clouds. It reminded Lurina of a time she had made potato chips by shaving potatoes with a potato peeler. The thin slices had clumped in a mound in the bowl, one on top of the other, much like this snowfall. In the first twenty minutes, the ground had turned totally white. She couldn't see the mailbox, now, and the old stump in the front yard was barely visible. Lurina sighed. What was done was done. But she could at least throw rock salt on the porch steps, in case anyone did come looking for her.

Lurina tugged on her down jacket and shoved her feet into warm boots. Then she lugged the bag of rock salt from under the kitchen sink and dragged it across the living room carpet and out onto the porch. Bitter cold stung her face and gnashed at her cheeks and nose. It was an effort to breathe. Lurina tugged at the string that sealed the bag of rock salt, then tugged again. "Dang thing's sure hard to open," she muttered. "Gotta get me a pair of scissors."

Inside, Lurina could not remember where she had put the scissors, or where she had stored the sewing box. Well, a knife from the kitchen drawer would do just as well. It was hot in the kitchen, and Lurina removed her scarf and down jacket and slung them over the back of a chair. Breathing hard from worry and exertion, she sat for a time and rubbed her temples. Where *was* that darned sewing box?

It was a large box, and she remembered her step-grandson, Wayne, carrying it downstairs the day he and his friends moved her bedroom furniture into what used to be the dining room. Where had Wayne rested that sewing box?

Joseph Elisha would know. He liked to sit and sew on buttons. "Soon's he gets in from tendin' his pigs, I'll get him to open that bag and spread that rock salt," she muttered, forgetting that her husband was dead.

For years she had lived right good without a man around, but once they'd married, Joseph Elisha had taken up the chores she hated: taking out garbage, clearing snow, and even hanging out clothes to please her, for she liked the smell of fresh air on sheets and pillowcases.

Why's he so long getting back in from those pigs? Lurina shuffled over to the kitchen window, from where she could see the backyard and the pigs huddled in a corner of their pen.

"Lordy, lord," she muttered. "He ain't moved 'em to the barn." She opened the kitchen door and stuck her head out. "Joseph Elisha," she called several times. Then, unmindful that she wore no coat, hat, or scarf, she stepped out onto the porch.

Layers of sparkling ice glazed the straw-colored pampas grass that grew along the rear of the house. At the edge of the woods snow bowed the branches of trees, and several large limbs had split and toppled under the strain of the ice. The snow lay thick, and not a single footprint marred its surface. The barn door was closed, and the wooden bar that served as a lock sat firmly in place.

"Joseph Elisha," she called again.

The pigs disengaged from their cluster and shuffled toward the sound of her voice. Without her jacket, the cold pierced her clothing and burrowed through to her breastbone. Her cheeks burned. She must get back inside. In the warmth of the kitchen she could think more clearly, figure out what to do.

Lurina grasped the handle of the kitchen door. It was cold as ice and refused to budge. She tugged and twisted it to no avail. "I done locked myself out," she said. "Gonna have to go around the front."

She grasped the snowy handrail and eased down the steps into snow that reached nearly to the top of her boots. Where was Joseph Elisha? Had he gone to the store to chat with his cronies? Surely not on a day like this. Had he gone to the market for bread or milk? There wasn't any milk in the refrigerator, if she remembered right.

"It's sure hard to walk in this mess," she said, holding her arms out wide for balance.

A few more steps and she would round the corner of the house. Hunched over with cold, her hands tucked under her armpits now, Lurina trudged on, each step in the heavy snow tiring her more. The snow, falling in large, flat flakes, lowered the visibility to nearly zero.

"Just a bit more," Lurina muttered. "Gotta keep movin' or I'll turn into a pillar of ice." Her shoulder struck something hard, knocking her off balance, but the snow cushioned her fall. It was pleasant to lie in this snug bed with its soft white walls, but instinct warned her of danger. "Gotta get me up."

When she tried to rise, though, there was nothing firm to push against, and she lay back, exhausted. The wall of the farmhouse loomed above her; snow dusted her face, and Lurina brushed the white powder from her cheeks and eyes. She'd best turn over and crawl.

Then she heard his voice: "Lurina." He had come. Joseph Elisha kneeled and smiled at her. He offered his hand to help her to her feet. Lurina smiled up at him, put her hand in his, and closed her eyes as light filled the space around them and a great peace settled over her.

West of Asheville in Haywood County, Wayne had awakened to a silent, white world that was both beautiful and treacherous. He'd been so busy studying that he hadn't heard a weather report in days, and he'd taken his roommate's report that a storm was coming as a joke.

Immediately he thought of Lurina. Surely she was at the ladies' farmhouse. But a phone call from Grace informed him that Lurina had refused to leave her home, and Grace urged Wayne to go to her. Wayne did not hesitate. He dressed warmly, threw a blanket, a thermos of hot coffee, insulated knee-high boots, and his cell phone into his truck, and started for Covington.

Even driving slowly through the mess of snow, slush, and ice was treacherous. None of the secondary roads had been salted, and the glare off the snow and the ice dangling from tree limbs and power lines made it even harder. His fingers and back ached from the tension of gripping the wheel and driving defensively.

Especially dangerous were the deceptive patches of black ice, which looked like dry road. Wayne's heart thudded in his chest as he skidded and barely missed hitting a truck. The forty-five-minute ride became a two-hour nightmare. When he finally reached Elk Road, Wayne maneuvered his truck onto the bridge across Bad River. Below, the river gushed over snow-capped rocks and snow lathered the banks, while the sky was a roof of white snow. Then the slippery wooden planks gave way to snow, and he crossed the pasture to the farmhouse.

Caps of white covered the roofs of the house and barn. Snow clung along the branches of dogwood trees and formed deep pockets in the crotches of their limbs. On either side of the driveway, spikes of perennials poked green blades from the blanket of white. Wayne shivered. He recalled a bitter cold and icy day years ago when the electric line into his grandfather's property had crashed beneath the weight of falling tree limbs, and the lights and heat had gone out. Their stockpile of wood had not outlasted the cold, and when the repair truck crested the hill four days later, he and Old Man, chilled to the bone, stood knee deep in the snow waving blue towels and cheering until they had no voices left.

The light in the living-room window drew him to Lurina's farmhouse, and Wayne could almost taste hot chocolate, could almost feel his hands and feet warming in the glow of the fireplace. Clutching the hand railing, testing each icy step before placing his full weight on it, Wayne mounted the slippery front porch steps. "This is one hell of a storm," he muttered. "Feels like the world's coming to an end."

The unopened package of rock salt near the open front door set alarm bells ringing in his mind.

"Miss Lurina?" Wayne made his way into the kitchen. There was her jacket hanging over the back of a chair. He searched for her in her bedroom, the bathroom, and upstairs. Where was she? The agitated snorting of the pigs, loud in the snowy silence, drew him out onto the back porch. Under the still falling snow Lurina's footprints were barely visible. Wayne's heart pounded as he followed her footsteps along the house.

Lurina lay peacefully in a bed of snow, covered by a thin blanket of white. Her eyes were closed. Alarmed, he gently brushed the snow from her face and called her name, again and again. She smiled, and when he took her hands to lift her, the slight grasp of her fingers assured him she was still alive. Wayne scooped up her small limp body, carried Lurina to his truck and, knowing he could never make it to the hospital in Asheville, headed for the ladies' house.

Grace met him at the door. "My God, Wayne, what happened?"

"I found her outside lying in the snow. Another half hour and I'd have been too late."

Grace issued orders. "Take her to the guest room, Wayne. Amelia, get her wet things off and cover her with the blankets from the chest at the foot of the bed. I'll call nine-one-one."

They dressed Lurina in a flannel nightgown that Grace had warmed in the dryer. Spoon by spoon, Lurina managed to sip half a cup of freshly made chicken soup before drifting into sleep again. When the medics arrived, they bundled her warmly and transported her to the ambulance.

"Will she be all right?" Wayne asked the medic, a friend from high school.

"We hope so. Looks like you got to her just in time."

"I'll follow you to the hospital," Wayne said.

"Better not. The roads are terrible, and when we get there they'll rush her off for treatment, and you won't get to see her for hours. Why not wait till tomorrow?"

"Her doctor is Dr. James Findley," Grace told the other medic, who asked questions and made notes. "If she wakes up, tell her that Grace will be there to see her soon."

At Grace's insistence Wayne stayed the night with them, and in the morning he drove Grace to the hospital in Asheville.

When they entered her room, Lurina extended her thin arms in greeting. She looked tired, but happy to see them. "I went out to look after the pigs. The door locked on me. I was trying to get around to the front door. What happened?"

"You must have fallen," Wayne said. "I found you lying in the snow."

"I saw Joseph Elisha. He said he'd come for me. I was sure surprised when I opened my eyes this morning and found myself here. Well, I'm okay now. Let's go home. I don't like no hospital."

"The doctor needs to discharge you; then you'll come home with me," Grace said. "You'll stay with us until you're stronger."

Lurina thought about it, then nodded. "The minute it warms up, you gotta take me to Reynolds Cemetery to see Joseph Elisha. I gotta explain to him why I couldn't go with him, how his own grandson stopped me from going." She gave Wayne a reproachful look. "Dead ain't so bad, you know. I saw a light, and it was all peaceful, and Joseph Elisha was right there waiting for me. I could go any time, and it would be all right."

Several days later, when sunshine melted the snow from all but the northernmost slopes, Wayne carried a frail Lurina up the hillside and set her down beside the grave of her husband. She shooed him and Grace away. "Now, you two just get you over there a bit, so's I can talk to him private like."

They waited by the gate to the cemetery. "What will you do when you graduate, Wayne?" Grace asked.

"I'll have my associate's degree in horticulture. Miss Hannah says her foreman is leaving and she's offered me his job when I graduate."

146

"What a grand idea. And the girl you were going out with?"

"Maureen? She's gone back up north to her family."

"I'm sorry."

"It's okay. I guess, truth was, we didn't have much in common anyway."

"I hope you meet a nice girl, someone from around here."

Wayne nodded. "I still got Old Man's land." He gazed at the valley below. "I don't come up here much these days. Dunno what I'm gonna do with it, being as the cemetery's here and all."

"Hold on to land. They say if you take care of land and property, it will take care of you. I believe that. Hold on to it, if you can."

Leaning on the tombstone, Lurina brushed a bit of remaining snow from the top of it.

"Joseph Elisha. I miss you a lot, and I been afeared of dying. You came to tell me there ain't nothing to be afeared of, that when the time comes, you gonna be there taking my hand, and we gonna walk off into gloryland together. It weren't my time to go yet. Only the good Lord knows when that time will be. Grace and Wayne done brung me up here. Wayne's a good boy—you can be right proud of him." She looked about her. "Grace, Wayne. Let's get a-going."

Wayne came over and swooped Lurina into his arms. As they descended the hill, Wayne said to Grace, "I've been thinking about how much has happened to me since you ladies moved to Covington. Knowing you all, and especially Miss Hannah, has changed my life. I have direction now, and you all done so much for Miss Lurina and my grandpa."

"That's what it's all about, Wayne. We do our best for those close to us," Grace replied.

19
LURINA MOVES TO MARS HILL

When Wayne kissed Lurina good-bye, she clung to him. "Boy, you done saved my life. Your grandpa would be right proud of you." She stepped back. "Off with you, now, and take care."

Then Lurina asked Grace to come in the guest bedroom and talk with her.

"Grace. I don't think I can live alone no longer."

"You can live here with us."

Lurina shook her head. "I been hearing about a right nice retirement place in Mars Hill, and that ain't far from you. Cookin's hard for me. The other day I left fire on the stove and burned the peas. Done that more than once, Grace. One time I fell asleep, and the house got so full of smoke, I thought it was on fire. Some days, I don't remember if I fed the pigs or not. The other day I got ready to go to church and sat there waiting for Pa to call me. Now, Grace, what does that tell you? A person's got to show some good sense and make decisions before someone else makes 'em for you.

"What I want you to do for me is to go over to Mars

Hill Retirement Community and talk to 'em, see what it'll cost me to live there. They'll feed me three meals a day in a dining room with round tables, and people are right friendly, I hear. I get mighty lonely at nights in that big old house."

She was right, of course, and yet Grace hated to see her move. "What about the house, Lurina?"

"Time to let it go. But before I do . . ."—she tapped her forehead—"Might be money in that old metal box Pa buried under the kitchen floor, too. You gotta help me dig that out, Grace, and count what's there, see what I got. Then, after I get me settled over there, you'll call the government and tell them they can have the place, so long as they don't tear it down while I'm living."

Grace didn't move or speak. Money hidden under the kitchen floor? Lurina hadn't said a word about that, or about burning her food, or forgetting things.

"You hear me, Grace?" Lurina shook her arm. "You okay? Don't look so shocked. A woman my age ought to be thinking about retiring, don't you think?"

Grace nodded. She knew that her old friend was right. For a while now, she'd worried about Lurina living alone.

"I'll go," she said. "I'll talk to them. Then, if you still want to do this, we'll go look at the apartments together."

"We got to dig up the box Pa hid," Lurina said.

If there was a box, Grace had no high hopes that it contained money, and the retirement home could cost Lurina $2000 to $3000 a month.

When Grace parked her car in the lot behind the retirement community several days later, she was greeted by a gracious and attractive young woman who introduced herself as Teresa. As they walked past the beauty parlor, the craft room, and exercise room, Grace wondered what Lurina would do with any of this. Still, having twenty-four-hour medical services available at the push of a button was a huge plus, and the dining room was attractive, as were the apartments with their large windows.

Grace shared lunch with Teresa and took the week's menu back to Lurina. Dinner included such items as fried okra, cream of potato soup, beef and cabbage soup, turkey with dressing, spaghetti and meat sauce, seafood platter, as well as a large variety of vegetables and desserts.

"I'm gonna like the food there," Lurina said.

"There's a box buried under Lurina's kitchen floor?" Max asked. "I don't believe it. How come she's never mentioned it to you before, Grace?"

Grace shrugged. "I don't know, but I promised we'd dig it up. Please come along; what's to lose? And you never know."

"I'm game," Bob said. "I'll need your help, Max."

"A couple of picks and shovels, and we'll know in no time. We'll cheer you on," Hannah said.

And a date was made for Saturday.

Lurina sat in the kitchen, her fingers gripping the

arms of the chair, her face flushed with excitement. "I watched Pa bury it. He wouldn't tell me what all he'd got buried in there. I used to think about it a lot, then I forgot about it. It was close to where the fridge is. When he planted it, he marked the place."

"What did he mark it with?" Bob asked.

Her eyes clouded. "I can't rightly remember."

The digging continued until half the floorboards had been removed, and the dank smell of soil, which had not seen the light of day or air for a long time, caused them all to sneeze.

"What a minute. What's that?" Bob asked. He leaned forward and cast his flashlight along a line in the earth. "It looks like beads."

Lurina jumped from her chair. "Beads! Yes, bright, shiny beads. Pa said anyone with a good flashlight wouldn't miss them. That there box is right below the beads."

The shovel clunked against metal. "I hit it. I can see it," Bob said.

Lurina could hardly contain her excitement as Bob and Max tugged and heaved and finally brought the box up onto the kitchen floor. Grace brought a broom and swept the dirt up as the men pried open the lock and lifted the lid.

"Come look inside, Lurina," Max said.

Lurina leaned over, reached in and removed a small box, which contained a safe-deposit-box key, an envelope wrapped in plastic with the name of a bank on it, and an envelope with the safe-deposit-box number. The bank had changed ownership several times, and Max asked who had paid the box rental for all these years.

"I paid it." Lurina clapped her hands. "Pa left me cash in the house, and told me every year on February the ninth to get me over there and pay for the box, and I done it faithfully. Grace, you took me a couple of times."

Grace recalled driving Lurina to a bank and waiting in the car while she went inside. It all seemed unreal, like a story.

But there was more inside the large box. They gasped when Bob removed a long box that contained bundles of hundred-dollar bills, and another box that held World War Two savings bonds, long matured and worth many thousands of dollars.

"Grace, I was gonna leave you a letter about this box and saying it was all yours when I was gone. Whatever's left when I pass is yours."

"Oh, no, Lurina," Grace said.

"Ain't no 'no' about this. You been a daughter to me."

"I think we better get over to the bank, see what's in the safety-deposit box, and open an account in Lurina's and your name, Grace," Bob said.

Lurina Masterson proved to be a very rich woman, with liquid assets totaling over two hundred thousand dollars, and within a month she was ensconced in a bright, cheerful studio apartment at Mars Hill Retirement Community.

"I don't need me no kitchen," she had declared. "With

all this community space to wander about in, all I need is a place to rest, watch TV, and sleep. And it's a relief that I don't got to feed those pigs no more. I did it for Joseph Elisha, and I loved them, but they're gonna be fine with the farmer Wayne found. He loves pigs like Joseph Elisha did and he'll see they don't go to the market for pork chops."

She sat on the bed in her new quarters. "I don't need to worry about cleaning nothing here, and my bed gets made up for me. It was getting hard to bend to make it up at home. These last months, I just throwed a blanket over me on the couch."

Grace realized how much her old friend had gone downhill since Old Man passed away. Lurina had done the right thing to move to Mars Hill Retirement Community.

Within weeks, the deed to the Masterson farmhouse was transferred to the Department of Parks, and the old house sat dark and empty. Then, a heavy chain appeared across the entrance road and a large NO TRESPASSING sign. Vandals smashed the windows, broke open the front door, and left behind beer cans, fast food wrappers and cups, and discarded condoms. Grace felt violated, as if they had desecrated her home instead of Lurina's. They tried to keep this information from Lurina, but gradually news filtered to her.

"You got to call those government people, Grace, and tell them what's happening to my house."

Grace phoned the park service, and was put on hold for so long that she hung up.

"Maybe they're short staffed," Hannah said.

Grace fumed and tried again, but all that day and the next, she never got through.

20
UPPING THE ANTE

One morning Grace awoke to the rumble of heavy machinery. Immediately, she knew what it was for. Yanking on her coat, she rushed outside to her car and headed for Elk Road. Parked on the side of the road, she watched Lurina's old house strain at its seams, split into smithereens, and collapse under the force of the wrecking ball.

"I swear I heard it sigh as it went down. A long, low, mournful sigh," she told Amelia later.

That week, bold headlines in the Madison County Sentinel read: MASTERSON HOMESTEAD FLATTENED.

Lurina cried as if her heart would break, and Grace took the matter to Emily.

"It was wrong to take such drastic action," Grace said. "I saw Lurina sign a contract with them that said that they would not remove the house until her death. They weren't even supposed to get that property until she died. She did them a favor giving it to them now, and that was the condition, the only condition."

"I'll make some calls to see what I can do, but it seems to me the damage is done," Emily said.

Grace raved and ranted.

"Leave it be," Amelia said at breakfast the next morning. "What's done is done."

Grace sighed. "You're right. But they shouldn't have done that." Grace stirred the pancake batter so hard, some of it flew from the bowl onto the burners of the stove. "I've been feeling weepy ever since Lurina moved." Grace flipped a pancake on the griddle.

Amelia passed her a plate. "You make the best pancakes, Grace. Where's Hannah? I thought she planned on being here more often, but she didn't come home last night."

"She does stay at Max's a lot."

Amelia's fork paused in midair. "I'm getting used to not having her around. It's kind of nice, just you and me here."

"Don't say that, Amelia. We've defied the odds, three women being able to live together all these years. We've worked out all kinds of problems as they've come up." Grace wiped her hands on her apron and took the chair across from Amelia.

"True, but I see more of you now, and we talk more. I like it this way. Are you saying you don't?"

"No, that's not what I'm saying. I like it both ways. You and I have gotten closer, and I value that, but I also miss Hannah." Grace studied Amelia, whose sapphire eyes seemed to be challenging her. Their Caribbean cruise last winter and afterward had been tense with arguments between Hannah and Amelia. It had gotten so bad that Amelia had told Grace that she might move out, when she returned from a trip to Maine.

Though Amelia and Hannah had reconciled their differences, Amelia was saying she liked it better with Hannah out of the house.

Grace changed the subject. "How are the Inman women doing since you convinced them to leave their place by the river?"

"They've made contact with FEMA and filled out applications," Amelia said. "They're in a mobile home and the kids are with them. The father's still working in Hendersonville, but he gets up to see them some weekends. FEMA tried to convince them to relocate to Hendersonville, but they're hell-bent on rebuilding on Old Bunkie Creek."

Amelia gave an annoyed snort. "There ought to be a law: no government funds or low-cost loans for people in flood zones who don't relocate. The floods will come and just wipe them out again."

"Like they pass laws to stop rich people from rebuilding on the sand dunes on barrier islands after a hurricane?"

Amelia pushed back her chair. "This started off as a pleasant morning. It's turning into a political harangue. I'm going over to Mike's." She left the kitchen. The front door slammed and moments later Amelia's van started up.

Grace sat at the table, staring at nothing. Then she put away the remainder of the batter. From the window she could see Bob's cottage. He was a late riser. She'd wait a while, then take the batter over and treat him to a pancake breakfast.

The house was quiet and a trifle cool. Grace went into the living room, flipped the switch on the gas fireplace, then sat and stretched her feet toward its warmth. Her mind wandered to Emily and Russell. They seemed distant from each other—the last time she had seen them they hardly addressed each other when they spoke, rarely looking at each other.

And Melissa! Emily never disciplined the child, and wily Melissa wound her father around her little finger. Grace thought about that day when Melissa tore Tyler's history paper, and how angry she'd been with Bob for banishing the little girl to her room.

Her mind drifted back through time. She remembered her remarkable experience on the balcony of their cabin when they'd taken their Caribbean cruise. She had felt at one with all things, with the universe, but she had never been able to share it with anyone. It had had a powerful effect on her. She was more tolerant of things and people, and she no longer feared dying as she once had. That was a blessing.

She thought about how in high school she'd wanted a car, and had gotten one when she graduated. She was engaged to Ted then, and it served as a wedding present from her parents. Her eyes misted, thinking of her several miscarriages, and she smiled remembering Roger's birth. Ted's death from cancer had devastated her, unleashing fears of being alone and financial concerns. She'd been very angry when Roger insisted she move to Branston, miles and miles from home, but without that move, she'd never have met Amelia and Hannah and moved with them to Covington. She never would have met Bob.

The clock on the mantel struck nine, rousing Grace from her reverie. Bob must be up and about by now. Taking the pancake batter from the fridge, Grace walked across the lawn to his cottage.

Bob held the door wide for her. "I'm glad you're here, honey."

"You look upset. What's happened?"

"Emily's gotten another threat. This time it's a banner hung over their front porch railing."

"What did it say?"

"It said, 'I've warned you. Drop the case, or else.' None of the neighbors saw anyone in the street. The babysitter saw nothing, and it wasn't there when Russell left the house this morning."

"I am really frightened for them."

"So am I."

Bob followed Grace into the kitchen, where she set about making pancakes.

"They went to the cops, who said they have to catch the perpetrator in the act," Bob said. "I feel utterly frustrated and angry. Russell's family needs protection, and they aren't getting it."

"Could it be the work of a prankster?" Grace asked.

"I doubt it. If it were just one time, yes, but this harassment is ongoing." Bob started in on his pancakes. "I suggested we bring the kids over here until this thing is solved. But Emily said she wasn't about to let anyone chase her or her family from their home."

"Not very caring of the kids, is it?" Grace asked.

Bob shrugged. "I guess maybe she feels it's not the kids who are being threatened."

"What if they break in, maybe have a gun, and the kids are there?"

"They're having an alarm system installed today, and Russell has a gun."

"He knows how to use a gun?" Grace was surprised.

"Certainly." Bob patted her hand. "Don't you worry. Russell is well trained by me."

The idea of a gun in the house with children sent shivers down her spine.

They moved into the living room, and Grace removed her shoes and stretched out her legs on the sofa. "I'd feel much better if the kids were here with us."

"What can we do? Emily nixed it."

"For an educated woman, she certainly can be thick-headed," Grace said.

"I get the sense that Russell feels that way, too. I sense a coldness between them." Bob waved a hand. "Forget I said that. Maybe she's having a hard time adjusting to living here, what with starting her practice over again, and now these threats."

Grace half sat up. "What are you thinking? The marriage is in trouble?"

"I certainly hope not. I think Russell would work darned hard to see that that didn't happen. But Emily's so absorbed in her work." He brought his fist down hard on the end of the recliner. "She's got a family, a beautiful little girl. We all love her. Yet she seems unhappy. Have you noticed that she hardly smiles anymore?"

"Yes, you're right. She does seem overly serious, and doesn't appear to enjoy the kids. They seem to annoy her."

"Maybe if she spent more time with Melissa, the child wouldn't be such a handful." Bob rubbed his chin. "Martin says Ginger didn't want children. He talked her into one with the promise that he and a housekeeper would raise Emily."

"What must that have been like for Emily?"

Bob did not reply.

Grace said, "I'm so worried about these threats. If Francine Randall is behind this, she must know she'd be the main suspect if anything happens to Emily or her family. She couldn't risk letting anyone hurt them, could she?"

"I hope you're right, Grace. I hope you're right."

21
A FINAL WARNING

At two A.M., when the phone rang in Russell and Emily's bedroom, Russell snatched it up and heard a muffled voice say, "Check your garage. Fast!" A high-pitched laugh followed, and the caller slammed the phone down.

Russell bolted from bed and dashed downstairs. When he reached the kitchen, he smelled smoke. The garage was awash in smoke. Russell reached for the kitchen phone and dialed 911. Moments later Emily stood beside him, her hair tousled, her blue eyes wide, her skin pale as milk. She sniffed the air and shivered.

"Someone's set a fire in the garage. I've called nine-one-one. They're on their way." Russell put his arms about her, but Emily pulled away, sank into a chair, and covered her mouth with her hands as if to stifle a scream.

Bob stuffed wet kitchen towels along the bottom of the kitchen door. "This'll keep the smoke out of the house for now. Go on up and get the kids, Emily. I didn't see flames and the fire engines will be here soon, but we'll be safer outside. God knows what's been set on fire or how fast it'll spread."

Emily left and was back with the children just as sirens and the flashing lights of fire engines, police cars, and an ambulance rounded the corner of their street.

Tyler carried a crying Melissa, holding her tight. Russell took her from Tyler and held her close, whispering, "It's all right, honey. Look at the police car." He pointed to the police car with its light whirling round and round. They watched the firemen pull yards of hose from the fire engine and head for the garage. "Everything's going to be fine," Russell said, hoping.

When the firemen flung open the garage door, swirls of gray smoke enveloped them, and they stepped back. Moments later, water streamed from hoses and ran down the driveway. It was over in five minutes, for the fire had been set in a bundle of old blankets in one corner and hadn't spread.

"It was meant to be a slow burn," a policeman said.

Russell handed a protesting Melissa to her mother, who handed her to Tyler. The little girl clung to him. Russell explained, "We had a phone call from someone who said we should check the garage." He recounted the other threats that the family had received.

Across the street, lights in houses had come on. Faces peered from windows and bundled in bathrobes, people huddled in doorways, to see what was happening.

Dick Felder, whose house was directly across from theirs, strode over and listened while Russell talked to the police and firemen. "You all okay? A terrible fright for the children."

"For us all," Russell said.

Dick said, "If Emily's going to take that woman to court, she should do it soon and get it over with. That'll call their bluff."

"Their bluff? A fire's bluffing?" Russell asked, both hands going to his head.

"He's got a point," the fireman said. "Maybe whoever's behind this is trying to bully your wife out of taking that principal and the school district to court. If they'd wanted to torch the house, they'd have poured gasoline on that stuff and they'd never have called you."

The firemen rolled up their hoses and prepared to leave. Still shaking, Russell shook hands with them and the policeman and thanked them all. Then he said good night to Dick Felder and took his family inside.

"I'm scared, Daddy. I wanna sleep with you and Mommy," Melissa said.

"You move around and kick too much. I can't sleep with you in the bed," Emily said. She reached for Melissa's hand. "Now, be a good girl. Come, I'll tuck you in."

Russell watched them ascend the stairs.

But Melissa was not to be put off, and the moment her parents' door closed, she slipped out of bed and scampered to Tyler's room, where she stood alongside his bed staring down at him.

Tyler opened his eyes, unsurprised to see her. "What's the matter, Melissa?"

"I'm scared, Tyler." Her voice sounded genuinely tearful. "Can I sleep with you?"

"My bed's too small for both of us."

Tears spilled from her eyes. She was a pest, and she used tears to get what she wanted, but seeing the fear in her eyes, Tyler felt his heart stir. "Tell you what. Let's get your pillows, a blanket, and your bedspread. We'll make you up a bed right here on the floor next to mine."

She nodded.

Without making a sound they collected what was needed, and soon Melissa lay on a bed of pillows, surrounded with cushions from the couch in the den, and tucked under a lightweight blanket.

"Tyler?"

"Mmm?"

"Can you tell me a story?"

Tyler raised up on his elbows and peered over the side

of his bed. "Don't push it, kid." He flopped back and turned over.

"Tyler."

"What!"

"I'll tell you a story, okay?"

"Okay."

"Far away above the clouds," Melissa began.

As Tyler listened to her soft voice he marveled, as he had many times, at her incredible memory for detail. He found himself actually interested in the fates of snowflakes Marili and Calvin, but suddenly she stopped.

"So what's the end of the story?" he asked.

"I don't know. I fell asleep."

"We'll ask Dad to finish it for us. Would you like that?"

Melissa bolted into a sitting position. Her voice was hopeful and eager. "Now?"

"No, tomorrow. Go to sleep now. Don't be scared, everything's going to be okay."

She was silent for a moment, then she asked, "Who made a fire in our garage, Tyler?"

"I don't know. But it wasn't a big fire. The firemen put it out fast."

"Why'd they make a fire in our garage, Tyler?"

He was on his elbow again and leaning over the side. "I don't know why, Melissa. But I'm sleepy and I've got school tomorrow, so how about hushing up and letting me go to sleep?" Then he added. "I'm right here, and I'll take care of you."

"Promise, Tyler?"

He sighed. Much as he sometimes resented it, he also liked the responsibility he felt for his sister. He thought of his mother, and tears filled his eyes. *She* would never have left Melissa alone tonight. His mom would have bundled them all into the master bedroom, made beds for him and Melissa on the floor just as he'd done, and they would have told stories and sung songs and gotten through the night together. Turning over, Tyler buried his face in his pillow.

In their bedroom, Emily rubbed her arms. "I've still got gooseflesh."

"Let me hold you," Russell said. For a while, she lay in the crook of his arm.

"I'm so upset. In all my years in practice, nothing like this has ever happened." Emily's fingers toyed with the edge of the sheet. "We could move to Florida." She looked at him. "Would you consider moving to Florida, Russell?"

It was many moments before he replied. "I don't want to uproot Tyler. You know that. Why don't you finish this case, or maybe even drop the whole thing? Then we'll talk about it." He disengaged his arm, which had fallen asleep and tingled, and turned away from her.

The specter of his lonely boyhood invaded his mind. When he was twelve, his mother had finally refused to follow his dad from military base to military base. She bought a house and they had settled in Atlanta. Before then, Russell had dreaded each move, each new neigh-

165

borhood, each new school. Making new friends hadn't been easy for him, much less pretending to his mother that everything was fine and that he was happy.

He had promised himself that when he grew up and married, he would settle in a small town, and his children would attend high school with friends they'd had since elementary school. They would feel that they belonged.

But when Emily had insisted on moving closer to Mars Hill, where she worked, he had agreed, ignoring Tyler's sullen looks. It had been a huge relief when Emily left the law firm in Mars Hill, and they bought a home in Tyler's old school district.

Lying there in the dark, he could not help but think of Amy—how, accompanying him on a business trip to the area, she had occupied herself by driving about the countryside. She had stumbled onto Mars Hill and fallen in love with the area. Russell exchanged his high salary, city stress, and business travel for life in the country. Amy had worked as a high school substitute teacher, while Russell set about building a profitable home business in computer software, computer repairs, and as a consultant to individuals buying new equipment.

The birth of Tyler had brought them a sense of deep contentment. Amy had wanted four children, but for whatever reason, hadn't had any more. Always the optimist, she'd handled it philosophically.

"It's not meant to be, Russell. Aren't we lucky to have our sweet, precious boy?"

Yes, thank God he had Tyler, and now Melissa. Thank God that his father had met Grace, whose generous spirit brought them all together into a large and loving surrogate family.

Move to Florida? The very idea knotted Russell's stomach, and he did not sleep the rest of that night.

22
ORDINARY AND EXTRAORDINARY MATTERS

Dark, ominous clouds piled one atop the other over Snowman's Cap. Rain followed a clap of thunder, and a gust of wind bent the branches of the crape myrtle bushes nearly to the ground.

Grace watched as Hannah left Max's house without an umbrella and raced across the road. The front door slammed. Water dripping from her hair, her clothes clinging to her body, Hannah entered the kitchen.

"Grace. I'm home."

In the interest of Hannah's happiness, Grace had resigned her heart to missing her friend. But at the sound of Hannah's voice, a genuine and robust delight raced through her, and suddenly the air seemed lighter, the thunder less ominous, and the room seemed charged with energy.

"I thought I could beat the storm." Hannah wiped her hair, arms, and face with a kitchen towel. "I'm going up to change. I'd love a cup of hot tea."

"I'll make us a pot," Grace said.

As she ascended the stairs, Hannah called over her shoulder, "I missed my bathtub. Max's tub's not nearly as deep as ours, and the hot water over there doesn't last a bath."

Shielded from the rain by a huge blue and yellow striped umbrella, Amelia arrived just as Hannah pulled out a chair and Grace poured her a cup of hot tea. "Hannah, you're home. How wonderful. Come to stay, I hope." Amelia set her umbrella on a mat in the foyer, entered the kitchen, and immediately embraced Hannah.

Is she acting, or is she really glad to see Hannah? Grace wondered.

"Muffins again? Darn. I want good old-fashioned sugar cookies, Grace. Please?"

"I'll make up a batch soon." *How good it feels to be together, the three of us.*

Later that night, when Grace lay in bed reading, her phone rang. It was Emily.

"I guess Bob told you about the threatening sign at our place, and the fire."

"He did. I called your house, but there was no answer. I'm horrified at what's happening. Do you think Francine Randall is behind this?"

"I do, but I can't prove that."

"What will you do?"

"I'm going ahead with prosecuting her and the school district. It looks like it will overlap Jerry McCorkle's trial. I was trying to avoid that, but I need to get this behind me fast."

"You feel you have a case, then?"

"Yes. There was a falling-out between Travis's parents and Francine Randall; they said they'd let him testify. He's admitted to hacking into that computer when the substitute teacher left the classroom."

"That's good news."

"Yes. Francine can no longer accuse Lucy of doing the hacking. And the school is responsible for having a monitor in that classroom."

"Why wasn't that substitute teacher fired?"

Emily's voice hardened. "Because the substitute is distantly related to Francine Randall. In these parts, one drop of blood and you're family forever and bound by some unspoken code to protect your kin, even if you never see the person or don't like him or her.

"There's also the question of why it took the regular teacher so many weeks to discover the problem when she returned. I don't know if I can get Francine Randall fired, but I can at least knock her down a peg or two, and bring this whole computer chat room issue to everyone's attention. Parents need to be alert to what their kids are doing."

"By pursuing Francine, you're guaranteed to have made an enemy of all the Randalls for life," Grace said.

"I know." Emily lowered her voice. "I've asked Russell if he'd consider moving to Florida."

"Florida? Leave Covington?"

"Grace, how can I go on living in a place where

people resort to frightening a family? The children are terrified."

"Maybe you'll feel differently when you win this case. Has Russell agreed to move?"

"Even if I get Francine Randall dismissed as principal and the school system pays the Banks family damages, the Randall name is powerful in these parts. We won't be safe." She paused, then asked, "You think I'm over-reacting, don't you?"

Emily's petulance reminded Grace of Melissa. She took a deep breath. "All I'm saying is, wait and see."

Emily's usually controlled voice suddenly sounded out of control. "I know what you're going to do. You disagree with me, and you won't support me in this."

"I don't recall your saying that Russell said no." Grace made every effort to stay calm. "What did he say?" She wanted to end this conversation. She knew she'd lie awake and think about it all night.

"That it's the last thing he wants to do."

"Well, why don't you wait and see what happens? Things have a way, given time, of working themselves out."

"Good night, then." Emily hung up and Grace faced a sleepless night.

23
WINDS OF CHANGE

The mall teemed with shoppers hustling along, dashing into stores and coming out with packages. Grace didn't see the tall, young soldier until she smacked into him. Had he not turned and grabbed her, she would have fallen.

"Mrs. Grace," the young man said.

"Randy! Randy Banks, is that you?" Still holding his arm, she stepped back and looked up. "Look at you. You've gotten so tall and handsome, and so grown-up in your uniform." She hugged him.

Randy tucked her arm through his. "Mrs. Grace, let's walk down to the food court, get something to eat, and have a visit."

Like all food courts, this one was bright, busy, and noisy. Once seated, Randy asked, "What would you like?"

"A small salad would be nice, with blue cheese dressing and iced tea."

"You sit. Let me get it." A short while later, Randy returned with her salad and tea, and a hamburger, fries, and an oversized soda for himself.

"Lucy mentioned you'd be coming home for a visit."

"I arrived yesterday. I intended to stop over at your place this afternoon, but I'm glad we bumped into each other."

Grace laughed. "I think you have that wrong, young man. It was I who bumped into you."

"Destiny at work," he said. "I was wondering how to get you alone to talk about Lucy."

"Yes. She's been so worried that you'd be angry with her. She was devastated when your mother wrote you

171

about that frightful business with the chat room on the school computer."

"Mother was confused by the whole thing, especially the police coming to the house. I'm not sure she even understands exactly what happened. Computers and chat rooms are as mysterious to her as aliens from outer space." He laughed. "I'm not sure she doesn't believe they're the advance guard of a foreign civilization."

"It was a frightening experience, Lucy getting caught up with that awful Jerry McCorkle, claiming to be a seventeen-year-old. And then the police cars with sirens blaring at the house, Lucy refusing to cooperate and the kids crying, scared out of their minds. I don't blame your mother for being confused and upset."

"You saved Lucy. Heaven knows what would have happened to her. I hear that McCorkle—or Ringo, as he called himself—is wanted for murdering an old lady."

"Yes, he is. A relative, an elderly woman, years ago."

"I sat down with Lucy last night and she told me the whole story. I assured her that I wasn't angry, and that I love her." He kneaded his cap with his hands. "I feel so darned guilty not being here when my family needed me. Maybe if I'd been home this would never have happened. Maybe Lucy would have come to me. When I think what that man might have done to her . . ."

He seemed close to tears. "Thank you for being there for my family, Mrs. Grace. Lucy and I talked about boys—their possible intentions, dating, and guys with cars, and being your own person and not listening to what other kids urge you to do. I'm getting her a cell phone. I want her to be able to call someone if she ever needs to."

"That's a good idea. Lucy is an innocent. She really believed Ringo when he told her he was mistreated by a stepfather and desperately lonely."

"Like a lamb being led to the slaughter."

"Afterward, she was very depressed," Grace said. "For a time she saw a counselor. That seemed to help, but I think what really helped was joining Hannah's garden club at school, making friends, and working with Hannah at the park."

"She told me. Bless all of you ladies for being so good to her—to my whole family. When I'm out of the army, I'll find a way to repay you."

"Just come home safe. There's nothing to repay, Randy. I believe it's important that we all help each other when we can. I love Lucy. I'll fight like a tiger to see that she isn't harmed."

"I know that." His thick dark hair was close cropped, and his deep-set eyes carried the weight of the world. "Being the only man in the family, it's hard for me to be so far away. And now, I'm going even farther away."

"Maybe there's a deferment you could get, since you're the only male in your family?"

He shrugged. "I'll ask, but I won't get my hopes up. They want every boy, man, and woman that they can get to volunteer. I did it for the long-range benefits, really, for when I come home." He was silent for a time. "My mother doesn't look well. She's worn out, I'd say."

"The last time I saw your mother was at your house

that evening, when the police were there. Something like that shocks your system—more so when you're older. It was very traumatic for her."

He nodded and sat silent for a time. "The girls are growing up. Aggie's so tall. I don't think any of them get much supervision. That worries me."

"Perhaps they don't. Your mother works hard. One child can wear you down; several are harder."

"Life can wear you down," he replied.

Grace studied his face, too young to bear those creases about his eyes.

"I wouldn't say this to Ma, but I'm scared to death of what I'm facing. You'd be surprised, Mrs. Grace, how many guys are eager to go to war. They talk about kicking butt. They think it's exciting. They're sure nothing will happen to them. The next guy might get it, but not them. I don't feel that way."

Grace's throat constricted. She took his hand in both of hers, and his blunt fingers extended beyond hers. "How mature you are, and wise. I'll pray for you."

Randy hesitated, then said, "I haven't told my mother, but my orders are for Afghanistan."

Grace gasped. "So soon?" Randy looked so vulnerable.

She patted his hand reassuringly. "It's okay to be scared. You'll do the best you can, and then you'll come home."

But she would pray for him. Oh, how she would pray for him.

24
NEW YORK, NEW YORK

Several days later, Amelia and Mike sat arguing in his workshop in Weaverville.

"I don't want to make this trip, Mike. Since nine-eleven, I haven't wanted to go to New York City."

"We have to go, Amelia. The gallery's clamoring for a show and a show means *you,* not just your work. People want to put nine-eleven behind them; they want to see beautiful things like your photographs and meet the photographer. A personal connection with you inspires them to buy, and selling your work is what it's all about."

"What if I tell you that it's not important to me anymore?"

"I'd say you were having a bad day. How can it not be important? Think of how many photographers would kill to be in your place."

"They can have it, and spare themselves the trouble of killing anyone."

"You're quite *contraire* today. Look." Mike pulled out the tickets he had picked up that morning. "We don't have to drive to Charlotte anymore to get to New York. There's a flight from Asheville to Newark, New Jersey. Our plane leaves at eleven A.M. That gives us plenty of time to take a limo to the city, check into the hotel, and get to the gallery before seven P.M. The exhibit opens at night, but we'll need to preview

175

it and meet the new owner."

"Use any excuse. Say I'm not well. Say anything you want, but I don't want to go."

"Our reservations are at the Mayflower Hotel on Central Park West, and I got tickets for us to see *La Traviata* at the Met, and the revival of *Oklahoma!* on Broadway."

"I'm not going, Mike." Amelia crossed her arms. "If you want to go, go ahead, but I am not budging from home."

"Come on, Amelia. You'll love it once we get there."

"Cajolery won't help. I hate flying. I hate traveling, and since nine-eleven, I hate it even more."

Mike waved the tickets and his voice softened. "Once we get there, it'll be great fun."

"Forget it." Amelia turned on her heel and walked out of his shop.

Mike persisted, and Amelia caved in. On a sunshiny day in the beginning of June, they boarded the plane for Newark. By any standards it was a rough trip. Air pockets, a thunderstorm, and a temporary loss of altitude decimated her courage and left her shaken.

"I'm not flying back," Amelia said. "I'll take a train or rent a car, but I will not fly."

The limo went through the Lincoln Tunnel into Manhattan and headed uptown toward Central Park. Mike peered out of the window. "The city seems less congested, doesn't it?"

"Not to me." Amelia had the sense of being squeezed

between concrete walls. But when they finally arrived at the hotel, the elegance of her room, which faced the tranquility of Central Park, helped Amelia relax.

The new owner had renamed the gallery Gallery Number Ten. Marvin Cohen, a suave young man in an Armani suit, welcomed them effusively.

"A great pleasure to meet you. Mr. Saunders regrets not being able to be here to greet you himself." Marvin waved his hand. "Family obligations. You know how that is."

Amelia's beautifully framed photographs hung against walls of the palest blush, and seeing her work displayed in such an elegant setting impressed her.

"We'll have a reception and preview this evening. The general public will be admitted tomorrow," Marvin said. He pointed to a delicate, finely wrought mahogany table and chair at one side of the room. "Buyers will want your signature on the prints they purchase. Tomorrow we'll be open from ten o'clock to four in the afternoon. Perhaps you and Mike would join Mr. Saunders for lunch in his private office. We're having lunch brought in from Sardi's."

"What if people buy a framed photo?" Amelia asked.

"We don't sell framed photographs. We'll frame their purchases if they wish, of course, but we keep the framed ones for our collection. We're planning to take your work on the road later this year. Oh, my." Marvin clapped his hand over his mouth. "I should have let Mr. Saunders tell you that."

Amelia shot Mike a swift glance. Would Mr. Saunders expect her to travel with the exhibit, to smile until her cheeks felt as if they would crack, stand on her feet and make small talk until she had no voice? This sounded like a repeat of the endless receptions she had attended with Thomas. And she had been younger then.

As they toured the rooms, Marvin described the reception planned for that evening. "Mr. Saunders has spared no expense. Nothing but the finest for you, Mrs. Declose." He lowered his voice as if giving them top secret information. "Mr. Saunders has engaged a string quartet.

"And the dress for this affair?" Mike asked.

"Formal, of course. If you didn't bring a tuxedo, I'll call and rent you one. Just give me your size."

"I brought a tux," Mike said.

Thank heaven I brought my black chiffon, Amelia thought.

Later, when they met to leave for the reception, Mike lifted her hand to his lips and kissed it. "My, God, you look breathtakingly beautiful. Ready to go?"

"I'm all butterflies in my stomach. Tonight's reception calls for a level of sophistication I'm not sure I have any longer."

"You can take the girl out of the city, but you can't take the city out of the girl." Mike opened the door of her room and led her to the elevator. "Amelia Declose will step into that room and knock everyone off their feet."

"We both will." Amelia smiled at him warmly and slipped her arm through his.

In the wee hours of the morning, in their pajamas and wrapped in lush terrycloth bathrobes, a deliciously tired Amelia and Mike sat shoulder to shoulder on Mike's bed and reminisced about the evening.

"You were right about tonight, Mike. When I stepped into that gallery, something clicked inside of me. I felt as regal as a queen."

"And you looked like one. You charmed everyone. Stay in New York awhile, and you'll be the belle of every art event."

"It was so refined, so elegant." She stretched her arms above her head. "I felt young and free and beautiful."

"Simon Blanchette, the art critic, couldn't keep his eyes off you."

"That Casanova!" She poked his arm. "You weren't without admirers, either, *mon ami*. Who was that handsome gentleman you were chatting with when the musicians took a break?"

"Samuel Frankel, one of the musicians. A violist. Mainly we were comparing and contrasting the viola and the violin. I used to dabble in the violin long ago. We agreed that the viola is the more full-bodied of the two instruments."

"You're something else, Mike. Getting to know you is like unraveling a skein of yarn. You studied the violin. You were a ballet dancer way back when. You've done so many things."

"For years I rolled like a stone from place to place, had no roots. When I became part of your extended family, I decided to settle in Weaverville and stay put."

Amelia squeezed his arm. "We all love you, Mike. Thank you for staying and for being my friend."

In silence, they sipped herbal tea from room service. From somewhere in the city a siren sounded, grew louder, then faded.

"At least half of those high rollers will be at the gallery tomorrow," Mike said. "We'll sell a lot of photographs. There's no telling where this could lead."

"Right back to Covington, Mike. I don't covet fame and the demands it makes on one's time and energy. I like my life as it is."

He waved his arm to encompass the plush room. "You mean, after all your work you'd walk away from all of this?"

"I may seem frivolous at times, but I am also serious and reliable, and I'm rooted in Covington. I love my life. These past months, I've neglected my work at the hospital. I miss rocking babies in the nursery, helping an infant survive against huge odds. The other day, the nursing staff celebrated a baby's going home. Since I'd spent hours with that infant, they asked me to join them. That meant a lot to me.

"Contrast that with people tonight. They're like fireworks; they sparkle briefly, then lose their pizzazz, fall back to earth, and disappear. They'll buy my work because they're betting it will prove to be a wise investment, not because they've fallen in love with it.

Although some will probably buy because they genuinely love the photo."

"I understand, Amelia. I really do." Mike sighed. "I've been caught up in the excitement, riding your coattails, you could say—living my own fantasies through you."

"I'm sorry, Mike. Looks like you made a lousy investment when you took me on."

"You're my friend, Amelia." He patted her hand. "My best friend, and I'm proud of you. I could never be sorry."

On Saturday, seasoned art connoisseurs and the general public poured into Gallery Number Ten. Amelia signed photographs, smiled, made small talk, and charmed everyone. At the day's end, she pried her stiff fingers from the pen and stretched them in and out.

Observing Amelia the night before, Simon Blanchette, the art critic, had perfunctorily labeled her frivolous, superficial—a woman addicted to adulation, whose attitude was in direct contrast to the sensitivity and intensity of her work. He pondered her relationship with Mike—one moment judging him gay, the next seeing him as her heterosexual lover and condemning the fact that Mike was obviously younger than Amelia. Mike had appeared possessive of her and rarely left her side at the reception.

Simon was in his late sixties, with two greedy ex-wives and four avaricious children, whom he had essentially divorced along with his wives. Why not? They had good stepfathers, better fathers than he had ever been. Recently, however, he longed to see his grandchildren. He imagined himself sitting in a well-worn chair with little ones clambering all over him, hugging him, calling him Grandpa.

Simon had recently terminated a two-year relationship with a celebrated and materialistic runway model, and was "off" women. Or so he thought until Amelia floated into that reception on Mike's arm.

In the gallery, today, Simon observed Mike wander off among the potential buyers, chat with this one and that, and return only occasionally to Amelia. The small touches and looks that would indicate intimacy were absent, and he deduced that Mike and Amelia were business partners.

Simon leaned against a column and studied Amelia: the way she held her shoulders erect when she leaned forward to sign a photo; the way her smile lit her face; the grace and charm with which she turned her head and lifted excited eyes to each new buyer.

White hair, even hair as beautiful as Amelia's, was anathema to Simon. It stamped one as old. Why didn't she color hers? He dyed what remained of his hair a pale ash. How old *was* she, anyway? It was hard to determine. Early to mid sixties? Maybe what he needed, and had so far assiduously avoided, was a woman closer to his own age. Nonsense! Why give up the lush young starlets and wannabe artists who would gladly share his bed? Spurred by their vitality, he could pretend, for a time and with the aid of Viagra, that he was still a young stallion.

Simon meandered from one photograph to another. The black-and-whites impressed him with their Ansel Adams–like clarity, but Amelia used people in her land-scapes. She captured them in deeply emotional poses, such as the woman in this photo, who stood at a gravesite behind a woman who seemed to be the weeping widow, her face a mask of grief and wariness. Was she the dead man's mistress? Momentarily he wondered, who will stand at my grave and grieve for Simon Blanchette?

He moved on to another wall of photos. Amelia's photographs abjured the ordinary: no run-of-the-mill cluster of trees by a stream, or cows grazing on a hill-side. When Amelia photographed cows, she literally faced the creatures. This cow staring at him had per-sonality, its deep dark eyes indifferent to the intruder and her camera, while another cow stood alert and guarded. He'd never thought cows capable of con-veying such humanity. If he kept looking at them, he'd never eat beef again.

Simon had previewed the show the week before and written admiringly about it. Usually he preferred avant-garde work, modern, ironic or satirical. It was odd that he should be so taken by Amelia's realistic and poignant photographs. His review of her work had flowed uncensored from his soul to his fingers and onto the computer. But then, the tragedy of nine-eleven had softened him in ways he was still discovering.

Simon stood over the table where the prints were laid out. He selected a photo of an old and wrinkled woman weaving. Light fell in shafts across her fingers. Then he sauntered over to the mahogany table for Amelia's autograph. *Am I imagining it, or did her amazing sapphire eyes brighten when she looked up at me?*

"This is one of my favorites," Amelia said as she penned her name across the bottom.

"Who is this woman?" Simon asked.

"Miss Claudine Banks. She's ninety years old, and she still weaves every day. Her daughter, who's seventy, threads the loom for her. Her wall hangings are much in demand at the Folk Art Center in Asheville."

Simon smiled and carefully slipped the photograph into a protective tube. "Good luck," he said and walked away.

That evening Mike and Amelia attended the Metropolitan Opera. The lavish production of *La Traviata* introduced a new Alfredo, a young Italian tenor touted as an up-and-coming Placido Domingo. His voice thrilled Amelia. Tears filled her eyes when she sprang to her feet and joined the wildly enthusiastic audience. "Bravo!" she yelled, and clapped until her palms hurt. *This is why we opera lovers keep coming back, for that special moment when the singer is so extraordinary that that performance is etched forever in our hearts and memories.* She had seen a *Faust* once with a Mephistopheles whose superlative basso/baritone and acting ability had exceeded all her expectations. It had been a sensuous and stunning performance, and like the performance tonight, it was one that Amelia would never forget.

The excitement of New York City swept them away. At the Whitney Museum on Madison Avenue, they watched a documentary film on the genesis of a quilt show. Created in the isolated hamlet of Gee's Bend, Alabama, the quilts illustrated the amazing creativity of the women who worked on them. The result was a collection of quilts with strong geometric patterns, rich colors, and a variety of fabrics, some as untraditional as old potato sacks. Amelia and Mike had been drawn to this exhibit after reading a review that had called the quilts "virtuoso performances in frugality" and "aesthetically inventive."

At the Houk Museum on Fifth Avenue, they browsed among sepia prints of amazing close-ups of butterflies and other bugs. The powerful photo of a daddy longlegs, with its pulsing body and shimmering legs, fascinated Amelia.

"What incredible patience to get shots like that. Wow!" Amelia sank onto a bench. The city had spiked Mike's energy and she could not keep up. "My feet are killing me, Mike. You go on to the International Center of Photography. I'm bushed. If we're going to the theater tonight, I need a good long soak in the tub."

Amelia relaxed, luxuriating in what seemed an endless stream of hot water. Fragrant bubbles surrounded her up to her chin. For a moment she considered calling

Grace from the phone above the tub, but it seemed too much effort to lift her arm. Just then the phone rang, intruding on her solitude. It was probably Mike. Amelia heaved up and reached for the receiver. "Hello?"

"Amelia? This is Simon Blanchette, the art critic. We met on Friday evening briefly, and again at the gallery."

"Oh, of course." Amelia sank into the water. "How are you?"

"Better and better every day."

A strange reply—like a mantra, Amelia thought.

Simon cleared his throat. "I'm calling to wish you well and a safe trip home."

"That's very kind of you."

There was a pause, then he said, "It was a most successful show."

"Thanks to the lovely review you gave my photographs, Mr. Blanchette. Thank you."

"Please call me Simon. Your work is very fine. I was pleased to review it."

"Thank you."

A longer pause.

"I may be in your area this summer. I visit my sister in Greenville, South Carolina, every year. Perhaps I'll stop by."

"It would be a pleasure to show you around."

"Well, fine. I'll ring off, then."

"Good-bye." Amelia replaced the receiver. She scooped bubbles about her like a blanket and sank low into the water. It was amazing that he had called. Flattering, too. This trip had been perfect.

25
STRANGER THAN FICTION

"No one really knows if it was an accident or not."

Mike and Amelia had returned from New York at noon, and were sitting in the living room with Grace and Bob.

"It rained, and roads get slippery up in the mountains—especially that curve, and there was no guardrail." Grace sipped her tea. "Most people think it was an accident, but others are certain it was suicide."

"Accident, my eye," Bob scoffed. "Where were the skid marks? That car sailed right off the road and over the cliff. Francine Randall didn't have a prayer of a chance of surviving."

"Francine Randall dead. That's so hard to believe," Amelia said. *While I was autographing photographs, Francine's car plunged over a cliff.*

"Her funeral was huge. Cars were parked up and down every street in Mars Hill for the church service, and the cars were a mile long to the cemetery," Grace said.

"And lots of McCorkles," Bob added. "They looked like a line of ants walking up the hill to the graveyard. I didn't recognize any of them, except for May and June, their husbands, and their mother, Ida."

"How ironic," Grace said. "Brenda says Francine Randall detested the McCorkles. She acknowledged a family connection only when she was pushed to the wall."

"I hadn't a clue there was any kind of connection between them," Bob said.

"Why'd they bury her in such a hurry?" Mike asked.

"The car burned. There was nothing left to view, I imagine," Bob replied.

"I'm absolutely stunned. Why would she kill herself? It must have been an accident." Amelia's mind filled with images: a patch of black wet road, the car skidding, Francine turning the wheel in a desperate effort to stop the slide. Had Francine felt a chilling terror, or had she grown calm and accepted the inevitable as she careened through space, falling, falling, brushing the tops of trees? Had she lost consciousness early or on impact, before or after the car burst into flames? Amelia pressed her fist against her lips. In her imagination she heard the thud of metal striking granite and saw orange flames. Unwittingly, her fingers clasped her scarf, which covered the scars she bore from the car crash that had killed her husband.

"Amelia," Mike said. "You look positively ill."

"I was remembering Thomas, and our car accident, and thinking about that poor woman. One minute everything is going along normally, the next it's sheer chaos, sheer hell."

Bob suggested, "Maybe the prospect of being sued, of having to appear in court and held up to public criticism or ridicule, was overwhelming. Once they knew that Emily was proceeding with a case against

Francine, the newspapers blew Lucy's story and Francine's connection with the McCorkles all out of proportion."

"I think that's an oversimplification," Grace said. "There's more to this than meets the eye."

Amelia buried her face in her hands. "Please stop talking about this. It's just too horrible."

Grace slid her arm about her friend's shoulders. "Of course. We may not have liked her, but Francine Randall's death is sobering. Who knows what goes on deep inside another human being? It's made me stop and think how vulnerable we all are. It makes me love you all more, and want to tell you that I do."

Thoughts of dying haunted Grace, and averting the long-term effects of diabetes became a near obsession. She decided to try the Atkins plan, and when she ordered a pork roast at the market, she requested that the fat be left on.

"They send it to us trimmed of fat," the butcher said.

"Please order me one without the fat cut off."

The man shrugged. "I'll do my best."

When Grace picked up the roast a few days later, a layer of fat had been tied around it.

Bob, who had just returned from golfing and had dropped in at the ladies' house, looked at the roast sitting on the counter. "I haven't seen fat like that on meat in years. It can't be healthy to eat like that."

She turned to him, angry at his words. "One bonus of this plan is that I *can* eat fat. I wouldn't have ordered a pork roast otherwise. It's too dry with all the fat removed." Grace pounded her thigh with her fist. "Look at me. I feel trapped in this body. The doctor says that losing weight will delay the long-term effects of diabetes, and this diet's supposed to make you lose weight quickly." She lowered her head into her hands. "Sometimes I think to the devil with dieting. I'm going to die anyway. We all die. What's a few less years?"

"Honey, how can you say that? Every moment of life is precious," Bob said, putting his arm about her. "I can't imagine life without you."

Grace lifted her head and looked into his eyes. "When I think of the complications of diabetes, I get really scared. I'm on a new blood pressure medication now, one that the doctor says, ever so casually, will protect my kidneys. I had no idea my kidneys were at risk until he said that."

"I'm sorry, Grace. I've been so wrapped up in golf and teaching, I didn't realize you were having such a difficult time."

"It's funny," Grace said, sinking into a chair. "Since I turned seventy—or is it since Francine died? I don't sleep well." Tears filled Grace's eyes. "I hate talking about my health, or lack of it."

"Then let's change the subject. Seems like everyone's got problems lately. Can I talk about Russell and Emily?"

"Sure, what about them?"

"Something is off-key in that marriage," Bob said.

Grace rubbed her arms. "I sense something's not

right. I get chills thinking that they might separate."

"Now, don't go jumping the gun, honey. I don't know anything for sure."

"You wouldn't say such a thing on a whim." Grace made a whistling kind of sound between her teeth. "I like to think of myself as fair and open-minded, but there are careers that make more sense for a married woman with small children."

"Like what? What career?" Bob asked.

"Teaching comes to mind, though I'm sure there are others. Teachers get home at a reasonable hour every day and don't bring home work."

"Teachers have papers to correct and lesson plans to prepare. Often they haven't time to finish at school, and they bring work home," Bob said.

"But not every day, and they have long holidays," Grace replied.

"That's true. You consider being a lawyer too time-consuming? How about being a clerk in a store? They come home dog tired, I'm sure."

Grace's adrenaline was pumping, gearing up for an argument. Why was Bob playing devil's advocate? She rose and began to wash the few dishes in the sink. Lately she found herself easily annoyed at things and at people. Her eyes traveled to the pork roast, not yet in the oven. She wanted to throw it into the garbage and might have, had Bob not been there. Could this diet be making her excessively disagreeable?

"I was a stay-at-home mom." Tears filled her eyes. "And for what? I devoted my life to Ted and Roger. I gave up going to college, gave up pursuing my interest in ancient civilizations, or taking a job outside the home." She stopped herself, her mind racing. *What's wrong with me? I'm ranting. If I'd wanted to go to college, I could have gone once Roger started school. Adults do that all the time. I was too scared to go, to try anything new. How can I compare myself to Emily?*

"The world is different today," Bob said. "Russell and Emily are adults, and they'll stay together or not regardless of what you or I do or say. I just worry about the kids."

"Tyler's not the problem. It's Melissa. I'd hate to see Emily move back to Florida, where she'll have that child in day care or with a nanny, a stranger. If we think Melissa's wild now, she'd be bonkers without her father. I can't imagine Emily taking Melissa. She hardly spends any time with her now."

Bob did not reply.

Grace went to the fridge and took out packages of sliced ham and cheese, lettuce and a tomato. She rolled a slice of ham around a slice of cheese and waved it at Bob. "Protein," she said.

"This diet thing is really affecting you, Grace. It's making you nuts. I love you just the way you are."

Grace ignored him. She bit into the rolled cold cuts. "Emily says she'd like to move the kids and Russell to Ocala. She thinks I might try to influence Russell against her plan. She solicited my cooperation."

"She couldn't have meant that." But he asked, "What'd you tell her?"

"That I hardly had that kind of influence."

"I think you do," he said.

"Ridiculous." The urge to argue was strong. The pain she felt at the thought of Russell and the children moving away was real. "I'd miss them, especially the children, so very much."

"Honey, don't go on like this. You're upsetting yourself. Let's give it time and see what happens."

Grace went to Bob and put her arms about him. "Hold me. I need the comfort of your arms."

26
SPECULATIONS

People gossiped about Francine's death, especially after word spread that she had bequeathed the bulk of her estate, a rather large sum of money, for Jerry McCorkle's defense, and a small amount to Lucy Banks. In the shops in Elk Plaza—the market, the beauty parlor, the video store, Craine's auto parts store, and the barbershop—people discussed the matter. They talked about Francine when they walked their dogs, whispered about her on Sundays before and after church, and conjectured about her death, as Frank Craine and Charlie Herrill did in the diner at Elk Plaza.

Frank said, "Francine Randall changed her will"—his hand rose and descended in a downward swoop—"then, she killed herself."

"But why?" Charlie asked.

"She done it 'cause she was guilty as hell about what

almost happened to that little girl, especially as Ringo's her kin," Frank said.

"Her kin, eh? Strange, her caring about Jerry. He killed old lady Hilda years back, everybody knows that. Just never been able to prove it until now. So why'd she go leaving money to pay his lawyers?" Charlie frowned.

"Maybe so we'd sit around like this talking about her, rest her soul." Frank shrugged. "I dunno. But I think she planned the whole thing, or she wouldn't have changed her will two weeks before."

The diner was almost empty except for two tables of out-of-town folks, or maybe they were new people from Loring Valley.

Frank lowered his voice and tipped his head toward the tables. "Them flatlanders come on up from South Georgia or Florida, or Yankees from up north. They buy 'em a place in Loring Valley, live there a bit, and can't stand the quiet life. So they sell and move, and you've never even heard their names. Then the next batch comes and does the same thing."

Charlie nodded, and Frank brushed crumbs, the residue of the double-thick piecrust, off his belly. A waitress deposited a huge plate of french fries for the strangers at one of the tables. Charlie's mouth watered looking at them, and the smell sent set his stomach rumbling. He looked away, then motioned for a refill of iced tea and gulped it down. If he ordered french fries, what with his high blood pressure and high cholesterol, and Frank mentioned it to Alma, and Alma told Velma, which she would, Velma'd let him have it good. Darn womenfolk and their gossip. It never occurred to Charlie that he and Frank were doing exactly that.

Through the bank of windows, Charlie could see people scurrying by. Some he recognized; others, he did not. He fished a toothpick from his shirt pocket and picked his teeth. "Time was, you knew everybody," he muttered.

The stranger at the closest table turned around and looked at Frank. "I couldn't help overhearing your conversation about Ms. Randall. You think she committed suicide?"

Feeling important, Frank said, "For sure, 'cos of guilt and shame over a lawsuit she had coming up. She was a mighty prideful woman."

"The computer thing and the girl from her school, you mean? I heard about that. A sorry business," the man said.

"Guilt, pure and simple, drove her to it." Frank nodded vigorously.

"She was one tough bird," the man said. "You'd go in to talk to her about your kid, and she'd get this steely look in her eyes. Nothing you said made a lick of difference. We had a son in her school. Had to take him out and put him in private school. That woman hauled him in her office every other day for one thing or another: too noisy, walked too fast in the halls, spoke out of turn, sassed a teacher, picked a fight, pulled a girl's braids." He rolled his eyes and shrugged. "A lot of it was just kid stuff, but she called everything he did criminal behavior. Maybe now she's gone, I can save a bundle and put my boy back in public school." The man turned and set about eating his fries.

Charlie wanted those fries. He wanted them so bad his stomach ached.

"Tightfisted old woman, that Francine," Frank said. "She lived alone, not even a cat for company. Who'da figured she had all that money?"

"She could have left money to the church or a children's home. That's what a decent person would have done," Charlie said.

Frank shook his head. "Old Francine knew that what she did would stir up folks, and they'd take sides one against another. We ain't had no trouble in these parts for years. You mark my words, Charlie, we're gonna see trouble when that trial starts. I think Francine, wherever she is, rest her soul, is laughing at everybody."

Brenda Tate agreed with Frank. "Francine Randall was a malevolent, extremely calculating woman." Brenda and Grace were having a quick lunch in the school cafeteria. "If I know her, she's splitting her sides laughing at all the talk and speculation round these parts. In her whole life, she never got this much attention."

"It's so confusing," Grace replied. "Her bequest to pay for Ringo's lawyers is very odd, don't you think?"

"They were kin of some kind. I think she set it up that way deliberately, sort of a slap in the face to the community. They'll hire Ringo some big-shot lawyer who'll rev up publicity and pull out all the stops. He can't win this case, but he can make allusions and suggestions, and hint at things that'll cause people to take sides. Could stir up plenty of ill will among folks around here."

"Why would that happen? Like what?" Grace asked.

"There are all kind of old scores that people feel they never settled. Remember, this is a Spartan county, with Spartan-minded folk ready to argue and even fight at the least provocation." She laughed. "Did I ever tell you that a writer once said that Marshall thinks of itself as ancient Sparta, and Mars Hill, because of the college, fancies itself to be Athens?"

"And Hot Springs?" Grace asked, thinking of the other small town in Madison County.

"Ah," Brenda said. "Maybe that's ancient Rome."

"Why?"

"Hot Springs was once a mecca for the rich and famous. It's gone way down but folks dream it will come back again."

"All the things about a place that outsiders don't know," Grace said. But it was Francine that interested her. "Do you think Francine was responsible for those threats against Emily?"

"If they stop, I'd say, yes. But you never know. Might have been pranksters, or someone trying to cast suspicion on Francine because of some grudge they had against her. Old grudges lie like they're dead, but someone's always biding his time, waiting for the right moment."

"I hope the threats are over. Emily's talking about

moving the family to Florida, where she had her practice."

"I'd hate to see that happen." Brenda stood and picked up her tray.

"I cringe at the thought," Grace replied, rising.

They walked toward the kitchen and placed the trays on the moving counter, where the trays disappeared through a rubber flap. "That always reminds me of a car wash," Brenda said.

Later that night, Brenda phoned Grace. "Wait till you hear this. I just got the news through the grapevine that Francine was seeing a psychiatrist. She was on medication for severe depression, they say. You hear that? Severe depression. That might explain the accident, or suicide, whichever it was."

Grace visited Hannah in her room later to share this information with her. Hannah said, "Nothing surprises me." Sitting in robe and slippers, she brushed her hair away from crimson cheeks. "I was just about to go to bed. I'm exhausted."

Tired from whatever you're doing over there with Max. Grace smiled. "Sleep well, my friend. I'm glad you're home tonight."

Back in her room, Grace rested her head on the back of her chair, closed her eyes, and considered that terrible illness called depression. She had experienced several short bleak periods in her life, when she had awakened at four or five A.M. with a heart like lead and slogged through her day shrouded by a gray veil and haunted by a sense of meaninglessness. Joy had been alien to her then, and she remembered wondering if she would ever smile, laugh, or feel enthusiasm for anything ever again.

Those frightening times had been short-lived, thank God. Self-help books, shyly selected from the local bookstore and hidden from Ted, who would have laughed at her, assured Grace that her depression was "normal depression," the result of losing her babies, and later of losing Ted. Time, and many hours of volunteer work at her church's soup kitchen, had helped pull her up and out into the light of life again.

Had depression driven Francine to turn her wheel and the car over that cliff? Grace had disliked the arrogant woman and had hoped that Emily would discredit her to the point where Francine would lose her job. Now she sympathized with Francine. You could hardly call it "living" with severe, unremitting depression and a sense of hopelessness dragging you down day after day, month after month. On the other hand, perhaps Francine had merely been driving too fast, and then it was too late. That could easily happen. Last winter, Bob had come very close to going over the cliff while coming down from his apartment in Loring Valley.

Bob had told her, "It was that fast." He snapped his fingers. "There I was, sliding toward the edge thinking it was aces for me, after all my years in the service. What stopped the slide, I'll never know. I'm not a praying man, but that day, as I sat there shaking and sweating, I sure thanked God."

Well, however Francine had died, whether by accident or by her own hand, the woman had had a conscience, at least. Francine had left Lucy something in her will. Grace wondered when the distribution would come and how much Lucy would get.

When she learned that information several days later, Grace, who never cursed, went about the house muttering "damn woman." The five thousand dollars bequeathed to Lucy would be doled out in halves for two years after she graduated from high school, to be used exclusively for education at a community college. But that was several years away, with not a word about interest accrued on the money during those years, or compensation for the stress on poor Mrs. Banks, or recognition of the danger Lucy had been exposed to. If Francine Randall had designated four thousand dollars a year for four years, it would at least have assured Lucy's education at the University of North Carolina in Asheville. Who did she think she was, trying to limit Lucy's opportunities from beyond the grave?

Well, Grace would take care of that. She'd talk to Amelia and Hannah and to Bob and Russell. She was sure that they would help her make up the difference when the time came, and Lucy would have a chance at a four-year degree and the brightest possible future. "That awful woman," Grace muttered.

That night, as she got ready for bed, the phone rang. It was her son, Roger, calling to invite Bob and her to South Carolina. "I'd like you to see how the house is coming along. Ask Max and Hannah to join you," Roger suggested.

And Francine Randall was, for the moment, forgotten.

27
SINS OF THE PARENTS

In his jail cell, Jerry McCorkle heard the news that Francine Randall was dead. Too bad! He'd had a good thing going, with all that hush money she'd been paying him this last year. Maybe that's why she'd up and killed herself—she was afraid he might walk up to her in some public place, like the courthouse, and call her ma.

He'd never have known she was his ma, if his drunken no-good pa hadn't come clean on his death bed and told Jerry that Francine was his mother. He was such a blasted stinkin' liar that Jerry hadn't paid him no mind to start with. But he wasn't no fool, not Jerry McCorkle. He'd brooded a while on what his old man said, then taken matters in his own hands. When his granny had refused to talk about it, he'd held a knife to her throat, and sure enough she'd admitted it was true.

Granny told him how Francine's family had paid his daddy cash in hand, every month since Jerry was born, to keep their mouths shut. They'd sent his daddy off to live in Alabama and supplied him with liquor all these years.

"Francine, the old she goat, was probably glad when Pa's liver gave out," Granny said. She hastened to add. "Can't blame your pa. Francine was a pretty thing back when they was younguns. She done give him the eye and turned his head right quick. I warned him not to mess with them rich cousins, who looked down their noses at the rest of us McCorkles. But your pa was wild, and he was sure good-lookin'."

Jerry had stood there stunned.

"They shipped Francine off somewhere till you was born. They wanted to give you for adoption, but I wasn't gonna turn no kin of mine over to no strangers." She chuckled. "Your pa brung you home from the hospital while they was waiting for the folks who were gonna take you to come up from Texas. Took you right outta your crib. We swore we'd tell everyone up and down Covington who your rightful ma was, and sure 'nough, Francine's high-and-mighty folks backed off right quick." She laughed. "I got to keep you and raise you myself." Granny had looked at him slyly, then, and rubbed her thumb and forefinger together. "With a bit of help from them Randalls, that is." He could still hear her cackle, high-pitched and mean.

When Jerry was little, he'd asked Granny about his ma.

Granny'd said, "Your ma done up and left after you was born. We heard she done went and got herself run over by a truck down in Georgia."

He hadn't wasted time mourning a ma he never knew, a ma who was stupid enough to get killed by a truck. So when Jerry learned that Francine Randall had left him most of her money to pay for his lawyers, he laughed, knowing his trial would be a blast and

202

could run on and on for a good long while. He laughed so hard he peed in his pants. His blasted, no-good mother had finally acknowledged him. She'da never done it aloud and spoiled her precious reputation. What a joke! She'd done gone and killed herself and left him guilt money.

Sometimes, late at night in his cell, he'd think what to do. Maybe he'd wait till he was in court, and then he'd tell all those high-and-mighty folk who his ma was. Or maybe he'd never tell no one, or maybe he'd write a book. Guys in jail wrote books. He'd be famous. They'd send Katie Couric to interview him. Sometimes, lying there in the stinking cell, he'd laugh so loud he'd wake up his neighbors. They'd yell at him to shut up and curse him, and he'd curse them back the way he'd wanted to curse Granny and Pa and Francine Randall, and all those Randalls with their fancy cars and fancy houses.

28
TEA AND THERAPY

Sweeping across the United States from the west, a storm with the force of an invading army drenched the central portions of Tennessee and marched on to the mountains of North Carolina. The storm extended into the upstate part of South Carolina and included the 1-85 corridor, closing sections of the highway. Secondary roads in North Carolina flooded. Water levels rose, flooded basements, and deposited an inch of silt inside houses constructed on flood plains. Without zoning, there were many places like that.

Two days after the storm, newspaper headlines read: RURAL ROADS FLOODED, IMPASSABLE. BRIDGES WASHED AWAY. HIGHWAY PATROL HANDLES HUNDREDS OF WRECKS. Madison County was especially hard hit. The county was comprised of mountain ridges and deep valleys. The slopes of the mountains served as reservoirs and water poured into the valleys, where it turned even dry streambeds into raging rivers. The scene Amelia had witnessed at Old Bunkie Creek was repeated again and again across the county.

Grace watched the rain from the window of her kitchen. Alma's twin granddaughters dashed out onto Cove Road carrying red umbrellas. They skipped and hopped along the road giggling, stomping in puddles, making huge messes of their clothes. Their grandfather, Frank, appeared, without umbrella or rain gear, and yelled at them to get inside. The girls ran on, and a thoroughly soaked Frank chased them down Cove Road. When he caught them, he scooped them up and headed home, a girl under each arm, arms flailing, legs dangling.

Watching, Grace remembered how, as a child, she used to sneak out into the rain. She had loved the feel of it on her face and arms, well worth the scolding and spanking her mother administered, or being exiled to her room without lunch or dinner.

And then a car turned into the driveway. Emily stepped out and, under cover of a huge black umbrella, hastened up the steps. Grace hurried to the door to let her inside.

"Cup of tea?" she asked as Emily deposited her umbrella in the stand and wiped her shoes on the rug in the foyer.

Emily shook her head.

"Mind if I have a cup?" Grace led the way into the kitchen and turned the flame up under the kettle.

"Well, I guess I'll have tea, since you are." The dark circles beneath Emily's eyes suggested sleepless nights.

Grace placed bright flowered mats on the table, plates for cookies, and her best china cups and saucers. "All I have to go with tea are fat-free cookies. They're sweetened with apple juice concentrate. It's a different taste, but they're quite good."

Emily waved her hand. "I don't need cookies. I want to talk to you." She walked to the window and peered out. "This darn rain won't stop, will it? I hate rainy days, and we've had so many this spring."

Emily's tension permeated the room. *Whatever she's come to say,* Grace thought, *I won't like it.*

"They picked up two creeps from Covington just as they were about to throw a dead dog on our lawn," Emily said.

"A dead dog? That's awful! Who are these people doing such a dreadful thing?"

"Two McCorkle teenagers. They're crazy people." She stamped a foot on the floor. "Grace, I can't raise my child here. I don't want Melissa going to school with the likes of the McCorkles."

"They're not all bad," Grace said. She set the teapot on the table. "In every community, there are some people whom one would prefer their children not associate with. There were kids in Dentry that I didn't want Roger going about with, and that was a long time ago. Who put those boys up to it, do you know?"

"Jerry McCorkle. They admitted it to the police."

"But he's been in jail for weeks."

"He has visitors." Emily's voice grew sharp and edgy. "He paid them, so they did it."

"He has money for such a thing?" Grace's hand trembled as she poured their tea.

"It seems that Jerry had plenty of money in the months before he went to jail. He threw it around like water. He told people he'd come into a windfall."

Grace watched the grains of Splenda run from the yellow packet into her cup. She stirred her tea and watched Emily's mouth tighten and her eyes narrow.

Emily stared at a spot on the far wall. Finally she said, "Things are not good between Russell and myself, Grace."

This was the last thing Grace wanted to hear. "Emily, dear, I'd . . . I'd rather not be involved in such a private matter, considering my relationship with Bob and all."

Emily dropped her head into her hands. "Who, then?" She lifted her head and brushed away the moisture gathering in her eyes. "I've no one else to turn to. You were there for me when Tyler acted out and made my life miserable, and Russell and I almost didn't get married."

Emily twisted her wedding band around and around. "There are times when I wish we had never gotten married."

Grace swallowed hard. "Do you love Russell?"

"Sometimes I do, and other times I wonder what I'm doing here." She tilted her chin up. "I don't know how I feel about him. It's so different from what I expected."

"In what way? What did you expect?" Grace asked, resigned to listening.

Emily heaved a sigh and stirred her tea. The time it took to sip the tea afforded her the opportunity to gather her thoughts. Like the attorney she was, she had anticipated several possibilities: Grace might refuse to hear her out, she might offer her a cup of tea, listen politely, then request that Emily leave. If that happened, Emily expected to employ all her powers of persuasion, to at least be granted a hearing. But Grace sat across the table waiting for her to begin.

"I'm listening," she said.

Emily braced herself. "I had a good practice in Ocala, but I was crazy about Russell or I would never have uprooted my life and moved here." She paused. "We were insanely in love—or maybe it wasn't love, just passion. I don't know anymore." She smiled weakly. "Not a good reason to marry.

"One day I woke up married, and another day I woke up pregnant, and then Melissa was born." Her eyes held Grace's. "How could I not know it would be like this?" She shook her head and sipped her tea. "I wasn't prepared to be a mother, that's pretty obvious. I haven't the

207

time to read books about mothering, and it sure didn't come naturally to me."

"Aren't you being rather hard on yourself? It seems to me you were quite motherly when Melissa was little."

"She was so tiny, so helpless, and so adorable. I wanted to be a better mother than mine had been. But I'm not even a good daughter. I hardly see my dad at a time like this, when he's adjusting to my mother leaving."

Grace sat silent, her hands resting on the table, her eyes fixed on Emily, with no hint of either approval or disapproval on her face.

"You know how undisciplined Melissa is. It's my fault. I resolve to spend more time with her and Russell. I look at my watch at four in the afternoon and tell myself I'm leaving this office by five, and when I look again it's seven, and I've missed another meal with the family. By then I'm tired, and I hope that when I get home Melissa will be asleep."

Emily's eyes skittered to the clock on the wall, then across the room to the window, and back to Grace. She chose her words carefully. "Sex was great until Melissa was born. Afterward, we hardly touched each other that way. I was exhausted. Many times I turned away from Russell, and after a while he stopped approaching me. At first I was glad, then too embarrassed to ask.

"I work late. Russell goes to bed early, and he's a heavy sleeper. Sometimes I ache to reach over and touch him, but I don't. I can't bear the possibility that he'll reject me. Other times, I hope he won't touch me."

Grace flushed, thinking of last night and the quiet pleasure that she and Bob had shared. "I imagine you'd miss that part of your life. Have you two talked about this, or been to see a counselor? From what I've read in magazines and seen on TV, couples with very busy lives such as yours often have this problem, and they say it can be fixed."

Emily rolled her neck slowly in one direction then the other, as if to relieve tension. "I don't want to take a problem like this to anyone around here."

"Counselors don't talk about their clients' problems."

"Can you really be sure?"

"Do you talk about your clients' problems, Emily?"

"Well, no. But how can you be sure about anyone else?" She lowered her voice. "I'm ashamed to admit it, Grace, but I don't respect Russell. He's not ambitious. Money has never been his goal. I make more than he does, and I have loftier ambitions: a bigger house, car, travel. Russell's satisfied with what we have."

"You knew this when you married him, didn't you?"

"Yes." She lowered her eyes for a moment and bit her lower lip. "I knew he adored Tyler, that parenting was very important to him. I thought once we were married, and if we had children, he'd be motivated to want more—for himself, for the kids, for me."

"I don't know what to say. I'm so sorry about all of this."

"It's so darn complicated. What came first, Grace: the pressures and demands of my work, or did I deliberately work long hours to avoid intimacy? I just don't know anymore. Help me, Grace. Tell me what to do about my life, my marriage, my daughter." Emily buried her face in her hands and wept.

I should comfort her, put my arms about her, be the mother she never had—but I can't. I'm confused, too. She's raised more issues than I can sort out at this moment: passion, love, loneliness, sex, money, family. And my loyalties and love lie with Russell and the children.

When Emily raised her head, Grace handed her a tissue and helplessly said, "I'm so sorry. I don't know how to help you."

Emily drew herself to her feet. "I better be going. I'm sorry I dumped on you, Grace. I had to talk to someone."

Grace looked into her puffy, red eyes and her heart ached for Emily. *Lord, I wouldn't want to be young again.* Moving to the sink, she ran cold water and dampened a hand towel, then ever so gently wiped Emily's face.

Emily grasped Grace's hand. "My God. If only you had been my mother." She burst into tears.

Grace placed her arm about her shoulders. "Give it some time. Things have a way of working out." But when she walked Emily to the door and closed it behind her, anxiety filled her and she leaned heavily against the door for many minutes. *Look at the odds against three women making a home together,* she thought. *It works because we want it to, because we have good will toward one another. Look at Bob's and my relationship. I don't want to marry, and he very much wants to. What are the odds of that working? Bob could have gone off and found himself a wife, men are at a premium at our ages. But we want it to work, so it does. Russell's a good man. Surely they can iron this out.*

Then she remembered reading an article in a self-help magazine. She'd pass on to Emily the idea that she should make a date with Russell, invite him for dinner at a nice, quiet restaurant, where they could be alone and talk. She and Bob would gladly babysit. For a moment, Grace felt better, then she upbraided herself for the sense of self-importance she felt thinking that she could help solve such complicated problems.

For a long while, then, Grace sat at the kitchen table staring at her hands without actually seeing them. Instead, she saw Emily twisting her wedding band.

An unromantic image of Ted in his boxer shorts lying next to her in bed snoring came to mind, and she searched her memory for the passion, the lust that Emily had spoken about. She'd had no experience of sex prior to their marriage.

"It'll just happen," her mother had said. "Natural like."

Grace's expectations had been vague and nonspecific, and afterward she often wondered what all the talk and fuss was about. How would she describe sex with Ted? Mundane, ordinary, practical? Certainly it had been essential if one wanted children, and Grace had wanted children very much.

Emily's visit upset Grace, and the day passed in a blur while she waited anxiously to speak with Bob, who was playing golf with Martin. When she told him about the conversation, his response was, "When sex goes, the marriage goes."

"You don't think they can fix it, then?"

"Frankly, no. Barriers get higher and higher and are harder to breach. It takes a lot of work." Bob leaned over and untied his shoelaces, then slipped his feet out of his shoes and put them on a hassock. "Russell's mother and I stopped having sex years before we divorced. After I was discharged from the army we shared a house and a child, but no sex and little communication for years while we waited for Russell to get old enough to where he'd understand." Bob shook his head.

"But children never understand. Their world's turned topsy-turvy when parents divorce. When the marriage ended, the hardest thing for me to accept was Russell's unequivocal loyalty and preference for his mother. Looking back, I think, why not? I was never there for him. Russell and I didn't have any meaningful contact for years. After Amy died, things changed when I moved up here from Florida. God, I'd hate to see them pick up and go to Florida."

"Emily said Russell wouldn't go with her. I sensed that one of her many dilemmas is what to do about Melissa if she moved alone."

Bob bent and rubbed one foot. "I don't give a damn if Emily goes, but for God's sake, leave the rest of the family intact. She's got no time for that child now. What's she going to do with Melissa in Florida?"

"I know. I'd like to see them work this out."

"It's not your problem to fix, remember that." He was silent a moment. "There are so darn many reasons why a marriage turns sour and goes celibate: infidelity, emotional or physical abuse, illness, loss of respect, fear of intimacy, or simply that one of the partners has a lower sex drive than the other."

"Emily said she doesn't respect Russell. He's not competitive enough, makes less money than she does."

Anger flared in Bob's eyes. He clenched his fists. "Who the hell does she think she is? She's got her nerve. Respect? How can anyone respect a woman who brings a child into the world and then ignores her, a woman who's never there for her family? I'd like to tell her a thing or two."

"I know. But we're not going to do or say anything about this. As you said, it's not our business. If they want to fix their marriage, they'll try. If not, it's goodbye, Emily, and hopefully not Melissa."

The anger in Bob's eyes subsided. "I almost wish you hadn't told me any of this."

"Believe me, I wish I didn't have it to tell."

29

TALK OVER DINNER

Emily acted on Grace's suggestion. She invited Russell for dinner at a quiet upscale restaurant south of Asheville. Accustomed to being adversarial at work, she prepared to present to Russell a systematized, reasonable, and toned-down version of her concerns. But once settled at a table and having ordered dinner, she found that all her planning vanished as conflicting emotions came into play. Her mouth felt coated with a fine dust and her skin grew hot and sticky.

"Russell, we need to talk about our sex life," she blurted and knew immediately that she had bollixed it.

He stared at her as if she'd struck him. "What?"

Wrong! Wrong! Wrong! Stupid.

He unfolded his napkin, spread it across his lap, and motioned the waitress to refill his water glass, which was already half-empty. Then his eyes focused on Emily. "What sex life would you be referring to?"

The muscles of her stomach tightened. "Don't play dumb. You know darn well what I mean."

Russell set his napkin on the table. "Emily, if you've brought me here to argue, I'm leaving."

A circle of sadness widened around her heart. Emily concentrated on the bar, visible behind a glass partition, where a man and woman on barstools chatted and blew swirls of cigarette smoke into the air. The man slipped his arm about the woman's shoulders and leaned in close. She threw back her head and laughed a low, throaty laugh. Were they married? Were they happy?

Overwhelmed by a sense of futility, of failure, Emily's eyes misted. "Russell, I didn't mean to . . . Please don't leave. I'm sorry. I'm frightened that our marriage is falling apart, and I don't know what to do about it. I'm so sorry. Is it too late for us, Russell?"

The waitress refilled Russell's glass. He smiled up at the woman, that warm boyish smile that had so captivated Emily when she had first met him. He never smiled at her that way anymore. In fact, he rarely smiled when she was around.

Russell took a long drink of water and reached for a roll.

At least he isn't going to get up and walk out.

"I don't know, Emily. I can tell you that I am not moving to Ocala. If you're hell-bent on this move, well, then I guess it's over."

"Do you want it to be, Russell?"

"I don't know. What we have isn't good for either of us, and certainly not for the kids."

"I was thinking maybe I could go to Florida for a while, let things cool off, see how we feel being apart."

"If you want to do that, fine. Just leave Melissa here."

"Damn it, Russell, she's my child, too. If I go, she'll go with me."

"Then I'll have to sue you for custody."

Angry, critical, challenging words made a beeline for Emily's mouth, then she remembered Grace's wise counsel to be calm, not to hurl accusations. After a

215

moment's silence, she said, "No, this is all upside down. I want our marriage to work. If we can work things out, I'm not going anywhere."

"Are you saying that you want to go back to Ocala because our marriage isn't good, and not because of those threats? All I've heard from you is how frightened you are, what a horrible place Madison County is, and how awful the people are." He leaned forward. "The people who mean anything in our lives, Grace, Hannah, Amelia, Max, and my dad, are wonderful people, and you know that."

She felt rightly admonished. "Yes. I know that."

"It's really about us then, isn't it?"

"I don't know how to be a wife, Russell. I'm sorry. The only model I had were my parents, and they were pretty cold and indifferent to each other and to me: my mother was gone a lot and my dad sulked. Until they moved to Loring Valley and Dad made a life for himself here, and . . ." She shrugged. "Well, no sense talking about all that. Mother's left." *If only my mother had been attentive, loving, less self-involved. If only my mother had baked cookies and welcomed me home after school with a smile, a hug, a mug of hot chocolate. If only my parents had watched TV together in the evenings, and gone up to bed together, and kissed good-bye in the mornings when Dad went off to work. If. If. If.*

"My parents weren't hotshots when it came to marriage, either," Russell retorted. "I was an army brat, remember, and my folks lived apart for years. It was actually a lot better, just Mom and me, before he came home to live with us."

The knot in Emily's stomach loosened. "Then I guess if we're going to have a decent marriage, we'll have to invent it, won't we?"

"I imagine so."

"My hours have been horrendous. I'm sorry about that."

"It's not so much your hours," Russell said. "It's how you act when you get home. If you walked in the door with your arms open and a smile on your face, we'd all rejoice. As it is, you look as if the garbage of the world's been dumped on you, and you've brought it home to dump on us. Sure, you ask how we are, but it seems perfunctory.

"Have you ever noticed how, when you get home early, Melissa stumbles over her words trying to tell you something that's happened to her that day? She can't get it out fast enough. She's afraid you'll walk away and shut yourself in the den. Do you ever listen to that child, read her a bedtime story, or put her to bed?"

Emily opened her mouth to speak but Russell raised his hand.

"I'm not finished. I'm the one who reads to Melissa. Tyler gets up with her and comforts her when she has a nightmare. He patches her cuts, holds her, and soothes her if she gets hurt when I'm not around. Frankly, Emily, the kids and I feel superfluous in your life. You're a self-contained unit. You need no one, or that's how it appears. If anything's had an adverse effect on our sex life, I'd say that's it."

Her list of complaints paled beside his grievances. He was right. Work was her refuge from an underlying discontent that she had brought to the marriage.

The waitress arrived with their dinners, and eating gave Emily time to think. She hadn't been happy in Ocala, either, but she'd never admitted that to Russell or to anyone else. Besides being attracted to him, marrying Russell had seemed the ideal alternative, the way out. Thinking about moving back to Ocala brought a sinking feeling to her heart.

"I want to stay here and work things out with you," Emily said. "If it's not too late." *I'll go to a therapist, get some help, find out what drives my dissatisfaction.*

Russell put down his fork.

A feeling of expectancy swept over Emily. She held her breath.

"I'd like that too, Emily. We have a family to think about."

Her expectation shriveled. What was he saying? He wanted to work it out for Melissa's sake? "Not just for the children," she said, unable to keep the edge from her voice. "I want to make it better for us."

He nodded. "Of course, for us."

Recognizing that enough had been said, they ordered dessert and coffee, and spoke softly of inconsequential matters.

On the drive back to Covington, Emily's mood fluctuated between hope and resignation, one moment fixating on the belief that this would not work, then certain they could work it out.

She thought about Melissa and what a difficult child she was. Had she been that way from the start, or had the problems started when Melissa began to walk, to get into everything? Emily had pushed the child away, ignored her for long periods of time, yelled at her. Melissa was almost three, and already she had failed her daughter, as she believed that her mother had failed her.

It was never pleasant for Emily to think about her childhood. Her mother had trivialized her concerns over things large and small, starting with nightmares and moving on to being bullied at school, the way her hair looked, her difficulties with friends.

"Don't be stupid and melodramatic," Ginger had said, waving the thirteen-year-old Emily away as she wept about a too-short haircut. Or, "You're pathetic. What makes you think you're the only child who ever got teased?" tossed over Ginger's shoulder as she walked out of the front door with a Scrabble set under her arm.

Melissa deserved better. But what did one do or say to a young child who was already spoiled rotten? Emily felt as barren of ideas as a dried-up riverbed.

That night, she and Russell made love, timorously approaching each other beneath the sheets. It went too fast and ended too soon for Emily, but the small familiar touches, the occasional murmurs of enjoyment, the renewal of physical contact with Russell comforted her and gave her hope, for them, and for herself.

30
A TIME FOR TRUTHS

"It would be nice," Grace said, "if we could spend some time without anyone having a crisis. It seems to me that since last Christmas, it's been one thing after another." She and Bob were sitting in his living room.

Bob looked through his newspaper for the sports page. "Martin and I had a good golf game yesterday."

"How's Martin doing with Ginger gone?"

"I doubt there's a difference. No, that's not true." Bob set down his paper for a moment. "There was a certain tension not knowing if he'd find her at home—or, if she were away, when she'd return. I think it's easier for him now. He's more relaxed."

Grace watched Bob sort the newspaper. *In a second, he'll lose himself in that newspaper again. I'll clean up the breakfast dishes and go home.*

When she had gotten home last night, Bob had taken her hand and led her up the front steps of his cottage. She'd had a moment of concern that Amelia might be home alone, and Amelia hated being alone at night. Bob saw her look toward the house and sensed her reluctance.

"Grace. Amelia's a grown woman. She doesn't need a babysitter."

"You're right, of course, especially since we had an alarm system installed. But I worry that she might feel abandoned."

"You like to worry."

Grace had acquiesced, and spent the night at Bob's cottage.

She said now, "I like babysitting the kids. We don't see them as much as we used to. Tyler was such a dear the other evening, don't you think?"

Eyes glued to his paper, Bob nodded.

"I'm so proud of him getting an A in history and science. Aren't you?"

Bob nodded.

"He asked if I'd work with him to bring that C in English up to a B. Of course I will." Grace pulled her chair closer to Bob's and nudged his arm. He lifted his eyes, smiled absently at her, then turned back to the paper.

"Tyler even tolerated Melissa with all her noise, and pranks, and running about. It was nice, the way he carried her up to bed when she fell asleep on the floor at her grandpa's feet, don't you think?"

"Yep," Bob said.

"Why do you think Melissa's wound so tight? She never stopped chattering or running around until she collapsed. I was quite worn out. Was Russell as active as Melissa when he was a child?"

"Hum. What?" Bob did not lift his head.

Grace jiggled the side of his paper. "What can be so interesting about sports this early in the morning? And how can you read with the TV on?"

"Scores. Details of games. Which player did what and when."

She sighed. "I'll never understand what all the fuss is about ballgames."

"Grace." He laid the paper aside. "You know how we all have quirks?"

"Certainly."

"Well, honey, reading my paper on Sunday morning is one of mine. Let's talk about Tyler later, shall we?" He reached over and kissed her cheek. "I love you. Now go away."

Somewhat mollified by his kiss, Grace stood. "All right, I'll be going now."

"We have breaking news," the TV anchorman said tersely. Across the screen, against a blue sky, a plume of smoke streaked earthward. "Breaking apart," were the next words the anchorman spoke.

"Oh, my God," Grace said. "No! The shuttle's exploded." She burst into tears.

Bob's paper was forgotten. "No," he said, "it can't be. They're due back today." He grabbed the clicker and turned up the sound. "Across Texas. Two hundred thousand feet up over Texas." He reached for Grace and put his arms about her. "This is terrible. Just terrible. Those brave young people—they were almost home."

Grace buried her face in his shoulder and sobbed. Tears ran down Bob's face. As they held each other, someone pounded on the door. Eyes wide and red from crying, Amelia stood on the porch.

"Don't stand there. Come in, Amelia," Grace said.

"Did you see it, hear the news?"

"We just did. Horrible. Those poor men and woman, almost home."

"And their families. Imagine their families waiting, and then to see that. Awful! Horrible!"

"Bob's in the living room. Go on in."

Amelia moved toward the living room just as the front door swung open again, admitting Hannah and Max. "We were just finishing breakfast when we saw the news," Hannah said.

"Bob's watching TV in there." Grace pointed to the right. "I'll bring us all some tea and coffee."

Max nodded and followed Amelia into the living room.

Hannah trailed Grace to the kitchen. "Do you realize, Grace, that in the last five years we've weathered good news, bad news, all kinds of important news together? When this report came on all I wanted to do was run home, and then I saw Amelia start over here, so Max and I came, too."

"I'm glad you did. It's best to be together at a time like this."

"Goodness, I miss living at home full-time."

"You're home more than you were."

"I adore Max, and I love being with him." Hannah's face turned rosy. Her hand skimmed across her hair. "Who would have thought at my age, in bed, it would be so . . . well, you know. It's a powerful thing."

Grace smiled. "It certainly is. We're lucky, you and I, to have another chance at love and passion."

"I'm at Max's more than I ought to be. The thing is,

when I stay overnight there, it's simpler to get dressed and go to work with him. And when I have dinner there it just seems natural to stay the night."

Grace's brow furrowed. "I know what you mean. It was easier for me to separate myself from Bob when he lived elsewhere. I spend too much time worrying about him since he moved next door."

Hannah nodded. "Living so close to Max unsettles me somehow, as if I *ought* to be with him. That's not what we planned. I was to live at home and he at his place."

"Nothing's as simple as we think it's going to be, is it?"

"No, it's not. Do you think that eventually we'll settle into a comfortable routine?" Hannah asked.

"I certainly hope so. I hate feeling guilty, eating dinner at home when I know Bob's alone. There are times when I wish he still lived with Russell or had his apartment in Loring Valley." Grace poured boiling water over tea leaves in the teapot and filled three mugs with coffee. "It's complex, these relationships with the men in our lives. I imagine, in time, it'll work out."

"I certainly hope you're right," Hannah replied. "However subtle they may be, men keep up the pressure for more of our time. I'd forgotten that."

Grace thought of Lurina who, old as she was, had complained of the same thing with Old Man. "Indeed they do. Unless they're immersed in the Sunday paper."

"And what about Amelia? She's had a big adjustment, also. She must feel we've abandoned her," Hannah said.

"Yes. It's been hard on her." Grace picked up the tray with the mugs and cups, and Hannah followed her into the living room, where they watched TV until the repetition of the event and the lack of a definitive explanation exhausted them.

"I must get away from this for a bit," Bob said, clicking to a sports channel. "When NASA knows more, they'll tell us."

"Agreed," Max said. Shortly after, he kissed Hannah, bade the others good-bye, and with long strides crossed the road to his farmhouse. Soon the ladies returned to their home, and Bob, with a sigh of relief, picked up the sports pages.

A hush descended on his cottage, and the aroma of fresh-brewed coffee from the mug on the table pleased Bob. But he had lost interest in reading, and instead thought about Grace and the changing nature of their relationship.

After years of levying pressure on her to live with him, he had come to accept her firm resistance. He'd grown accustomed to living alone and enjoyed his freedom. It was actually nice not to account for his goings and comings, and being able to read all night, if he chose, without worrying that his light bothered Grace. There was no pressure about routines—fixed mealtimes and other domesticities such as where he hung up his clothes or towels.

After moving to the cottage, fretfulness that had no specific focus weighed down his spirits. There were moments when he wondered if he'd forgotten to do something with Grace or to tell her something. And it sometimes annoyed him, after a day of golf, when all he wanted was to kick off his shoes and stick his feet and stinky socks in the air, drink a beer, and read his paper, that Grace would arrive with dinner or to visit. The look on her face, the way she wrinkled her nose, sent him scurrying to put his shoes back on and set aside his paper. He felt piqued at having to defer gratification, to pay attention to Grace at times when he would have preferred being alone, and he berated himself for his self-centeredness. Keeping him up nights, now, was the problem of how to tell this to his dear, sweet Grace and not hurt her?

Bob rested his head back and closed his eyes. Immediately, images of the streaks across the blue sky, the reporter's stunned and disbelieving voice, further unsettled him. As he looked back, his own life seemed inconsequential—all his years in the army as naught measured against these dauntless, inspired men and women who had braved outer space. When the space program was in its infancy, he had never hungered to participate, and had considered the whole business a huge waste of time and money.

Bob shifted in his chair. Enough of this kind of thinking. He'd been brave enough in his day, had paid his dues in service to his country. He'd done time in Korea—not on the battle lines, but even that had taken guts. Then his bravado faded. There were many forms of cowardice, after all, one of them being his inability to share his changed perspective with Grace.

In the beginning of their relationship, passion and a pulsing energy had infused his every waking moment. He ached for communion and a merging with Grace, and his need to see, to touch, to hold, to love her, had resonated within him when they were apart.

Grace had acquiesced in most matters, except moving in with him—until the fire that burned her home brought her to stay in his apartment. When the ladies moved back to their new farmhouse, Grace stayed with him. But after a few short weeks, when she tearfully poured out her dissatisfaction and stated her desire to go home, a weight had lifted from his shoulders.

Bob reached for his coffee. He loved Grace with a surety and quiet confidence that was no longer based on sex or dependency. Before Grace, he had lived in a perpetual state of discontent. She had anchored him to herself, to Covington, and to his family. Unwittingly, she had served as his angel of peace. But at what cost to her?

Bob slapped the side of his head. How egocentric he was. What if Grace felt the same way he did? What if her attentions to him were habit driven and interfered with the things she really wanted to do?

Back and forth Bob went. He had a duty to be true to himself, didn't he? Yet it was hard giving up both the idea and the reality of Grace's devotion. On the other hand, there were times when he wanted to yell, "Leave me alone"—like her late-night call inquiring if he was all right because the light in his bedroom was on at two A.M. He resented the surveillance. What was she doing up at that hour, anyway?

He could bury his feelings, but wouldn't that be a disservice to them both? How to bring up the subject, though? Bob sighed and picked up the newspaper.

The following afternoon, Russell dropped Tyler off at the ladies' farmhouse.

Slouching under the weight of his backpack, Tyler walked into the house and sloughed his pack onto the kitchen table. He flopped into a chair. "It's always so nice and cozy here. Good to see you, Granny Grace."

Grace placed a slice of Vienna cake in front of him and a glass of milk. "It's good to see you, too, Tyler."

Tyler swiftly downed the milk. "Thanks—I sure was thirsty. I get real thirsty in school. Sometimes there's such a line at the water fountain, I can't take the time to get a drink."

Grace refilled his glass and joined him at the table. "How about taking a small bottle of water with you to school?" she suggested.

His eyes went to his backpack, and he shook his head. "I've got enough to lug."

Grace backed off. If Tyler were thirsty enough, he'd find a way to have a drink. "Well, what's the English assignment today?"

Tyler tipped the backpack, disgorging notebooks, pencils, and textbooks, which he sorted through until he located a notebook with ENGLISH scrawled in large bold letters across the front.

"I'm supposed to do a character sketch of a person I know." He rested his hand over his heart. "It's got to be 'from the heart, and no making it up,' Mrs. Earl says." He opened the notebook. "I was gonna write about Grandpa, and then I got to thinking about Emily."

That grabbed Grace's attention. "Emily? Why Emily?"

"It might be cool to write about how a person starts off so nice and how they change."

Grace leaned her elbows on the table and studied Tyler's face. "How has Emily changed?"

"Before I tell you, Granny Grace, you got to promise me two things."

"What two things?"

"First off, if Emily makes Dad move to Ocala, I'm not going. I'll live here with either you or Grandpa." His voice hardened. "I am not gonna leave my home, and my friends, and school. She made me do that one time, but not again."

Grace nodded. "I hear you, Tyler."

"You gotta promise not to say anything to Dad about what I just said. It could stir things up and make matters worse. You know what I mean."

"You have my word," Grace said. "And the other thing?"

"I want to tell you how I really feel about Emily, but you must never, ever tell anyone, especially Dad or even Grandpa. Okay?"

"It's a deal." She extended her hand and they shook hands.

Tyler ate a bite of cake, took a swallow of milk, and settled back in his chair. "When Dad first married Emily they seemed happy enough, with a lot of kissing and hugging stuff. But after Melissa was born, everything changed. Emily changed. Sometimes she'd look at the baby as if she didn't recognize her, as if she were wondering what she was doing sitting in that rocker holding a baby. If Dad wasn't home, Melissa would cry a long time before Emily went to her. Sometimes I'd go, and Melissa'd be cold and wet and shivering, her little face all scrunched up and red and puffy, and her chest heaving from crying. I'd change her and hold her until her body went from hard and stiff to soft. Even now, I can comfort Melissa, like if she falls and hurts herself, better than anyone. Maybe she remembers."

His vulnerability touched Grace. So this was where his usual kindness toward Melissa originated.

"Granny Grace." Tyler looked at her with an intensity and understanding far beyond his age. "I know Melissa's a handful. Sometimes she's downright mean, but when I think about her lying there alone, cold and crying so hard I thought she'd burst, my heart goes soft. Melissa probably doesn't remember all this, but I do. I think how alone she must have felt, maybe even scared and abandoned, like I felt when my mom died." He looked away for a moment. "I don't really like Emily very much. I wish she'd take herself back to Florida and leave Dad, Melissa, and me right where we are." His hands became fists. "I don't want her to take my sister. If Emily went back to Florida, she'd dump Melissa in some stupid day care with strangers. If everyone thinks Melissa's rambunctious now, she'll be off-the-wall nuts if she's taken away from her home and Dad and me."

The same thing Bob had said. Grace agreed but kept her counsel. "I won't say a word about any of this to anyone. Truth is, Tyler, I'm worried, too. Emily's confused and unhappy. Maybe if she were happier she'd be able to cope with Melissa. Maybe she wouldn't want to go back to Florida."

Tyler thought a moment, then cocked his head. "What would make her feel better, do you think?"

"I don't know. Maybe if she relaxed more, worked less, worried less, smiled more, and spent more time with Russell and you kids."

"Good luck. That's a mighty big order, Granny Grace."

Grace straightened her shoulders. "So, you want to write about Emily?"

"No. I don't." He slouched across his scattered books. "Telling you how I feel is more than enough about her." He rolled a pencil back and forth, back and forth on the table. "Writing about her would be what Aunt Amelia would call hanging out my dirty laundry." Tyler grinned. "Aunt Amelia sure is a character. I remember the time everyone was out half the night hunting for her in Pisgah Forest, and then another time she nearly froze to death walking in a snowstorm over in Barnardsville.

The cops found her and brought her home, remember, Granny Grace?"

"Sure. I'm surprised you remember. You were what, seven?"

"Yep. Seven, almost eight when she got lost in the forest."

"I don't think she'd let any of those things happen to her today."

"Aunt Amelia's changed. She was really uptight when she first came here and kind of snooty. She's not anymore. She tried to teach me photography, and she didn't get mad when I told her I didn't want to learn it."

"We grow and learn many things, and hopefully we change those behaviors that no longer work for us, Tyler."

"You've changed, too. You're brave, Granny Grace. You went back in the house when it was on fire and saved Aunt Amelia's antique fans, even though you lost all the porcelain clowns Grandpa gave you." He pulled back from the table and shoved his books to one side. "You ever replace those clowns?"

"A few. Your grandpa gave me a lovely porcelain clown tossing a hoop for Christmas."

Tyler smiled. "I remember how shy you used to be when I first knew you. Boy, you've really changed."

Grace smiled. *He's sweet, and dear, and thoughtful, and I love him.* "Darling boy. Being a part of your family has been a most wonderful experience. It's helped me be a stronger, better, happier person than I was when I came to Covington."

"Is it true, Granny Grace, that you drove Aunt Hannah's car from Pennsylvania at forty miles an hour?"

She laughed, remembering. "It's true. I'd never driven a car on an interstate. I'd lived in a very small town."

The long hand of the big clock above the refrigerator clicked, signaling its approach to the hour. "Goodness, it's four already. Decide who you'll write about, and go ahead while I peel potatoes for dinner." Grace rose and headed for the pantry.

"I'll write about you," he said. "I know you the best of all."

"Oh, Tyler, there must be someone else." Grace stopped, the bag of potatoes in her hand, and looked at him.

"Nope. You're it."

She rested the bag on the counter near the sink. "Well, all right, then. I'm proud you've chosen me."

31
REALIGNING THE MARRIAGE

Emily's conversation with Russell, their one night of lovemaking, and her well-intentioned resolutions proved insufficient to quell the discontent that nagged at her. She had expected that marriage would fill the void. Instead it gaped, a huge hole within her, and marriage was proving to be a box over which she could not see.

Why couldn't she enjoy her husband and child, and Tyler, too? Russell asked very little of her: a modicum of quality time, gentleness, a smile, attention paid to the children. Even early on, when she had turned from him in bed, he had not pressed her but had waited patiently for her to take the lead. That had annoyed her. She wanted him to persist, to pursue, to ravish her. But Russell wasn't a ravisher. He was a decent, reliable man who had loved her. They'd been married less than four years, and she couldn't say that he loved her or even liked her much any longer, and she had grave doubts about her feelings for him.

After their dinner at the restaurant, Emily vowed to be all that she believed Russell hoped for, all that she considered she ought to be for him and the children. But when she stepped into the house in the evening, the walls closed about her. Melissa, with her constant demands for attention, irritated her. Tyler's silent disapproval, the way he turned from her, his ability to quiet and calm Melissa when she could not, made her uncomfortable, even jealous, and augmented her feelings of inadequacy.

Then Russell suggested that they have dinner out again, and with a heavy heart, she agreed.

Russell looked at her across the table and his voice was soft. "I love you, Emily. If it's something I've done or said, please tell me. Give me the opportunity to change."

This she had not expected. "It's not you, Russell.

You're a dear, good man. It's me. I haven't a clue how to be a decent wife or mother."

"It's not a question of decent or good or bad, Emily."

"More caring, then, more appropriate to what the roles suggest."

"You seem unhappy at home. Only your work brings you satisfaction."

"You're right, Russell, and I don't know why." Tears filled her eyes. "It's not what I wanted or hoped for when we married, believe me."

"You're saying your expectations were not met in our marriage, that I failed you?"

"Oh. Russell, it's not you, or the kids. It's something inside of me, don't you understand?"

"And you think moving to Ocala will change that, make you happy?"

She dabbed at her eyes with a handkerchief from her purse and shook her head. "I don't know. I just don't know. Where else would I go? I wouldn't leave you and stay here. What would be the sense of that? I know people back in Ocala. Maybe I can pick up my practice again."

The waiter set their dinners on the table but neither of them picked up a fork. "I've been thinking," he said. "Maybe you could go to Ocala for a few months and see how you like it. If you do, would you consider leaving Melissa with us for that time? Let's not consider it a formal separation, just a realignment, trying a new tack. What do you say?"

Emily picked up her utensils and began to cut her

steak, and the vigor with which she attacked her dinner felt like a slap in the face, since he could hardly swallow his mashed potatoes. *She's steely and insensitive. Whatever the outcome of this, I can't let Emily walk away with my daughter.* "Will you at least think about my suggestion?"

Russell looked around the room and wondered about the lives of their fellow diners. Who among them was happy? Who was not? Was that family enjoying the evening? The youngest, a boy of about two, began to scream. People at nearby tables cast disapproving looks, reminding him that this was how it was when they took Melissa out to eat. As he watched, an argument ensued between the parents, seemingly about who would take the child from the table.

Surreptitiously, Russell eyed a couple in a booth across the way. They avoided each other's eyes. The man tapped his leg under the table; the woman drummed the top with polished fingernails. Obviously bored! But surely that young couple leaning toward each other across their table and talking animatedly were in the flush of new love. How would someone observing him and Emily evaluate them?

At the table next to theirs, a man stood and headed toward the restroom. His female companion's eyes roamed the room, settling for long moments on a good-looking young waiter, then on a man at another table, then moved on to Russell, whom she eyed quizzically before looking away.

People married with high hopes for the future, Russell thought. His longing for companionship and union had been answered with Amy, and, he had thought, a second time with Emily. But he had struck out with Emily. Russell felt suddenly ill, and Grace's voice sounded in his mind. "A cup of tea will settle your stomach. Try it. You'll see." Russell beckoned their waiter and ordered tea.

Emily sopped up the juices from her meat with a chunk of roll. What she would do, what she would tell Russell, was the hardest thing she had ever done, but she felt at a dead end here in Covington. How would she ever know what her life could be, should be, if she didn't return to Florida? There, in her mind, at least, she'd had the ideal working situation.

Russell sipped the tea, and his stomach did begin to settle. But it was not until he had paid the bill, and they were walking across the parking lot to the car, that Emily finally spoke.

"I'll take your suggestion. I'll go to Florida for several months and I will leave Melissa with you."

At home that night, Russell slept downstairs on the couch. It was early when Emily awakened him, her heart in her mouth. Before coming down she had gone into her daughter's room and stood over the sleeping child, curled in a ball, her arms about her teddy bear. If she had ever dreamed of a child, it was Melissa, yet having a child hadn't lived up to her ideal of motherhood. She hated herself that her own daughter, and

Russell, and Tyler, her life here, was not enough.

Downstairs, she told Russell, "I'm going to the office. I'll prepare an agreement regarding Melissa. If it suits you, we can sign it. It'll take me three weeks to clean up my business and transfer all my pending cases to another lawyer. I'll try Ocala for six months, and then we'll see."

Russell's emotions spun and collided. He had gotten what he'd asked for. Was it what he wanted? The pleasant thought that her departure would end the tension in the house was quickly overshadowed by a deep, gut-wrenching loneliness. How could he want her gone and still want her here? Russell stared up at his wife, and realized that he had already begun to mourn the loss of her.

All he could manage was, "Fine, Emily, you do that." Then he sat up, gathered the sheet about him, grabbed the blanket and pillow, and headed for the stairs to dress and get on with his day.

32
A DAY IN SALEM, SOUTH CAROLINA

Max drove the four of them to visit Roger in his new Subaru. In the back seat Grace snuggled close to Bob, relieved that he was not driving. Bob had a way of precipitously shifting lanes that made her cringe. Sometimes he drove above the speed limit or drifted toward the center of the road, and he often braked at the last moment at red lights. With Max at the steering wheel, she could relax and enjoy the view of fields backed by mountains that seemed to guard the valley.

From the front seat came Max's voice. "Why didn't Amelia come with us?"

"The art critic who gave her work such a terrific write-up is coming in from New York. Mike said that he was quite taken with Amelia when they met," Grace replied.

"How nice for her," Max said. "She must feel like odd man out these days."

"Yes," Grace said. "And that troubles me. What if my two housemates were busy with the men in their lives, and I had no one? Amelia has always wanted a meaningful relationship with a man."

Hannah wrinkled her nose. "And when she finally found someone, he turned out to be no good. I knew about Lance, what a bum he was, from day one." She turned to look at Grace and changed the subject. "So Emily's really leaving?"

Grace wished Hannah hadn't asked; she wanted to forget it and enjoy this trip. "Melissa will stay, while Emily goes off to decide what she wants to do."

"That woman doesn't have a clue what she wants to do. She's not satisfied with anything," Bob said. "She doesn't deserve that little girl, or Russell and Tyler. She'll not meet up again with a man as decent as Russell."

"That little girl, if I remember, is quite a handful." Max slowed the Subaru as an ancient pickup, loaded with crates of chickens or turkeys, pulled from a side road onto the road ahead of them. Max braked hard. "Wonder how far he's going at thirty-five miles an hour?"

"Take a deep breath, summon up your patience, and enjoy the scenery," Hannah said, before returning to the earlier topic. "Emily's a foolish woman. I agree with you, Bob, she won't find another man as tolerant and patient as Russell."

"Maybe she doesn't want or need anyone in her life," Bob said. "Some people are like that. They ought never to marry."

"I thought I liked being alone for a long time. It's nicer to have someone." Hannah smiled at Max and patted his leg.

"Even an old codger like me?" Max grinned.

"Even an old codger like you."

"When does Emily leave?" Hannah asked.

"Sometime within the next two weeks," Bob replied.

Grace squeezed Bob's hand. It was her way of asking him not to go on talking about Emily.

He looked at her. "Honey, ignoring what's happening isn't going to change anything. It's for the best, as I see it. In six months the kids will have a chance to settle down, and hopefully, Emily will see that there's no place for a three-year-old in her new life."

"You make it sound so simple." Grace withdrew the arm she had slipped through his. "Can't you see how hurt and disappointed Russell is? And Melissa's very confused."

"And Tyler's happier than I've seen him in months," Bob said.

Grace's strong commitment to family drove her on. "All the avenues have not been explored. They haven't tried counseling. If Emily handled divorce cases, she'd have more respect for mediation counseling. She'd know someone who specializes in mediation."

"Isn't mediation about compromise in settling financial, custody, and other family matters more amicably in a divorce case, rather than a counseling tool?" Bob asked.

"I hardly see where counseling does anything," Max said. "Married folks have their ups and downs. You muddle through and stay married, or you don't."

"Can we talk about something else, please?" Grace asked.

Hannah straightened and faced the road. "Oh, good," she said. "That truck's turning off."

The truck creaked and leaned as it slowed then turned onto a single-lane dirt road. Max speeded up, and no one spoke for a long while.

Glimmering in the sunshine, Lake Keowee came into view. Sprawling homes on spits of land thrust into the lake. Mountains rose in the distance. They drove on for several miles, passed the sign to Lake Jocassee, and took the turn onto the Piedmont Forest Nursery road, which led to Roger's land in Salem.

Finally they found his driveway and drove across the rutted dirt road down to the nearly completed house. An enthusiastic Roger welcomed them, standing in the doorway of a solid ranch-style house that sprang from the landscape as if it were the capstone of forty instead of six acres.

The kitchen, great room, and dining area all spilled one into the other. French doors opened to a spacious covered porch overlooking bottomland, a river, and planted fields across the river. Beyond it all, the haze-covered North Carolina mountains framed the view.

The house was a split-bedroom plan: two bedrooms on one side, one on the other. "For guests," Roger said as he opened the door to a large, bright room with a view of the mountains. He took his mother's arm. "Come, I want to show you the rest of the house and the view of the river from the porch. Look." Roger pointed down.

No trace remained of the thick, bushy barrier that had concealed Little River. Clearly visible now, the river, driven by copious rains and melting mountain snows, rushed steadily along. Sparkles of sunlight flicked across its surface. A rectangular gazebo with a shingled roof had been erected along its bank.

"It's built right where you said it should be, Mother. You were right, it's peaceful sitting there by the water. The river's always different. Takes your mind off all your problems." He looked out to the far hills and whispered, "Charles would have loved it here."

"Does the river flood the bottomland?" Hannah asked. "How rich the soil must be."

"They say it floods occasionally. I haven't seen it come close to cresting its banks, but yes, it's rich soil down in that bottom. I've had it tested and a bit of lime was all it needed. I plan on planting a large garden, then canning and freezing the vegetables I grow."

Grace pictured her son in a hot kitchen, an apron tied about his waist, sweat running down his forehead and beading across his upper lip as he lifted jars of carrots from the steamer. She smiled. *If Charles were looking down from heaven he would be smiling.*

"Lenny's a vegetarian, and I'm slowly cutting back on meat." Roger patted his stomach. "I feel better already."

"Who's Lenny?" Grace asked.

"Dr. Leonard Meadows, professor of horticulture at the university. We met when I took his class. He's been trying to make a vegetarian and a Unitarian out of me since we became friends."

"How nice you've found someone," Hannah said.

"Oh, we don't live together," Roger said. "That's not what I want right now."

"It's good to have a friend with common interests," Hannah said.

Roger led them back inside. At the end of the great room closest to the kitchen, six folding chairs surrounded a table. A straw basket and a Styrofoam ice chest sat on the wood plank floor. "I haven't had a final electrical inspection yet, so the appliances aren't on, but I've got a picnic lunch for us. We can eat in here or take it out onto the porch, whichever you prefer. The sun's moving behind the house now, so the porch is shaded this time of day."

"There are six chairs, Roger. Are you expecting someone else?" Grace asked.

"Yes, Lenny. I thought you'd like to meet him, especially Hannah—the horticulture and all, you know."

"We'd all like to meet him," Bob said.

Max wandered about the house opening and closing doors, knocking on walls, kneeling to run his hands along the smooth grain of the floors. He pulled down the steps to the attic, climbed up, poked his head into the opening and climbed back down. "Nice finishes. Good work here," he said. "It's built solid to last."

Roger handed his mother a red-checked tablecloth, which she spread over the table, and set out plastic plates and utensils. Together they emptied the picnic basket of tuna, egg, roast beef, and pimento cheese sandwiches, as well as crocks of potato salad and cold slaw. "Not very original, but everything is fresh from a good deli in Clemson," Roger said.

The sound of tires crunching stone could be heard. "That must be Lenny."

Grace moved a step closer to Bob, and he put his arm around her. "Relax, honey. It's okay. Roger needs a friend."

Why do people say "need" when "want" is a better word? Grace brushed strands of hair from her face, and turned to greet the man entering the front door.

Stocky, with reddish-brown hair and freckles, Lenny was not a handsome man, but he was certainly a vibrant and energetic one. His gray-blue eyes danced as if with some deeply felt pleasure, or as if he knew the biggest, most exciting secret and would soon share it with you. He moved across the room shaking hands with everyone and smiling his wide, generous smile. Grace noticed that Lenny did not embrace Roger, he merely smiled and slapped him on the back in buddy fashion. Grace liked him immediately.

Hannah responded to Lenny with obvious interest. They strolled out onto the porch, and Grace heard talk of organic fertilizers, companion planting, and varieties of fungus-resistant tomatoes best suited to the climate.

"Let's eat," Roger soon called.

They crowded about the table, shoulder to shoulder, and chatted lightheartedly. Lenny told them stories about Clemson's theater, greenhouses, traffic, and ball-games, and related funny stories about his classes. When they were done they walked down to the bottomland, all but Max and Bob, who headed up the hill to explore the rest of the land.

"Marigolds planted in sufficient amounts around tomatoes will help considerably in protecting them from insects," Lenny said, as he offered Hannah his arm down the rough dirt track.

"I quite agree. Last year, I didn't plant enough of them around my tomatoes." Engrossed in plant talk, Hannah and Lenny continued across the field and away from the river, leaving Grace and her son alone in the gazebo.

"I like your friend," Grace said. "You must have learned a lot about planting from him."

"The man's a font of knowledge. When I started in his class, I was the dumbest student and the oldest. Everyone seemed to know what was going on but me. The vocabulary took me forever to master with all those Latin names. It was a huge relief when I got a C on my first exam. Now I ace them." He stuck his thumbs into his armpits, stuck out his chest, and grinned. "You're looking at an A student."

"I'm so proud of you, and happy for you, Roger."

"Lenny's a great guy. He's generous of spirit. Our friendship's developed slowly."

Does a mother's concern for her child ever diminish? When Roger was a young man, parent-bashing had been popular, and whenever her son was dissatisfied or unhappy, Grace had blamed herself. Had she been too harsh with him, demanded too much or too little of him, discouraged him, or not encouraged him sufficiently? Had she, with her own anxieties, contributed to his? When he was a child, had she doted on him and coddled him excessively? As an adolescent, had she traumatized him by minimizing his fears? And down to the root of her concern: had she been responsible for his being gay? Roger would of course insist that she was not.

Grace thought of Charles, who, with his strength and quiet calm, had diffused the uptightness characteristic of Roger. When he passed away, it had appeared to Grace that Roger's need for attention and all his latent insecurities had been unleashed.

Before his move to Salem, Grace had found her son increasingly self-centered, uptight, and downright mean, shown in his deplorable behavior and abrupt dismissal of Mike. But now, as they sat here watching Little River drift along, she felt that her son's tension and restlessness seemed gone. The lines about Roger's mouth had softened. His eyes no longer vacillated between steely and haunted.

Roger sat with his feet up on the rail, his body relaxed, his hands hanging loosely over the arms of the chair, and Grace's heart swelled with pleasure. *He's letting Charles go. Maybe Lenny's provided the curative balm Roger needed? But Roger seems to have been victorious in some internal battle that's enabled him to be truer to himself than he's ever been. It's enabled him to strike out on his own, to buy this land long before he met Lenny Meadows.*

Looking back, Grace knew that Charles had played the role of father to Roger. Perhaps Roger's need for a caring father had now been satisfied, for the friendship between Lenny and Roger seemed to be one of equals—brothers rather than parent and child. And they were close in age, not twenty years apart as Roger and Charles had been.

Grace relaxed. Chatting with her son was a new pleasure for her, and when he asked, she told him about Emily and Russell's separation and her concerns for the children. She spoke of Amelia's successful show in New York and the reportedly charming Mr. Blanchette who was, at this very moment, visiting Amelia in Covington. She told him of Lurina's mishap in the snow and her moving to a retirement community in Mars

247

Hill, and she showed him the cameo pin that Lurina had given her. Finally she said, "My goodness, I haven't shut up, have I?"

"It's good to get the news," Roger replied. "I've come to care for your friends. I'm sorry about the old Masterson place being bulldozed. They could have repaired it and used it as a museum."

"We were all very upset. Emily spoke to the people at the Park Service. They apologized profusely and said someone had misread the instructions for the care of the property. What could we do? The place was gone, and Lurina is quite content at Mars Hill and didn't want to pursue a lawsuit."

Light as air and comfortable as an old pair of slippers, silence settled about them. Intermittent breezes, fresh and cool, touched her face. Contentedly, Grace stretched her arms above her head.

Then Roger said, "Look, Mother, the way the water licks away at the bank. I've been told that the river's about a foot wider than it was fifty years ago. In geological time, that's instantaneous." He snapped his fingers.

Geological time. He would never have thought or talked about geological time, or rivers, or the land before. The changes occurring in her son were absolutely wonderful.

"Water is so very powerful," Grace said. "I've never been comfortable with large bodies of water."

"I'm surprised you took a cruise. That's water on every side stretching to the horizon."

Grace squared her shoulders. "You'd have been proud of me. I told myself, 'Now Grace, you can't be an old scaredy cat all your life. What's going to happen will happen and to heck with it.' I did have one scary moment, going down an unsteady gangplank to a small boat that took us across the harbor to St. Thomas, but Hannah and Amelia bolstered my courage. When I got back to the ship that afternoon, Roger, I stepped from the boat onto that swaying gangplank like I'd done it all my life. I felt as if I'd climbed Everest."

He laughed lightly and slapped his thigh. "Well, good for you, Mother. Good for you."

Inside she felt warm and happy.

Roger's eyes traversed the bottomland and followed the hill up to the house. "This was the right move, the right time and place for me. I never told you, but I took your advice after Charles died. I drove up into the mountains and parked in an isolated spot, then cried and screamed until I thought my heart and lungs would burst."

Deeply touched by his words, she offered a silent prayer of thanks.

"I raged. I cursed Charles for dying and leaving me. But then I forgave him. I cursed and forgave my father for never being there, for the unspoken contempt I knew he felt for me, for my lifestyle. It's not what he wanted, what he'd hoped for in his only child, his son. I understood and forgave him. In the process, I realized that I never wanted to be an engineer or a businessman, that I wanted an off-the-beaten-path, simpler, quieter life." He waved his hand toward the river. "I found it here and the local shopkeepers, bankers, and farmers I run into have been incredibly welcoming and helpful."

"There's something I like about this area. It's softer, more pastoral land, and they say it's warmer down here than where we are," Grace said. "Walhalla is a nice small town."

Hannah and Lenny had reached the far end of the field and turned around, and would soon join them in the gazebo. Behind them, their footprints branded the soft dark earth, marking their passage. Hannah returned, her face flushed from excitement and warmed by sunshine, and pulled a chair into the shade at the edge of the gazebo by the river. Lenny settled into a lounge near Grace, and the conversation turned from the personal and particular to the impersonal and general, to varieties of vegetables and fruit: blueberries, raspberries, blackberries, and figs, with canned preserves as the end product.

Grace thanked the universe for the moment and the gift of happiness, for this perfect day.

33
SIMON VISITS COVINGTON

Simon Blanchette scrutinized the landscape from the window of the plane as it approached and landed at the Asheville airport. Totally at home in a forest of skyscrapers, Simon felt oppressed by the acres of trees and hills that sprawled to the horizon. Inside the terminal, fellow passengers sauntered to the escalator and the luggage carousel. The airport, though neat and orderly, lacked panache. He had entered the hinterlands.

Dressed in a dark suit and tie, a tourist in a town he already considered unsophisticated, Simon searched for Amelia among the clusters of people. She was nowhere to be seen, and for a moment he regretted having arranged this trip with the sole intent of visiting a woman he hardly knew.

Then he saw her and his gait quickened. Mike stood alongside her, his hand outthrust in greeting, as was Amelia's. *Surely he merited a hug.* Mike took his luggage tags, and Simon felt ridiculous standing there, swapping banalities with Amelia.

"Did you have a nice trip?" "Was it bumpy?" "You didn't have too long a wait in Charlotte, did you?" she asked.

And he asked, "How have you been?" and "How is your work going?"

When Mike returned with a suitcase in each hand, Simon took one and they walked out to the parking lot, where Mike deposited the bags in the trunk of the van.

Amelia urged Simon to sit in front. "So you can enjoy the scenery. It's an hour's drive and very pretty." She got into the back seat.

Simon would have preferred to sit beside Amelia, to inhale the scent of her perfume, to feel the warmth of her beside him, but Mike was her friend and not a hired chauffeur. Simon removed his jacket and tie and slid into the front seat, and they were off.

The ride to Covington was beautiful *if* you enjoyed the country, which Simon did not. Recollections of a summer at his grandparents' rustic retreat in the Catskills, of insects feasting on his skin, of his grandfather's tales of snakes and bears filling his nightmares, still sent shivers down his spine. He should have checked into the Haywood Park Hotel in the heart of Asheville, as his travel agent had suggested. But no, he had allowed Amelia to persuade him to be the guest of herself and her housemates, two women he had absolutely no interest in meeting. Now, it seemed, Mike had assumed the role of travel guide.

"That mountain over there is Cold Mountain, as in the book of the same name," Mike said.

Simon had never heard of Cold Mountain or read the book, and he didn't care. The name repelled him. The occasional comment from Amelia, directed to the scenery or the weather, offered no reassurance that he had made the right decision in coming.

"What's it like living in the country?" Simon asked Amelia.

"Relaxing, pleasant," Mike said. "It's a long drive when we go into Asheville to a show or a concert, or a gallery opening. Otherwise, it's a quiet, easygoing way of life. My studio's not five minutes' drive from my town house, which is great. I used to live on the other side of Asheville. Amelia insisted I relocate closer to my work. I'm glad I did." His proprietary manner offended Simon.

The man was gay, after all—which to Simon, for all his apparent sophistication, meant that Mike should take a back seat to a stud like himself.

"You don't live in Covington, then?"

"I live twenty minutes from Covington, in Weaverville, ten minutes from Asheville."

"I love living in the country. My life's busy, not boring as you might think," Amelia said. "I volunteer at the hospital one afternoon a week, and shooting and preparing photos for the local gallery consumes my time. I love my work. I enjoy the countryside, and the people are interesting and generally quite nice." Her eyes sparkled. "Would you like to join me one day while you're here, weather permitting?"

"You trek about in the woods?" Simon asked.

"Not when it's raining, snowing, or too cold. But there's no rain predicted for the next week, and it's certainly not cold."

Simon changed the direction of the conversation. "I'd like to see your work, your most recent work. May I?"

Mike replied, "Amelia spent all last summer and fall photographing a family that lived up a cove, the way folks did in this area fifty years ago. Those are heartrending photographs of a family totally dependent on one another for almost everything." He shook his head. "But Amelia's having second thoughts. She feels as if she'd be exploiting the Inmans if she uses the photographs."

Simon was incredulous and a trifle curt. "Surely you signed an agreement, got permission from them to use the photos?" He swiveled around to see Amelia.

"Yes, of course I did." Amelia took a deep breath and continued. "But things happened. A flood swept away the bridge to their place, and the water destroyed every-thing they owned. They were forced to move to a trailer park. The father works about two hours away from the family now and only gets home some weekends. Everything in their lives has changed."

This glorious, sensitive woman, Simon thought, *can make a cow look as if it speaks English and can give a wrinkled old woman with gnarled hands dignity. I'd lather my body with insect repellent and follow Amelia into the woods, rather than have her think I'm a sniveling wimp.* "Have you considered that since they've lost everything, the Inmans would benefit from any monies you paid them? I agree with Mike. You ought to print those photos. What a unique opportunity you've had to record before and after the flood. You could show the effect it's had on the parents and chil-dren."

"There's Mars Hill College." Amelia pointed to their right.

The redbrick buildings appeared and vanished in a moment as they left the town and drove into sparsely populated countryside.

At the farmhouse, Mike proffered excuses: his mother, in Ohio, expected a phone call from him by three, and it was almost three, so he departed.

Amelia explained that her housemates were in South Carolina. "Grace's son bought a place there, and they're down visiting. They'll be home later, probably not before dinner."

Simon followed Amelia out onto the front porch. "This reminds me of home, when I was a boy. We lived just out of town and my mother enjoyed sitting out on her porch, rocking, watching the neighborhood go by." He didn't say that he had fled his hometown as soon as possible.

"Sit and rock. I'll get us some drinks. If anyone goes by and waves, just wave back. I'll be back in a jiffy." She returned with a scotch and soda over plenty of ice for him and, for herself, a tall glass of iced tea.

"It's delightful sitting here," Simon said. "And you are charming and as lovely as I remembered you."

How exciting, being with an interesting man who obviously likes me. The urge to impress him was irresistible. "My husband was an executive with the International Red Cross. Most of my married life was spent overseas—London, Rome, Paris." *Why am I saying all this? Why would he care?*

Simon rolled the glass in his hands, making the ice clink against its sides, then he drank deeply.

"Would you like a refill?"

He shook his head. "One before dinner's my limit."

That's good. He doesn't drink too much.

"Paris, the city of love. Did you enjoy Paris?"

"Ah, yes. I was young then. *Voyager c'est vivre.*"

He leaned toward her. *"Vous parlez français?"*

Her pronunciation suffered from disuse. She shook her head. "Very little. I've mostly forgotten."

He shrugged. "I met my first wife in Paris—an artist, and very successful. She was older than I was by a number of years and very well connected." He laughed. "She took pity on a languishing art student. When it became clear that my talent did not lie with the brush, I switched to the pen."

"Do you love your work?" Amelia asked.

"I do, but even more, I adore the city that offers me such a grand playing field for my work, my game of life."

"New York?"

"Yes. New York. I love everything about it." He downed the last of his drink and looked at her over the rim of his glass. "Its energy, its vibrancy, its zest for life attracts me as the nectar of a flower attracts a butterfly."

A warning bell sounded in Amelia's mind. *And your interest in me may be as ephemeral as a butterfly's is to a flower.*

Frank Craine's truck rolled slowly down Cove Road. He waved at them, and they both waved back.

"Nice and homey," Simon said and gave the rocker a shove. "I have a twentieth-floor apartment overlooking Washington Square." He leaned forward and set his empty glass on the porch railing. "Amelia, my dear, can you imagine what it would be like, sitting on my balcony of a summer evening with the city spread out below you?" He looked off into the distance and spread his arms wide. "Muffled sounds ascend from the pavement below. You can hear music from the square, and traffic, and sirens, all calling 'Life. Life.'"

He swung his feet up on the railing. "I hope you don't mind. It's been a long day, lots of airport walking." They rocked a while in silence before he said, "Paris, London, Rome. They can't hold a candle to New York City."

Frenetic New York? In her imagination, Amelia peered down from the dizzying height of twenty stories. Below her the trees, the grand arch in Washington Square, the people and cars were Lilliputian. Her mind traveled the length of the city, across proud buildings lit like stars.

For the next hour, Amelia listened while Simon talked about his life in New York—the museum and gallery openings, the important people that he hobnobbed with—and was surprised and relieved that the world he spoke of held no attraction for her.

"I never attend a play unless I have complimentary front row seats for opening night." As Simon held forth about his box at the opera and the chic weekend parties he attended in East Hampton, Amelia studied him.

What exactly had I anticipated that this encounter would bring? Am I so fatuous that the idea of having a man in my life could take possession of my reason? The life Simon describes, the tag-along role I would be expected to play, sounds so much like my life with Thomas, and that had not been satisfying. No man but Mike ever encouraged me to try new things, to pursue my own interests. They all made excessive demands on my time and energy. I've just come into my own, become a person in my own right, and I'm not going backward. Never again.

There were certainly moments when she watched Max and Hannah together, or Bob and Grace, and she pined for companionship and love. But increasingly Amelia relished the life she had built here, filled as it was with good friends and satisfying work.

Simon was no different, no less self-involved than Thomas or her erstwhile infatuation, Lance, had been. His eyes flashed and sparkled when he spoke of being courted by the directors of a gallery or museum. *He's besotted with himself,* she thought, and sat listening politely, smiling occasionally, nodding at the appropriate moment. In reality, Amelia wanted to tell him that he bored her, that she considered his life shallow, his goals vacuous and meaningless, and that his coming here was a waste of both their time. But saying that would be foolish, inappropriate, and unkind.

Who am I to judge or condemn Simon? Didn't I once espouse Thomas's values and believe that being seen at the right soirees by the right people was of the ultimate importance? Thomas's work had been primarily fundraising and public relations, and heavily dependent on socializing with rich and powerful people. *I'd forgotten the sense of consequence, the imperative nature of each cocktail party, each dance or dinner party; forgotten the misery I accepted and endured of standing on my feet in pointed high heel shoes until my toes cramped. I'd made inconsequential small talk until my voice died in my throat, and all this to please Thomas.* Looking back, Amelia judged herself to have been a compliant fool. Never again.

She smiled to think how her interests had broadened since coming to Covington, her values clarified, and her life expanded. Her self-esteem had undergone a metamorphosis on many levels.

She and Lance had met on a foggy night on Elk Road, when Lance Lundquist's car accidentally hit hers. Hurtling into her life, he had charmed, flattered, and wooed her. Feeling seventeen again, Amelia had trusted him, cast aside her doubts, and allowed herself to love wildly and recklessly. When it was over, after he had lied to her and betrayed her, after he had disappeared and the memories of him no longer throbbed and pulsed within her, Amelia had labored to mend the scars.

When time had passed and Amelia could think rationally, she had reevaluated her life and found it to be good just as it was: supportive friends, a successful, creative career, volunteer work, a meaningful life. No man, not even elegant, brilliant Simon Blanchette, would ever again be the puppeteer manipulating the strings of her life.

Simon rubbed one foot against the other and continued talking about his life and desires. Amelia half-listened, her mind drifting to her friends, to the quilt on her bed that Hannah had brought back from her honeymoon, and to her exquisite antique fan collection that Grace had risked her life to save from the fire. Her heart quickened with a deep sense of identity and belonging.

In another lifetime, vanity might have clouded her thinking. But now she wore no blinders. She knew who she was and what she wanted, and it assuredly was not Simon. He was handsome, rich, and powerful, and Amelia understood that initially her interest had been sparked by his flattery. But their disparate goals and values and his self-centeredness created a distance between them that widened with Simon's every word. She wished him gone, and when the phone rang, Amelia gladly excused herself and took the call in the kitchen.

"Amelia, this is Grace. We've had such a great day, but long. Everyone's tired and Hannah wants to go to the botanical gardens at Clemson University tomorrow. We're going to stay over at the Hampton Inn in Clemson. Here's the number if you need us." She gave Amelia the number. "Is your friend there? You having a good time?"

"He's here." Amelia fell silent.

"Say no more," Grace said. "I'm sorry. Take care of yourself. We'll see you tomorrow afternoon."

Bless Grace for her intuition, Amelia thought as she hung up the phone. She would call Mike and the three of them would go out for dinner. With Mike's help she would get through the remainder of Simon's visit and hopefully not offend him. After all, with one lousy review he could affect the sales of her work.

Amelia felt relief the following morning when she

came down to make their breakfasts and Simon, in suit and tie, informed her that he had received an urgent phone call and must leave that very day.

He grimaced. "Business, you know. One can't always do what one would like." But his half-smile and his eyes belied his words.

"Oh, I am sorry." Amelia returned the lie. "I'd looked forward to taking you on a field trip, and it's going to be such a nice day today. I so wanted you to meet my friends. They'll be back this afternoon."

"Perhaps another time," he said.

Mike drove them to the airport, and they walked Simon to the farthest point allowed visitors, then stood waving and smiling farewell.

"He seemed somewhat out of sorts. What happened? Why'd he leave so soon?" Mike asked as they strolled back to his van.

"Let's just say we each had more important business to attend to," she replied.

34
OF MEN AND WOMEN;
OF THIS AND THAT

Haze lay in wisps atop the mountains, and the sky glowed golden as Max's Subaru rolled slowly around the corner into Cove Road. The day in Clemson had been long and pleasant. Last evening, once the decision had been made to stay overnight, the women insisted on stopping at a Kmart for sleepwear, and they had dined at a lovely new restaurant on Lake Keowee and watched the sunset across the water.

Lenny Meadows had given them a tour of the Clemson campus and the botanical garden, and taken them for lunch at a quaint, old-fashioned restaurant in a town close by. On the way home, they had stopped for ice cream at Aunt Sue's on Highway 11. Grace broke the Atkins program by indulging in her favorite peppermint ice cream flecked with chunks of chocolate. Her energy, somewhat capricious anyway, plunged and she dozed with her head on Bob's shoulder until Hannah's voice awakened her.

"Careful, Max. Remember, there are little kids playing out on the road these days," Hannah said.

"Seems as if Alma's grandkids have been here for a long time. They ever going to leave?"

"I imagine when their son gets a job, they can move out," Grace said.

Max shook his head. "That's all you hear about these days—people being laid off."

"Some people have no one and no place to turn to. The little girls are adorable, I watched them running in the rain the other day. Poor Frank came out to get them and got soaking wet."

"It must be hard on Alma. At our age, kids can really wear you out," Hannah said. "Since Andy's walking, he wears me out. Good thing Laura started him in day care, where he's got other kids to play with."

"Does their mother work?" Bob asked. "Alma's daughter-in-law, I mean?"

"Maybe she did, but right now she's pregnant, and the baby's about due."

"There's been another factory closed over in Haywood County, a small appliance plant, I think," Bob said. "With so little industry around here, it's tough when even one factory shuts its doors."

"It worries me for everyone," Grace said. "And I don't see how a war is going to help."

Max and Bob shared similar feelings about the women in their lives and had spoken of it on their walk around the land near Roger's new home. The two men had walked slowly, in deference to Bob's knees, to a higher point on the land, where they had settled down on a boulder.

"So how's married life?" Bob asked.

"Not like I expected."

"Which was what?"

Max fixed his gaze on the horizon, where the mountains were bathed in blue haze. "I got used to living alone, you might say. Got set in my ways." He looked at Bob and shrugged. "Bella was a fine woman and we got along well, but we had our own lives. She had her art. I had my cows. She never set foot, not once in all those years, in the barn. Never asked about my business." He fell silent and kicked a pebble with the toe of his shoe. "I expected that Hannah would want to be mainly at her own place, and life would pretty much continue as it was." He chuckled. "She sure fooled me. I love her, but I do miss my privacy."

"I think, for Hannah, falling in love with you came as a shock, and once she tipped the bucket it toppled right on over."

"It's not that I don't return the feeling," Max said. "I guess I'll get used to the changes." He placed the ankle of one leg on the knee of the other and turned slightly away.

"Quite nice here, don't you think?" Bob said. "I'd never have figured Roger for a country boy."

"People surprise you all the time," Max said. Silence again.

"Well. As for Grace and me, I admit my life was easier when I was out of Grace's line of vision. That woman worries about everything. If I read late into the night, she sees my light and either rushes over or calls to ask if I'm all right. So I lie there waiting to see her or hear from her, when I should be relaxing. Frankly, I'd like to ask her to cool it, and I don't know how to broach the topic."

Max shifted on the boulder and cleared his throat. "Suffice it to say that in my whole life, I don't think I ever had as much sex as I do now."

"Wow!" Bob grinned. "That's not my problem. With me it's a question of time—the time and privacy to do what I want when I want to. It could be as simple as doing the crossword puzzle."

"Sex takes time," Max said.

"True. True." Bob had no clue where this conversation was going. The two men had never spoken of personal matters. They talked about the price of beef, the weather, sports. Bob would occasionally ask how the Covington Homestead buildings were coming. Max would invariably invite him over to see the place, but somehow, after the opening Bob never got around to it. Except for the women in their lives, they would probably never have met. But here they were, and for all intents and purposes they were as good as brothers-in-law.

Still, Bob was mighty uncomfortable with this conversation. Why should he be? He'd had plenty of raunchy and raucous conversations with guys in the service. He'd laughed at plenty of off-color jokes and talked about women. But that was different. Raunchy talk had been mostly half-truths with raunchy guys about raunchy women. Bob rubbed his hands together to wipe off bits of debris from the boulder. "Shall we walk?"

They ambled along. Their steps took them across the dirt road to a gently declining hillside bordered by small sturdy trees that offered Bob support as he walked. After a time they found themselves in a small bottom alongside the river. The stone walls of an old building—a storage room, or a one-room house?—sat to one side on a rise among the trees. As if they were the stitching that held the fabric of stones together, thick stems of leafless vines entwined and hugged the crumbling walls.

"I wonder who built that room and when?" Bob said.

"And why?" Max raised an eyebrow. "It's such an isolated place and hard to get to."

"Notice how loud the river is and how shallow down here? Very shallow." Bob walked to the water's edge. Across the river, an isolated red barn and old farmhouse sat beyond a well-tended pasture. Just past the bottom-land, where the river turned a bend and vanished, the bare gnarled roots of trees burrowed into crevices in the cliff face. Their limbs and branches canted out over the river. Max looked at his watch. "We probably need to start back."

Bob nodded. Perhaps they would talk again about the women in their lives. *Odd,* Bob thought as they moved up the hillside, *we love these women, yet we don't need them full-time.*

The reason centered around the way one lived one's life, the fullness of it. If you were actively engaged in meaningful work and play and felt loved by someone, you were generally happy. You needed less from individual people. Max lived a very full and busy life. Anna tended to his everyday household concerns. Bob's days were full, also. He had mastered the household appliances long ago, and he had a good friend, Martin, with whom he could speak freely and openly. His knees were much better with the new medication, and golf provided him delightful recreation and just enough exercise. Teaching two mornings a week at the College for Seniors kept his mind fresh.

Initially he had needed Grace to fill the holes in his life. Grace, so rich with friends, and so happy tutoring those kids at Caster Elementary School, had been a decidedly self-sufficient woman. It was he who had been the needy one. Over the years in Covington, his life had broadened, eliminating the urgency for the constant companionship of a loving woman. So what was going on with Grace now? Why the hovering and the late-night phone calls, and the dropping in at odd hours?

Bob stumbled. Max caught his arm and steadied him. "Watch those knees," Max said.

"Thanks," Bob said. "Sorry. Guess I wasn't paying attention. The medication helps me walk without pain, and until this minute I haven't had any difficulty. Guess when you don't have pain, you forget there's a problem"

"It's trickier walking uphill than going down," Max said.

Bob made it to the top by taking it slowly and being very careful where he placed each footstep. Just before they reached the top, Max asked, "So Emily's really going to Florida?"

"Yep. I hope she never comes back."

"That serious, eh?"

"To me it is."

Before Emily left for Florida, she visited Grace. "I'm off," she said, "and I'm not sure what the devil I'm doing. Maybe time will help me gain a perspective of what I really want, where I want to live." Emily screwed up the corners of her mouth. "Dad's furious with me. I believe he's taking his anger at Mom out on me."

"Where *is* Ginger?" Grace asked

Emily shrugged. "Last I heard she was in Reno, Nevada. Why Reno, I haven't a clue. Maybe she's just traveling, doing the Scrabble circuit." She placed her hands on her hips. "What am I doing, Grace?"

"Giving yourself time and space to think. Maybe you can find a good therapist you can trust in Florida and talk to her. Meanwhile, consider this period as a respite, a time for introspection. You'll find the answers."

"I will try to find someone to talk to. I can't just sit there and brood."

"That's right. And remember, you can always come home, ah, back here. Don't worry. Russell, the kids, all of us will be here to welcome you with open arms."

Emily's brows shot up. "If I come back, Grace. If."

"Well, *if,* then. But I hold the belief it will be *when.*"

Emily hugged her. "I am going to miss you. You've always been good to me."

"Write to me." Grace smiled at the young woman. "I'll write back."

"Take care of Melissa, please. I kissed her good-bye and said I'd be gone awhile, but I don't think she understood."

"I'll be here for her and your family."

"Thank you." Just before she left, Emily turned. "By the way, Ringo's trial is finally set to begin July seventh at the courthouse in Marshall. If I have to, I'll be back for that. If they need to talk to Lucy Banks and they don't need me, will you take her?"

"Of course I will."

Life can worry you the way a dog worries a bone, Grace thought, as the days passed and she fretted about what her responsibilities were toward Bob, and why it had become an issue for her since he had moved into his cottage. Too many evenings, of late, Grace stared from her bedroom window at Bob's cottage and brooded about his returning to an empty house, eating alone, sleeping alone. One night she noticed that every window was brightly lit. Something must be wrong—Bob had taken ill! Pulling on her robe, jamming her feet into her shoes, she started for the door to check on him.

But at her front door, Grace stopped. *What in heaven's name am I doing? This nonsense must end. Bob's not a child, and he isn't making demands or nagging me to be with him.* Bob had lived with his son before Russell had married Emily and then alone in an apartment in Loring Valley. When they parted each day he'd been out of sight, and she had simply put him out of her mind and gone about her business. Why not now?

Grace turned and went inside, where she sank into her favorite chair by the window in the living room. She peeked at the cottage. Had he turned off some of the lights? It was as hard to resist checking on Bob, as it was not to nibble on a sugar cookie fresh from the oven.

Grace rose and trudged back up the stairs to her bedroom. It was such a pleasant room, the nicest room she'd ever had. The handmade quilt that Hannah had brought back to her from her honeymoon lay across her bed. It pleased her every time she looked at it. Though it was too warm this time of year to cover herself with it at night, she had folded it so that the beautiful pattern showed and kept it lying neatly across the foot of her bed.

It struck her, then, that to assure her peace of mind, she would erect a visual barrier between the farmhouse and the cottage. Not a hard stone wall, but something soft and easy on the eyes. She would plant Leland cypress between the two houses! They would grow tall, keeping Bob's place out of sight and out of mind.

And what, pray tell, would she do while she waited for them to grow? Grace pulled down the window shade, folded her bathrobe, laid it across the back of the chair, moved the quilt to her chair, and slipped into bed. In every last bone of her body, she was tired. Moments later, she was fast asleep.

At that same moment, across Cove Road, Hannah's head lay in the crook of Max's arm as she stared at the high ceiling and wondered how to cope with this driving passion that so consumed her. It was marvelous feeling vital and alive, but so unexpected. The intensity of her carnality astounded her. Yielding as she had to this intoxication, she felt increasingly out of control, dependent and vulnerable, and robbed of time at home, where Grace, her closest and dearest friend, was drawing closer to Amelia by the day.

A faint hum of anxiety settled over Hannah. She tended to a dogged single-mindedness, which she considered a major flaw in her character. A good example had been that time after she left Bill Parrish. It had never occurred to her to enlist her daughters' help or to encourage them to see themselves as part of a triumvirate, planning and working together to overcome economic problems and adjust to a greatly diminished lifestyle. In her effort to educate herself and support her girls, she had single-mindedly focused on work, on earning money, on practical things. She had relegated her relationship with her daughters to the far back burner of her life, with dire consequences. At a time when they needed comfort and reassurance, a mother's attention, warmth, and love, she had established a hard, uncompromising household with strict rules of behavior. And she had never talked to them, never explained or clarified the situation with their father, or why she had so frantically bundled them up against the cold and fled from their home that dreadful February night. With her brow perpetually furrowed with worry, and her mouth a tight unsmiling line, her daughters had deemed her cold, austere, and inflexible, and as soon as they could, they had left her.

Miranda, just out of a secretarial course Hannah had insisted that she enroll in, had married at nineteen. Laura, after taking several computer courses, had packed a knapsack and departed without a good-bye or a backward glance.

Hannah didn't have to look far for other examples of that dogged determination and inflexibility that had consumed her when she got her teeth into something.

Ignoring Grace's wise counsel, her age, and her inability to stand on her feet for hours, Hannah had plunged into business and invested in a greenhouse in which she planned to grow ornamental plants for the wholesale trade. As predicted, the work overwhelmed her, and within a year she had sold the greenhouse and the business to Wayne Reynolds.

Then there was the fiasco with Sammy, Miranda's son and her oldest grandson. Several summers ago when they were teenagers, Sammy and his brother, Philip, had visited her. A drunken Sammy had wrecked his car, injuring both himself and Philip. When the policeman said "drunk," the word flashed red in her mind and screamed *Bill Parrish,* Sammy's no-good, alcoholic, abusive grandfather.

Grace had urged, "Give the boys a few days in the hospital to recover. Give your daughter time to make arrangements and buy a plane ticket."

"No!" Hannah had been adamant. "Miranda must come *now.*"

In retrospect, her demand that Miranda fly down to Asheville and take the boys home, bandaged, stitched, and in casts, appalled her. Bless Miranda for being the tolerant and forgiving woman she was, and thank God she herself had learned, through Grace and Amelia, to say, "I'm sorry."

Now, as she lay alongside Max, a sobering thought sent Hannah's heart plunging. Absorbed as she was in Max, she hovered on the brink of alienating her year-old grandson, whom she adored, as she had alienated her daughters. Even though he was now part-time in day care, Hannah realized that her recent contacts with Andy had been brusque, hurried, with quick, inattentive hugs while her mind raced elsewhere. Andy, fiercely determined to recapture her attention by any means, had begun to throw his toys at her, even a stick from the garden. Thinking of a future without a loving Andy beside her was unbearable. She must do something about it, and soon.

35
COMING HOME

Andy clutched the side of the playpen that had been set up in the ladies' living room. His pants drooped. He bent his knees, straightened them, bent them again, and wailed. He favored wailing to crying, it seemed to Amelia, and he had powerful lungs.

She lifted her head from her mending. "What's the matter, Andy, sweetie?" His playpen days would soon end, for he could climb out. Amelia finished sewing the button, bit off the end of the thread, and held the blouse up for closer inspection. "There. That's better. What do you think, Andy?"

The child looked at her and wailed. A mournful wail, she thought, but then wails were just that, weren't they? He'd been the easiest baby. He had hardly ever cried, and this wailing was new behavior. Was he angry? And if so, at whom?

Amelia was alone in the house with Andy. His parents

were away for the weekend. They babysat Andy some weekends, so Hank and Laura could enjoy time alone. Grace had run to the market and Hannah was apparently moving back home, for she had appeared earlier with a load of clothing on hangers and after the briefest greeting had hastened upstairs. Then Hannah made several trips to and from Max's place lugging boxes and books. *Max can't possibly know about this, or he would never let Hannah carry everything herself,* Amelia thought.

At the sound of the front door opening, Andy stopped wailing. "Gamma," he said, and then another mournful wail spilled from his mouth.

Hannah set the box down, hurried to him, picked him up, and held him close. Andy snuggled against her shoulder and nuzzled her neck. "Gamma," he said.

"I'm here, baby. We're going to have the best weekend, you and I, aren't we?"

Determined little fingers plucked at her glasses.

"Not Granny's glasses," Hannah said.

"He's been wailing. Not screaming or crying, just wailing. Have you ever heard him do that before?" Amelia closed the sewing box and folded the blouse.

"Gamma." Andy patted his grandma's cheeks with his palms.

"Not so hard, baby. Gently, like this, see." Hannah took one of his hands and ran it lightly against her cheek. "Do it like this, gently."

Andy arched his back, looked into Hannah's eyes, and wailed.

"I can't say I've heard him do this before," she said. Gently she let Andy slide along her hip and leg and down onto the floor, where he pulled to his feet, and tottered away toward the stairs. Hannah started after him.

"Bob's coming over with gates for the bottom and top of the steps. That ought to stop Andy for a while," Amelia said. "Until he can figure out how to unlatch the gates. He's smart, so that won't be too long."

Hannah felt piqued. He was her grandson, and it was her job to protect him from danger. She started to say she didn't need Bob's help, then stopped. "That's very nice of him," she said.

"Bob's great with Andy. Calls him a pistol," Amelia said.

Amelia's easy familiarity with the life and well-being of her grandson annoyed Hannah. *Get a grip. You're jealous,* she cautioned herself. *You've been oblivious to what's been going on for several months. Just be glad your friends care about you and your grandson so much. Be appreciative of the fact that they've picked up the pieces for you here at home.*

Hannah looked down at the child now toddling toward the fireplace in the living room. She hastened to him and scooped him into her arms. "You come with me, little fellow. We'll go see Anna and give Aunt Amelia a rest." Her eyes met Amelia's. "Thanks for everything. I have one small box left to bring home." Hoisting the baby on her hip, she left the house and crossed Cove Road.

• • •

Had Amelia and Andy not been there when Hannah entered the house with that first armload of clothes, she would have paused in the entryway, drawn a deep breath, and appreciated the familiar smell of home-baked bread. Welcomed by the thick comfort of the entryway rug, she would have lingered in the foyer, her eyes taking in the cream-colored walls, the walnut coat stand, the mahogany sideboard, the hammered silver-frame mirror above it. She would have stopped to study her eyes and face in this mirror and seen the satisfaction and pride she felt at her decision to come home. Hannah would have climbed the stairs slowly, her foot-steps silent on the carpeting, glided her palm along the banister, smelling the lemon polish that kept the wood smooth and shiny, the way Grace liked it. In her room, she would have dawdled for a time, perhaps even thrown herself upon her bed to lie quietly and relish the solace and calm of home. She had done none of that, merely hastened into the house and upstairs to her room with arms burdened by clothes and other items.

Now, as she strode across the road for a last check of things deliberately left behind—a nightgown, robe, slippers and undergarments, a change of clothes, a hair-brush, lipstick, the body powder Max loved—she sang to Andy. Andy responded by leaning in close. Then he arched his back, forcing her to use both hands to steady him.

"I gonna miss you, Señora Hannah," Anna said as she opened the door for them.

"I'm not going anywhere. I'll be here many evenings."

"Maybe you no come. Maybe you and Señor Max no be together." Her eyes questioned Hannah.

"Nonsense, Anna. We're married. We're together, but it was never the plan for me to move in here. I have obligations." She nodded toward Andy. "This is one of them."

Andy waved his arms and stretched toward Anna, and Hannah released him to her.

"You see, Señora Hannah, he like me *mucho*. You could stay, and he could come here. I take care of him."

"You're wonderful with him. He's grown so much, hasn't he?" Hannah said. "He's just over a year and walking already. Soon he'll be talking."

"Why Miss Laura put him in day care? I could take care of him better," Anna muttered. "I don't tell nobody, but Jose and me, we got a son."

"Oh? I thought you didn't have any children."

"We no talk about him. He not a good man." She bit her lower lip and looked away. "He steal when he was boy. Now he a man, he work with bad men." Her voice fell to a whisper. "He grow marijuana in the hills. He hide from police when they come." She shook her head, her eyes tired. "He make big sadness for Jose and me."

"I'm sorry," Hannah said. "This must hurt you very much."

Anna nodded. "But Jose and me, we have good life in America. We no want trouble, so we no talk about Manuel. We try no think about him."

"I won't tell anyone, not even Señor Max," Hannah said. "So don't you worry."

Anna set the squirming Andy on the floor. "I make you cup of tea, Señora Hannah?"

"No, thank you. Can I leave Andy with you for a minute or two? I want to make one quick trip upstairs, make sure I left a toothbrush and some other things, and then I'm off."

"I make bed like you like it, three down pillows for you, yes?"

"Yes. Thank you, Anna. You've been more than kind to me."

Anna's voice took on a conspiratorial tone. "Missy Bella, she come in my dreams. She tell me she happy about you and Señor Max."

Hannah started for the stairs. "Really? That's nice. When you see her again, say hello to her for me. I was very fond of her."

Anna's eyes lit up, and she broke into a wide smile. "I do that, Señora. I tell Missy Bella what you say."

"I thought Hannah would explode when I mentioned Bob was getting and installing the gates for the stairs," Amelia said to Grace, when she returned a few minutes after Hannah left with Andy. Bob followed with the gates in hand. "But she was great. She thanked me several times for babysitting Andy."

"The boxes?" Grace asked. Four boxes almost blocked the doorway into the kitchen.

"Hannah's moving home," Amelia said. "She took

Andy and went to Max's for something or other."

"Bloom must be off the rose," Bob said.

Grace ignored him. Her eyes grew wide with pleasure. "She told you she's moving back home?"

Amelia leaned against the living room doorframe, her hands crossed over her chest. "She's been back and forth for an hour or so, taking clothes upstairs, bringing in bags, and those boxes. Who'd imagine you could accumulate so much stuff in so short a time? Andy seems to understand what's happening. He wails when she's gone, and when she returns he's happy as a clam."

Bob shoved one gate under his arm and started upstairs. Soon they heard him muttering to himself as he wedged, adjusted, and screwed the childproof barrier into place.

Moments later, Andy straddling her hip, Hannah recrossed Cove Road thinking about Anna and her son. How sad to have a son who turned out to be a bad seed and broke your heart, as Manuel had surely done to Jose and Anna. They were such good, decent people, hardworking and honest. How proud Jose must have been when the boy was born. It must have been a cause for celebration. And Anna must have been thrilled to give him a son. But in jail while just a boy? How old had he been? She should have asked Anna. No—that would have been insensitive. If Anna had wanted to say, she would have. She wondered if Manuel knew where his parents were, or if he even cared.

Hannah's mind turned to Max. She'd mentioned taking most of her things home, of spending less time at his place, and he'd smiled and said, "Do whatever makes you happy. I'm here across the road, ready and waiting any time you want to come over."

She hadn't said specifically, "Max, today I'm moving my things back to the farmhouse." When he got home, she wouldn't be there. Would he be upset? She should have explained in more detail why she felt she must do this now and why. She had intended to do so at some unspecified moment at work, when they were alone in her office.

"I need more balance in my life," she had planned to say. "I need to pay more attention to Andy. He's acting up. I need more time with Grace and Amelia." She would never admit feeling out of control, or that her need for him was almost more than she could handle. One evening when he was needed in the barn, she'd been appalled at her feelings of jealousy about his cows. Jealous of a cow! He'd laugh if she told him that, of course, and she'd laugh, and they'd hold each other close, but she never had. She would not tell him how much her passion for him frightened her.

Years ago, once the trauma of life with Bill Parrish was behind her, Hannah had succeeded in bringing balance and calm to her life. No more seesawing, no more highs, lows, and chaos, she had promised herself. Life was better lived in the middle. And then she had met Dan and her resolve vanished. But Dan was married and that had restrained her. Now there was no reason for restraint, which struck her as amusing, considering her age.

Hannah reached the farmhouse. Grace's car was there and Bob's. She felt a thrill of pleasure, shifted Andy on her hip, and started up the porch steps.

Later that night Andy fell asleep in his playpen in the living room, and Amelia disappeared with Mike to a dance performance at the Civic Center in Asheville. With Grace keeping an eye on Andy, Hannah luxuriated in a hot bath, washed her hair, and slipped into pajamas and a robe before joining Grace downstairs in the living room.

It had begun to rain again. If the rain kept up, her plants would develop mildew and root rot. Dampness permeated the house, and her hair would never dry before she went to bed. A mug of steaming hot apple cider sat on a table by Hannah's favorite chair. Grace's mug was filled with what she described as a smidgen of coffee and lots of half-and-half, permitted on her Atkins program. The program was working for her; Grace's face was thinner. So were her buttocks. Her slacks bagged at the rear, and around her knees and ankles.

Grace seemed to be praying, her head bent forward, eyes closed, and her fingertips touching. "What are you doing?" Hannah asked, slipping into her chair and reaching for the mug of cider.

"I'm checking the muscles and joints of my hands. I just read that on top of everything else, if you have diabetes, you can have trouble with your hands. So I'm checking to see if I have what they call stiff-hand syndrome. If everything touches . . ." Now she pressed her palms together. "See, like this. Then I know I'm okay." She lowered her hands to her lap.

"You can make yourself crazy with all this stuff," Hannah said. "I had no idea there were so many complications with diabetes. Nobody talks about this. How'd you find out?"

"An article in a magazine. I wish doctors would hand you a folder of information right in the beginning." She sipped her coffee. "On the other hand, maybe they don't because it would be too overwhelming. Maybe people need to find these things out piecemeal, like I have. After all, it took me a year before I even accepted the fact that I had diabetes. It's still not easy for me to say, 'I'm a diabetic.' " She leaned forward and plucked a piece of something curled and brown off the carpet. "This looks like dried apple—probably something Andy cast away."

She continued, "There are three things you can get that affect your hands. There's stiff-hand syndrome, called Dupuyten's Contracture." She rolled her eyes. "I can hardly pronounce that. It has to do with the tendons in your fingers shortening so you can't open your hand fully. There's also carpal tunnel syndrome."

"You're kidding. I thought that happened to typists or people whose work required repetitive hand motions?" The hot cider was warming her. Hannah finished the drink and set the mug down.

"It seems you're more likely to develop any one of these things if you have diabetes," Grace said. "It was actually this article about hands that got me going on the Atkin's program."

"How's the program going?" Hannah realized how disconnected she had become from her friends' lives.

"I'm not walking around starving for food or craving tastes. I have trouble with breakfast, though. I can't abide cooking eggs, or eating tuna or cold meat for breakfast. I ordered crackers from Atkins, and I load them with cheese and have my smidgen of decaf and half-and-half, and that fills me up. I've lost ten pounds, and I feel much better."

Max's knock, and his voice at the door, interrupted them. "Hello. Hannah there?"

"Come on in. We're in the living room," Grace called back. Then she stood up. "I forgot, I locked the door. I'll let him in."

Moments later, Max stood in the doorway in his work clothes, khaki pants and a plaid flannel shirt. Removing his boots at the door, he followed Grace into the living room. "I hear you've moved out," he said to Hannah.

"Yes. Remember we talked about it the other night?"

"I guess I didn't realize it would be this soon."

"I'll leave you two alone." Grace started to rise, but Hannah waved her to her seat. "Goodness, no. I told Max I felt I wasn't spending enough time at home, and when I realized how Andy was acting up and trying to get my attention, I decided the time had come."

"I would have carried over your things," Max said.

"I know you would have, sweetheart, but the spirit moved me, so I just did it."

"You left some things?"

"Certainly. Do you think I'm not coming back? I'll live here and visit with you, like we originally said, rather than living with you and visiting over here."

He looked bemused. Hannah reached over and took his hand. "You look so tired, darling. Max, honey, we'll try it this way for a while and see how it works, okay?"

"It's fine," he said. "I just wanted to make sure you were all right. I see that you are, so I'm off. I've got to update the farm books and get some tax records ready for my accountant. This year we took an extension." He stooped to kiss her. "See you tomorrow at work," he said. "Bye, Grace. You okay?"

"I'm just fine, thanks."

"So what's going on?" Grace asked after he'd gone.

"We had a plan for this relationship, if you remember. We were to live in our own houses, but it's gotten all out of kilter. I feel as if I no longer have a life outside of Max. That's fine for a twenty-year-old but not for an old crone like me."

"Old crone, my eye." Grace giggled. "Max too much for you in bed?"

Only to Grace could she speak her heart. Hannah got up. "You got more cider?"

"In a pot on the stove. If it's cooled, just reheat it."

Hannah disappeared into the kitchen and returned in a few moments. She shoved the hassock close to her chair, sat, and slung her legs up onto it. "It's too much for me, and it's *all* too much—maybe for Max as well, though he's never said so."

"Which means?"

"I guess you could say Max turned out to be the great love of my life." She leaned forward, her eyes happy. "I never expected anything like this. Grace, he could be dirty and smelly from the barn, and I look at him and my stomach turns to water." She laughed. "Me, of all people. I thought that part of me was resting in peace."

"It's an amazing thing, isn't it," Grace said, "how a stimulus can awaken our senses. It could be an idea that triggers our energy and creativity, or a man who triggers our sexuality. I guess people think if you're seventy, that part of your life's over." She smiled and leaned toward Hannah. "We're here to testify it's not, aren't we?"

Hannah nodded. "Am I blushing?"

"Yes, you are."

They laughed.

"This whole thing is overwhelming, and it scares me. I'm haunted by the feeling that if I love Max too much, I'll lose him."

"I've come to the conclusion that that kind of thinking is something we all had drilled into us, the whole idea that happiness is too risky to feel or speak about. It's probably an old Puritan ethic—like if it's not hard work it's not worth doing, or grin and bear it. I don't believe there's any truth behind the belief that loving deeply means losing the other person. Hundreds and thousands of couples love deeply, marry, grow fat and old together, and proceed to live quite long lives. Enjoy the heights, I say."

"Maybe they're cautionary tales because no one can live at such a high pitch of emotion," Hannah said. "Too high a voltage will zap you, you know."

"I think that in time, even great passion lessens, grows calmer, more sedate. But that doesn't mean the love isn't deep and abiding."

Hannah gazed at a round bowl filled with red carnations, arranged by Amelia earlier that day, on the coffee table. Amelia had also replaced her photographs of people, which had hung over the fireplace, with landscapes that Hannah had never seen. "When did you get the new clown?" she asked, nodding at the glass clown that sat on the table near the flowers.

"Bob gave it to me this morning. He called it an 'unbirthday present.' I love that, don't you? An unbirthday present."

"It's pretty. Very delicate. I'd move it before Andy gets hold of it." Hannah relaxed, glad to have this time alone with Grace. She'd missed their talks. "Was it like that, all fire and passion with Bob and you at first?"

Grace shook her head. "No, it was more a gentle simmer than a rolling boil. Pleasant and satisfying, but not earthshaking, if you know what I mean."

Outside, the rain came down in buckets. The lights in the house flickered, and flickered again, and Hannah tried to remember where the flashlights were. But Grace would know.

Grace continued, "Bob and I have a relationship that's comfortable for us both." Her eyes and face were as open and honest as they had always been. "That's what matters. I'm no expert on this, but it seems to me that trouble comes when partners have different sex drives, like Ted and I did. He was much more interested in it than I was and my lack of responsiveness really bothered him. How could I tell him that sex with him was boring? So I didn't. But it sounds as if you and Max want the same thing, so I say, have a good time and enjoy yourselves."

"You make it all seem so simple, Grace. I love that about you. You make what seems so complicated, simple. I want to be with Max, but it's interfering with my time and other interests.

"You, Amelia, Andy, and my daughters have all been high on my priority list until these last few months. What I need is balance. When it comes right down to it, a good balance works best for me."

"I've missed you, Hannah, but I understood you want to be with Max. If you decide to move back over there, I'll understand."

"You're a dear and a great friend," Hannah said. "But I've brought my things home. This is where I live."

36
THE PROBLEM WITH MELISSA

Grace received a note from Emily. Old haunts in Ocala, she reported, had fallen to the wrecking ball and been replaced by strip malls and restaurants. Emily made no mention of work. Grace attempted to discuss the note with Bob, but he shook his head. "Spare me. Russell and the kids are doing fine without her."

Wrong, Grace thought. Things are not so great for Russell. A perpetual sadness dimmed his eyes, and he rarely smiled. Melissa's behavior had deteriorated. Only Tyler went about his business smiling and genuinely happy. At least two evenings a week, Russell and the children had dinner with them, either at the farmhouse or at Bob's cottage.

"I am worried about the family, but especially Melissa," Grace said to Bob one evening after a particularly challenging dinner. Melissa had spilled not one but two glasses of milk, one of which splattered Tyler's shirt and soaked his trousers. In retaliation, he had shoved her hard, dislodging her from her chair and causing her to tumble to the floor.

"Dammit, Tyler, you're older. Exhibit some control," Russell had said, his voice harsh.

"I have a lot of control," Tyler said. "More than some people around here."

"Mind your manners, young man," Bob had snapped.

"I take care of Melissa a lot. More than any of you know, and I always have. Sometimes I think she's just plain nuts."

Melissa continued to scream until Russell grasped her by the shoulders and shook her. "For God's sake, will you shut up."

For a moment the child stared at him, wide-eyed and silent. Then her screaming resumed.

"How can she shut up if you shake her?" Grace asked.

"How would you handle it?" Russell shouted at Grace.

"I don't know, but not like that, certainly."

"Enough, all of you." Bob stood, towering over the table. Immediately, Melissa stopped screaming. "Russell, I think you owe Grace an apology. No one's more caring of your children than she is."

Frustration and embarrassment crossed Russell's face. "I'm so sorry, Grace. I was just upset," he mumbled. And shortly after, Russell and Tyler gathered up their things and a now-quiet Melissa and departed.

"Leave the dishes. Leave everything," Bob said "I'll take care of it all later. You come in the living room with me."

Grace followed him from the kitchen. "I'm very worried about Melissa. The child is obviously deeply troubled."

Bob picked up the newspaper.

Grace yanked the paper from his hands, crumpled it, and slammed it to the floor. "I didn't come in here to watch you read the paper!" Appalled by her own behavior, she waited for his reaction.

"Let's not argue," Bob said. "I'll talk to Russell."

"I can talk to him myself. I don't need a mouthpiece." Grace sank into a chair. "I can see that it's easier not to know everything that's happening in your children's lives."

"You feel too much," Bob said. "You take too much to heart."

"I guess I do." She retrieved the crumpled newspaper

and attempted to smooth it on her lap. "I'm sorry I crumpled your paper."

"It's just a newspaper. If I miss a day, it's no big thing."

To Grace, behaving like a petulant child was a big thing. "I'm so sorry for snapping at you, Bob, really I am."

"What say we skip having them over for a week or so?"

"We can't do that. They need us now. They're having a hard time. We can't abandon them even if it's hard on us." Her hands moved across the paper like an iron smoothing a rumpled shirt.

"And if we lived three states away, what would they do?"

"We don't live three states away. They need us, and I won't desert them."

"Grace, honey, we need a break from Melissa. I can't go through another meal like tonight. I don't have indigestion often, but I sure do tonight." He rubbed his stomach.

"I don't feel great, either," Grace said. "I wish I could wave a wand and bingo, Melissa would be as sweet and gentle as she looks when she's sleeping. She can't put it into words, of course, but I don't think Melissa's ever been able to count on her mother, or trust her, and now she's gone. It's all enough to drive any child nuts."

"Melissa didn't trust her mother? She couldn't count on her? Why do you say that?"

Grace looked away. She'd given Tyler her word. "Things Tyler told me."

"Like what?" His voice challenged and demanded a reply. That rankled Grace.

"I promised him not to say."

"Would you call Tyler a reliable source, Grace? He's never liked Emily."

"That was early on. Then he liked her a great deal. All I'll say is thank God Tyler's always been there for his sister."

"I can't talk about this any longer, honey. I'm pooped. I'm going to turn in early. You staying over?"

"Not tonight." Bob could clean up the kitchen and turn off the lights. He could go to sleep and forget whatever was troubling him. She'd stew and fret all night. Without kissing him good night, Grace walked from the cottage.

"See you tomorrow," he called.

Grace stalked across their yards in a state of high dudgeon, and even after she'd soaked a long while in a hot bath, her annoyance persisted. Ted used to call her a busybody. She'd resented that. His life had touched so few people. Hers touched, perhaps, too many. Ted never extended himself for anyone. He had sidestepped major life issues: his son's lifestyle, their increasingly distant relationship, practical matters like purchasing life insurance, and he had assiduously avoided sustained contact with anyone, family member or not, who expressed even a hint of a problem. Because she listened to people, Grace had been, and still was, drawn into other people's lives, and she preferred to live that way, even if some nights she could not sleep.

Maybe, she thought as she dried her hair, *there's something else going on with Bob.* It was getting clearer to her that he no longer needed her. That ought to be a liberating idea, yet instead Grace took umbrage. Why didn't he need her?

Grace tried to read, but the lines of print blurred, and she closed her eyes. The lower half of her hair, still damp from the bath, felt clammy against the pillow. The familiar smell of bath powder suddenly seemed cloying.

The image of Melissa's face came to her mind, and in that instant Grace knew that she must take the child to a therapist to get help sooner rather than later. She would discuss this with Russell and offer to pay for it, if he agreed. She would ask Brenda if she knew of a child counselor and make an appointment for Melissa.

Within two days, Grace had Russell's approval, the name of a therapist, and an appointment. Melissa was quiet and angelic on the drive to Asheville, and Grace marveled that she could be so sweet, yet in a second turn into a screaming disaster.

Grace liked Dr. Anne Wilson immediately. She was older, motherly with graying hair, and welcomed Melissa with a hug. *The child,* Grace thought, *is in good hands.*

37
THE TWISTS AND TURNS
OF JERRY MCCORKLE'S TRIAL

The trial was much publicized on local television, in the newspapers, and by word of mouth. It attracted not only the lawyers, judge, jury, witnesses, and policemen, but farmers, shopkeepers, housewives, the genuinely interested, the morbidly curious, and a civics class from a local high school. Each morning, they converged at the courthouse. Those unable to obtain seats in the courtroom clustered in and about the Zuma Café across the street with coffee cups in hand, and exchanged current news or related the latest gossip.

"Jerry McCorkle's pleaded not guilty. The nerve of the man!" one woman said.

"His friend Bryan Henn, the one who ran away after they killed old Hilda, got born again and he's come home to set it right, to tell the truth. Praise the Lord," an old farmer said.

A woman said, "I hear Jerry's lawyers quit him, packed up and went back to Raleigh, where they came from."

Someone replied, "He'll get him another set of fancy lawyers what with all the money Francine Randall left him."

"If they can't get him on the murder of old Miss Hilda, I hope they nail his behind for trifling with a fourteen-year-old girl," an older woman said.

"They say he's so mean in jail, the inmates won't eat at the same table with him."

"I heard he beat up a guy."

"I heard a guy beat him up."

And so it went, day after day, while traffic snarled on Main Street, and all the parking spaces this side of the French Broad River in Marshall had filled by eight A.M.

Before leaving for Florida, Emily had turned Lucy's case over to Fred Kennedy, a colleague, and it was Fred who called to inform Grace that Jerry McCorkle, aka Ringo, had pleaded innocent to Hilda McCorkle's murder, and that he had hired other defense attorneys. "From Atlanta, this time," Fred said. "These guys are sharp. They'll try to discredit Bryan Henn. We're going to need Lucy's testimony regarding Ringo's near abduction of her. That will help establish the man's duplicitous character and criminal intent."

Grace agreed to talk to Lucy and to bring her to a meeting in the judge's chambers. Grace had visited Marshall once, years ago, when they first came to Covington. She had wondered why a town pinched between a vertical, rocky hillside and a wide, rushing river had been chosen as the county seat. Why an imposing two-story, redbrick courthouse with Corinthian columns across the front and a cupola and clock tower had ever been erected at that location.

"Politics, I guess," Harold Tate had said. "Being as it was on the river, and that was the selfsame route folks used to bring their animals to market down in South Carolina. The trail was probably where the railroad tracks are today. They had a tavern down there back then."

"Why's the judge needin' to see me? I'm real scared, Mrs. Grace," Lucy asked, as they drove along the French Broad River toward Marshall. "Am I gonna have to see Ringo?"

"No. I assure you he won't be anywhere around. Court's not in session today. We'll go directly to the judge's private office. The judge will ask you a few questions, and we'll come home. Just listen carefully to his questions. Think before you speak, and if there's anything you don't understand, say so, and he'll explain."

"You sure?" Lucy couldn't stop biting her fingernails.

"Fred Kennedy said that's what will happen."

Lucy looked at her with frightened eyes. "I'd never have come without you."

Grace smiled and stroked her hair. "Try not to worry. Mr. Kennedy says the judge is a very nice man, kind and patient. Keep in mind he's got your welfare at heart, not Ringo's."

"What if a bunch of newspaper people are waitin' outside? I don't want my picture took," Lucy said. "I seen on the TV how they rush a person and yell all kinds of questions at them."

"Look at the street. There's hardly a car in sight, and there's the courthouse. You see anyone about?" Grace asked.

Lucy shook her head. "No, ma'am. I don't see nobody."

They parked, then walked up the steps and between the columns. In the lobby they were met by Fred Kennedy and a tall policeman, who ushered them upstairs and into the courtroom with its semicircle of folding wooden seats that reminded Grace of old-time classroom chairs. They circled the judge's bench, past tall windows with a view of the steep hillside, and went into the judge's chamber. An American flag stood in one corner. Portraits of two of the judge's predecessors, solemn bearded men, hung on the wall behind his desk.

Judge Herbert Baird rose and stepped from behind his desk to greet them. It surprised Grace that he was young, maybe forty, for she had expected a white-haired, older man in a black robe. Judge Baird wore a business suit and a tie with tiny white dots.

Clearly intimidated, Lucy pressed against Grace.

"It's okay, Lucy," Grace said.

"Please have a seat." The judge smiled at Lucy. "Well, Lucy, how are you? You getting on well in school?"

"Fine, sir," Lucy said, and, "Yes, sir." She twisted her new white handkerchief and braided it between her fingers. Her feet tapped the ground, making her knees bob up and down.

He spoke softly, gently. "Lucy, I asked you to come here today because we need your help. Will you tell us everything you remember about . . ."—he consulted his notes—"Ringo, Jerry McCorkle, and the computer at your school? I need to know who opened a chat room, and when you started using it. Don't hide names or protect anyone; the truth is what matters here."

He leaned forward, cupped his hands, and rested his chin on top of them. "Take your time. Now, let's begin with who messed with the computer and opened that chat room."

Grace watched the tapping of Lucy's feet slow, and her eyes settle on the judge's face. *He's so young. Is he wise and experienced enough for this case? What am I thinking? That's reverse age discrimination on my part—he's young, so he's not wise? Is everyone who's old wise? Of course not.*

Lucy talked, at first hesitantly, then more rapidly, and the judge nodded encouragement. When she faltered and stopped, he said, "That's all right, Lucy. You're doing just fine. Take a deep breath and go on whenever you're ready." His eyes were kind, and when Lucy, sometimes crying, had told it all, he said, "Thank you, young lady. You've given us a clear picture of everything. You've been a great help."

And that was it. Grace and Lucy were escorted back through the courtroom, down the stairs, and out into the street to Grace's car.

"That wasn't bad," Lucy said once they were on their way. "The judge was nice. But I sure hope I don't have to go back." After a time she said, "Mrs. Grace, I felt ashamed telling about Ringo. How could I have believed all those lies he told me? Do you think Judge

Baird thought I was a real dingbat?"

"I think he admired your courage and appreciated all the details you gave him," Grace said. "I would never have been able to remember the sequence of things the way you did."

They rounded a curve. To their right, a narrow creek spilled over rocks on its way to join the French Broad River. Up, up they went, driving in silence, circling past small homes tucked into coves, past neat red barns and weatherworn ones, and past cows grazing in meadows. Finally the road flattened and widened, and they turned and headed toward Weaverville.

"Why'd they want me to go to the judge, anyway?" Lucy finally asked.

"Well, it's like this. Ringo's lawyers say he's not guilty of murder."

Lucy swung about to look at Grace. "Not guilty? But his friend came back and told the police about what Ringo did, didn't he?"

"Yes, but Ringo's lawyers are trying to discredit that friend. He did, after all, run away, and for years no one knew where he was. And it's their job to defend Ringo. That's what they're being paid for."

"You mean lawyers defend people they know are guilty?"

"I'm afraid they do, Lucy. Ringo's lawyers are called defense lawyers, while lawyers like Mr. Kennedy prosecute criminals. Mr. Kennedy might want to use your testimony to prove to the jurors the kind of really bad person Ringo is."

"The law's complicated, ain't it? I mean, isn't it?" Lucy asked.

"Yes, it is."

"I sure don't want to go back to that courthouse."

"You won't have to." Grace hoped she was right. Fred Kennedy had assured her that he'd do everything possible not to have her in the courtroom. They seemed sensitive to her age, and the judge clearly understood her fear of Ringo.

Jerry McCorkle paced the small sterile room, stopping only to pound his fists on the cold metal table. He shouted at his new attorneys, "I ain't gonna stay here and answer no more questions. I done told you I ain't killed no old lady, and if I did, it's my word against Bryan's."

The older of the two attorneys, James Connelly, said, "Behaving like a damn adolescent delinquent isn't going to help any of us. Your friend Bryan's taken a lie detector test and passed it. He's given graphic details about what happened that night. I suggest you get a grip on yourself and settle down. We're representing you, not prosecuting you, and we have to ask you the hard questions."

The younger lawyer, Sam Spender, shuffled papers on the table. "The police file says you spent the night of the murder with a girl, but you refused to give her name. We need to know her name and where she is now. If you're not guilty, she's your alibi."

Jerry flopped into the hard metal chair he had vacated

minutes ago. His eyes narrowed and a smirk settled about his mouth. "What I got to tell you is better than any girl's name. It's gonna blow this case in pieces all over this here county."

"Well, tell us." James Connelly leaned against the wall and crossed his arms.

Jerry snorted and tipped his chair back. "You know who's payin' your highfalutin fees?"

"Your trust fund."

"Ever wonder why someone like me's got a trust fund?"

"Frankly, no," Connelly said.

"Ever heard of Francine Randall?"

"Only that she set up the fund."

"Well, you're gonna hear plenty more about her now, and what I tell you's gonna knock your socks off."

Connelly moved to the table and snapped shut his briefcase. "Mr. McCorkle, see here——" But he was cut off in midsentence.

"What I'm gonna tell you will make that damned jury weep so hard for me, they'll forget about Hilda McCorkle."

"Out with it, then." Sam Spender leaned across the scarred metal table.

"To start with, Francine Randall was principal of the middle school, and she done gone and killed herself." Ringo nodded his head. His lips curled in scorn. "Run her car right off a cliff."

"What is this woman to you?" Connelly asked.

"That woman's dead, I done said. She was my f——

mother, only I ain't never knowed it until about a year ago."

The men exchanged a quick glance.

"I grew up thinkin' my ma was dead. Granny raised me. And my pa, he was a drunk lived down in Alabama. When he's dyin' he tells me Miss Fancy Pants, rich old Francine Randall, is my ma." Ringo smirked. "She was principal of the school I went to, just like all the kids round here. I got sent to her office regular, too, and she ain't never said a word, never even looked at me kindly. Even if I knew nothin' about who she was to me, she knew I was her kid. Way she came down on me, you'd never guess it, though." Jerry threw back his head and laughed. "Anyways, when I found out, I quick let old Francine know that I knew, and she didn't want no one else to know." He put two fingers across his lips. "I cooperated and kept my mouth shut." Then Ringo rubbed his thumb and forefinger together. "You get my drift?"

They nodded. Blackmail.

"Then Francine up and killed herself, but before she did, she made that there trust. She never married or had no more children. Musta' been guilt from lookin' at me thinkin' how if she'da raised me up, I'da made something of myself." He sneered. "Her family paid Granny all those years to keep her mouth shut. You're smart fellows. You can find ways to twist things, right?"

"You're not one for assuming responsibility for your actions, are you?" Spender said.

"I *ain't* responsible. I wasn't raised right. I ain't had

no opportunities to better myself." His eyes were hooded now, and mean. "If you don't say it in court, I'll stand right up there and look that judge in the eye and tell everyone the truth about my ma and how *I* am the victim."

Fred Kennedy received a call from Judge Baird's office. He phoned Grace immediately. "Looks like this is going to be a protracted affair. Ringo's second set of lawyers pulled out."

"What does that mean?"

"Just that it's going to take time to find someone who'll defend a sleaze like Ringo."

But inevitably the call of the almighty dollar outweighed truth, honor, and justice. Within three weeks, Ringo's new team of lawyers were in place. According to Fred, this group was completely indifferent to who Jerry was or what he did or said. "All they see is dollars. I think we may have to use Lucy's testimony."

"You're not going to put her on the stand, are you?" Grace's stomach tightened.

"No. As much as I can, I keep my promises. But she'll have to come in and go through it all again for videotape."

That afternoon when Hannah brought Lucy home with her from Bella's Park, Grace said, "Lucy, Mr. Kennedy called. He'd like you to come back to the judge's chamber and retell your story, so they can tape it to show to the jury, if they have to."

The color drained from Lucy's face. Flinging her arms about Grace, she molded her small body into Grace's and sobbed as if she had been beaten. When she could manage, she said, "Mrs. Grace. I can't. I just can't. Don't make me go back there. Please!"

Grace held the child close.

Lucy lifted a tearstained face to Grace. "This ain't never gonna end, is it?"

"Of course it'll end. Everything ends. They're just asking you to talk to the judge in his chamber again, and they will videotape you. That's all. You won't even know there's a camera there after the first two seconds. And Mr. Kennedy said that the tape will not be played in court, Only to the defending attorneys, and then maybe to no one else, once they view it," Grace said.

Lucy's arms slipped from about Grace's waist, and she sank into a chair at the kitchen table. Grace handed her a box of tissues and a damp towel to wipe her face.

"I don't want to talk about it again or have some strange person taking my picture," Lucy muttered. "The people on the jury'll know everything, and they'll go outta that courtroom and gossip with their friends, and pretty soon everyone about these parts is gonna be talkin' about me and makin' fun of me. I know how people are."

"If you don't help the prosecution, Ringo might go free," Hannah said. "You don't want that to happen, do you?"

"No, I don't." Lucy shook her head vehemently. "But still, I can't do it."

"Maybe you ought to talk to your mother, Lucy, and ask her what she thinks you ought to do," Grace said.

"I dunno." Lucy turned from Grace and stared at a spot on the table. "I gotta go home now. You gonna drive me, Miss Hannah, please?"

"Certainly."

The television in the Banks living room blared. Myrtle Banks took comfort in the sound and in the familiar faces of her daughters as they stared at cartoon characters performing ridiculous antics. This wasn't the first time Myrtle had numbed her mind with meaningless cartoons. When her husband died, she'd sat for days in front of the set, hardly paying attention to what was on. Lucy and Randy had taken over then, cooking and minding the younger ones. Now that Randy was off to war, she felt dead inside. She'd begged him not to sign up, but he'd said nothing was gonna happen to him, that all his friends were going and they'd all get educated afterward.

The lemon oil Aggie had used earlier to clean all the wood tables in the living room caused the wood to shine, and the smell of a pot roast simmering on a bed of grilled onions lent the small house the sense of stability that Myrtle needed. Arguing with Lucy wasn't gonna help none, she knew that. But Mrs. Grace was right: Lucy must help the good lawyer put bad people like Ringo in jail. If Grace had been unable to persuade her daughter, though, how could she?

Myrtle had listened and tried to understand the complications of the case. But fear and the sense of help-lessness, such as she had felt on that dreadful evening when the policemen came and Lucy dashed out into the dark, caused her mind to go numb, and her legs felt wobbly. Lord, she needed Randy now, and he was gone to some god-awful place on the other side of the world. Myrtle offered a silent prayer for her son.

Then suddenly, Myrtle felt herself slipping, slipping from the chair, and then she was on the floor and the kids were standing around her, and Audra was crying.

"Mama, Mama, speak to me. Are you all right?" Aggie asked.

It was then that Lucy walked into the house and with Aggie helped her to her feet, and to the couch, where they lifted her legs and placed a pillow beneath her head.

"Ma. You hurt?" Lucy asked. "Ma, talk to me. Ma."

Myrtle found her voice. "I ain't hurt none. Just had one of those dizzy spells I get sometimes. You gotta go with Mrs. Grace, Lucy. You gotta go," she whispered.

As much as she cried, as much as she resisted, Lucy understood what was at stake and what she must do. The next morning, she informed her mother she would abide by her wishes and go with Mrs. Grace.

A week later, Lucy and Grace walked down the main street in Marshall and climbed the steep stairs to the courtroom. It was hard, very hard, and it seemed to Lucy that the questioning was more intense, and that she was asked to remember even more details. The judge seemed impatient at times, which upset and confused Lucy and made it even harder for her to concentrate.

"Maybe . . ." she would say.

"Not maybe. It either is or it isn't," Judge Baird said. "Either Ringo made the first contact or you did. Now which was it?"

"I guess . . ." She lifted her eyes to the judge's face. "He did."

"What did he say?"

She shrugged. "Something simple like, 'Hi there, how are you?' "

"And what did you write back?" the judge asked.

Lucy nibbled the edge of her lower lip. "I musta said something like 'Hi, I'm fine. How about you?' I'd never been on any chat room before, sir."

Fred Kennedy took over the questioning. "Lucy, it's very important that you be as specific as possible."

"I'm trying, Mr. Kennedy, but it's hard to remember exactly." Tears brimmed in her eyes.

Grace reached over and patted her hand. "Take your time, dear."

"I felt sorry for him. He said he was seventeen and that he got beat every day, and that he was unhappy and thinkin' he'd just kill himself. I believed him. I told him about my life, about Pa dying and Ma sending us to live with those awful cousins down the mountain, and about how good Mrs. Grace and the ladies were to me."

"What did he say when you told him about the ladies?" Fred asked.

Lucy lifted a defiant chin. "He said I wasn't to tell them nothing about him or about our writing to each other. I told him plain out that he ain't had no right telling me who my friends should be."

The attorney pressed her. "And he said?"

She looked apologetically at Grace. "That I wouldn't need no old ladies for friends 'cause I'd have him, and he was all I'd need."

"Would you say that he tried to separate you from people you trusted and loved?"

"Yes, he did that," Lucy replied.

"What did you do then?"

"I didn't tell Mrs. Grace nothing about Ringo, and I didn't tell him any more about her, or Miss Hannah, and Miss Amelia."

"You love Mrs. Singleton, Lucy?"

"Yes, sir. I surely do." She looked over at Grace. "Mrs. Grace, she's helped me from the first day we met when I was in elementary school and having trouble reading."

"When she found out about this, why didn't you listen to her?" Judge Baird asked.

Lucy hung her head. "Ringo kept telling me how much he loved me and needed me, and how, without me, he was gonna walk away in the forest and throw himself over a cliff. I believed every word he said. I had to try to help him."

"You felt responsible for him?" Fred Kennedy asked.

"Yes, sir, you could rightly say so."

It was hot in the judge's chamber. The session was

taking longer than she'd anticipated, and Grace's cotton blouse stuck to her back. To distract herself, Grace studied dust motes swirling in the shaft of sunlight that fell across her lap.

When it was over, Grace and Lucy returned to the car. "I'm exhausted," Grace said, "and you must be, too. You worked hard to answer all their questions. I'm proud of you. You did well, Lucy."

Lucy crossed her arms over her chest. "Mrs. Grace," she said. "If they were to mess up that video, I'd let them lock me in the jailhouse before I'd go back there and do that again."

38
COUPLES ONLY FOR DINNER

As they drove off to a concert in Asheville, Amelia and Mike waved good-bye to Bob and Grace, who sat on Bob's front porch. "Amelia looked stunning tonight, didn't she?" Grace asked as Mike's van turned onto Elk Road.

"Yes, very nice," Bob said. "And soon we get to have dinner—just you and me and Max and Hannah. What time are they coming over?"

"About six. It doesn't matter, really. I made corned beef and cabbage, and that's always easy."

"And delicious," Bob said.

Grace's brows drew together for a moment. "Amelia loves corned beef and cabbage." Then she laughed. "You know, in a way, Amelia is like corned beef and cabbage. It doesn't take much to make corned beef taste great, and it doesn't take much to make Amelia look great."

"I would have thought Amelia would remind you of something French, like soufflé."

"That, too. But it's more the reliability of corned beef and cabbage and the reliability of Amelia's looks that I meant."

"Since we're equating looks with food, what food are you?" Bob teased.

She thought about that. "I guess I remind me of a good, hearty vegetable stew."

Bob laughed and kissed her cheek. "Or maybe a good chicken soup, the kind that heals. And I'm steak, right?"

"You guessed it." She rose and started inside.

"Where are you going?"

"I'm going inside to set out the flowers for the centerpiece."

"Why all the fuss? It's only Max and Hannah." Bob followed her.

She turned to him and stood in the kitchen doorway, her hands on her hips. "Men! Now, you go find a place to roost. I want everything to look great because it *is* Hannah and Max, and we're entertaining them as a couple for the first time."

Bob ambled off and moments later Grace heard the voice of some announcer calling the plays of a ballgame. They all sounded alike to her, but football was the most raucous of all.

Grace arranged white daisies from a flower shop in Mars Hill in a low bowl and set it in the center of the table. She scrutinized the flowers from all sides, and when she joined Bob in the living room he shut off the television so they could talk for a while. They had agreed that the men would not huddle around the set, and the women in the kitchen or on the porch.

Soon the doorbell rang.

"For you," Hannah said, handing a bouquet of roses to Grace. Max handed Bob a bottle of red wine.

"How beautiful they are." Grace burrowed her nose in the roses. "And fragrant. Thank you, Hannah."

"Come in, come in. Drinks, anyone?" And Bob was off to mix scotch and sodas for himself and Max.

When they sat down to eat, the corned beef melted in their mouths. "There's something so satisfying about a meal like this," Max said. "I'd like another helping of everything."

They chatted easily about how the day had gone for each of them.

Max had waited hours for a man to arrive to repair one of the milking machines. "It just infuriates me when a repairman says he's coming at one, and he gets there at three-thirty."

Hannah had overseen the planting of rosebushes, while Bob had golfed with Martin.

"And I cooked," Grace said.

"A marvelous dinner." Max patted his stomach.

"Room for apple pie and ice cream on the front porch?"

Outside, it surprised her when Bob brought up Emily. "Emily's letters seem to indicate she's settling in down there. What's she done now, Grace, taken work in some agency that deals with abused women?"

"She says it's temporary," Grace replied.

"Personally, I don't think she'll come back, not even to get Melissa, which is fine by me," Bob said.

"But somewhere down the line," Hannah said, "Melissa will blame herself for her mother leaving. That's what kids do."

"I worry about that, too," Grace said.

"She'll grow out of it. She's got three terrific grandmas," Max said.

"Not the same," Hannah said. "Doesn't compensate, nor does it explain a mother abandoning her family. Emily's one self-centered woman."

"She's a troubled woman," Grace said.

"Then she should go to a therapist and get untroubled," Hannah replied.

"How is Tyler with all of this?" Max asked.

"Tyler's happy as a sunflower after a rain shower," Hannah said.

"Melissa has fewer nightmares since she's been going to Dr. Wilson," Bob said. "Grace was right on about this one. Dr. Wilson says she doesn't have ADD, like her pediatrician thought. It's emotional. The child needs lots of love, a good swat on the rump, and time out when she goes out of control."

"Thank God she's getting the help she needs," Hannah said.

They were silent for a time. A full moon brightened the yard, defining every shrub and flower.

"What's the scoop on Jerry McCorkle's trial?" Max asked, changing the subject.

"Jerry created one heck of a scene in the courtroom last week. Did you see the pictures in the *Sentinel*? Judge Baird had him bodily removed. He behaved like a raving madman. It took six policemen to drag him out of there," Bob said. "Jerry started shouting about Francine Randall being his mother and how she'd killed herself because he found out and was blackmailing her, as if that would get him sympathy. By the time he got done cursing the woman and blaming his own miserable life on her, he'd produced such a negative effect on that jury that I think it sealed his fate even more than all the testimony Bryan Henn gave about Hilda's murder."

"Fred Kennedy told me yesterday that his associate Lance Hobbs is thinking of winding up the prosecution without using Lucy's videotape," Grace said. "Hobbs thinks he can go for a conviction of murder from the evidence supplied by Bryan, plus Jerry's outrageous behavior. His rantings scared everyone in that jury box. I don't think one of them wanted to see him out on the street again. Kennedy said if Jerry hadn't been in leg irons and restrained by guards, he'd have attacked the closest person he could get his hands on."

"I certainly hope he gets his comeuppance," Hannah said. "Life in prison's too good for him."

A car drove past. "There go Alma's son and daughter-in-law," Grace said.

"Seeing those young people out of work, and how hard it is for Frank and Alma having five extra people living with them, makes me realize that our little community's a microcosm of what's going on around this country," Bob said. "The unemployment figures are frightening."

"It all seemed so idyllic when we first moved here," Grace said.

"It's still idyllic compared to what it must be like for folks in cities, where it costs an arm and leg to survive," Max said.

After a time, the women rose. "Hannah and I are going home. You two go watch your ballgame on TV," Grace said.

The men did not protest.

Walking home, Hannah said, "I think the guys want more privacy, more time away from us, just as much as we do."

"You think so?"

"Yes. I think that after all those years, Bob finally got used to living alone. And Max certainly had time to adjust to being a bachelor, with all his household needs tended to by Anna."

"That would take the pressure off me," Grace said. She told Hannah about wanting to plant a hedge of tall pines.

"It would be years till they grew tall enough to hide Bob's place from your bedroom window," Hannah said.

"My mother used to say, 'wait long enough and things will change,' but do we have time to wait?"

"Do you think we should talk to the men about how we feel, and find out what they're thinking?" Grace asked.

They were walking up the front steps now, and turned to the cottage and waved. Bob had shifted to the rocker alongside Max and seemed to be arguing; his hands were cutting the air, his head wagging side to side.

Hannah shook her head. "I think we should go about our business and carry on as we choose. If it comes up we can inquire, and if it never comes up and no one's pouting, we'll know everyone's content with the situation."

Grace smiled. "Want a cup of tea before we go to bed?"

"Sure. I heard on Larry King the other night that tea's excellent for you. Let's do it fancy and have it in china cups in the living room." Hannah opened the door for Grace, and they entered the house.

39
AFTER THE CONCERT

Amelia and Mike waited in their seats until the theater in Asheville emptied sufficiently to allow easy egress up the aisle and through the lobby. They crossed Haywood Avenue and ambled along the sidewalk across from Malaprop's Café and Bookstore. Cars leaving parking garages moved past them in a steady line.

"I enjoyed the concert so much," Amelia said. "The Russian pianist was marvelous, didn't you think?"

"I get a kick out of your enthusiasm, about as much as the concert itself," Mike said.

"I do go on like a ten-year-old, don't I?"

"Don't ever squelch that little girl in you, Amelia. It's part of your charm. It's why all sorts of people let you take their photographs. If I approach them, they glare at me and turn away."

"They don't really, do they?"

"They really do."

She looked at him, puzzled. "Not if you take the time to chat with them and make them feel comfortable. That's what I do. I don't just walk up and take their pictures."

"Frankly, I haven't the patience or the interest in people that you do. That's why I'm strictly a nature photographer."

"And a fine one, too." She slipped her arm through his. "It's time you had a showing of your work."

"I don't need that sort of thing."

Amelia didn't believe that one little bit.

They rounded the corner. "By the way, Amelia, what did you decide about the Inmans?"

"I've been up to Laurel Community to visit Mrs. Inman and her mother. They didn't move back to Old Bunkie Creek. Alvin Inman got a job closer to where they're living, and the children protested about leaving Laurel Community. They loved going to school and have made friends. The oldest boy joined the summer softball team, apparently he's got a mean pitching arm. Leeanne pouted, as she always does, but her mother seemed pleased at their change of fortune."

"How do you feel now about doing a book of photos centered on their lives?"

"I talked with them about the book and how I felt, and Alvin wants to stand by the deal. He says he signed a contract with me, and that's all there is to it, and his word is his bond. He said that it might help the family, and that I should be sure to include the flood pictures and come back anytime and take photos of them in their new surroundings. He seemed pleased with the way things are now. He invited me to photograph him on the tractor he drives for a large estate farther up the mountain. He maintains the property and seems quite proud of that, and he beamed when he talked about his son's athletic ability. I get the sense that for Alvin, and those kids especially, the flood opened a world of opportunities." She paused and shook her head. "But seeing them in changed circumstances seems to nullify the whole intent of my book, which was to show a tight-knit family living as their grandparents did."

"Perhaps it's really about resilience and the human spirit," Mike said. "The kind of post-nine-eleven thing you were looking for originally?"

She tipped her head and looked up at him. "Maybe it is. I need to think about it some more. If I decide to do it, I'll shoot Alvin on his tractor and the kids at school. If it still makes a good story, maybe I'll go with it."

"Fair enough," Mike said.

Across the street, the door of the Uptown Café opened, discharging a cluster of women dressed in purple and wearing red hats. They brightened the night and the sidewalk.

"Another group of you gals." Mike bowed to the women as they crossed the street and passed him and Amelia. "They seem to be having fun." Mike turned to look at the laughing group, who were clearly having a great time.

"That's what it's all about, fun: eat, drink, travel, laugh, have fun," Amelia said.

The women turned the corner and the street grew gray and empty. "By the way," Mike asked, "are you still going to Maine? And if so, when?"

"I hate it when you press me for decisions," Amelia said. "I had to put off going in May because of New York, and it's been one thing after the other ever since. If I work with the Inmans, I won't have time to go at all, will I?"

Mike rolled his eyes, and they moved on. Cars cruised the street, seeking places to park. Mike's van was parked just ahead, and they picked up their pace.

That night, Amelia sat down and wrote a letter to Maggie in Maine.

Dear Maggie,

I find myself in the throes of photographing for a book to be published next year. The work, plus developing and selecting the final photos and the

words to accompany them, is exceedingly time con-
suming. When I get on a roll, so to speak, I find it's
best for the project if I stay with it.

Once more I must delay my visit. Perhaps I can
come in the fall, once this book is in the hands of the
publisher and behind me. I do so appreciate your
inviting me. I'll stay in touch.

Love, Amelia

40
RUSSELL AND EMILY

Russell eased from the chair alongside his daughter's bed and tiptoed to the door. Before exiting her room, he glanced back. Melissa lay on her side, her lips pursed and slightly open, her hair damp and curling about her cheek, her face still flushed from crying. It was two in the morning, and he had just gotten her back to sleep after a nightmare. Her screaming had jarred him from a deep sleep.

To Tyler's delight, Russell had moved him into the master bedroom in the front of the house and moved himself into Tyler's room, across from Melissa's. Russell had discovered that Tyler had been getting up several nights a week to soothe and comfort his sister. Would he have known this if Mrs. Franklin, Tyler's homeroom teacher, had not called to ask him why Tyler fell asleep in class? Russell hadn't noticed the dark circles under his son's eyes. Shamefaced, he admitted to not noticing anything, and realized that he had slept through his children's nocturnal travails.

Russell closed Melissa's door softly. *It must be hell to be afraid to go to sleep,* he thought. In the kitchen, he scrutinized the contents of the fridge and rejected milk, leftover pork chops, and macaroni and cheese that Grace had brought over. There was chocolate chip, rocky road, and vanilla ice cream in the freezer. He liked coffee ice cream and plain old chocolate. From the top shelf of a cabinet, Russell took a bottle of scotch and poured himself a stiff drink. He rarely drank, but somehow he needed a drink tonight.

Yesterday Emily had called, and he'd hated the way she sounded—bright and almost chirpy, like a silly bird in springtime. "How are the kids?" she'd asked.

"Melissa's not doing great. She still has nightmares."

Emily made light of that. "Oh, lots of little kids have nightmares."

"Did you?"

"Well . . ." She hesitated. "No, I guess not, but I had friends who did. They outgrew it. So will Melissa. Don't spoil her, Russell. Don't go in to her, and she'll stop having nightmares. She's probably crying to get your attention."

That advice flew in the face of the counsel of Dr. Wilson, who urged him to go to his daughter to comfort and reassure her.

"They will stop, in time," she had assured him. "Melissa's doing very well. It's amazing how verbal she is and how able to get to her feelings."

"You don't think her nightmares could possibly be

related to not having a mother?" Russell asked Emily. He hated the tone of his voice. It was not how he wanted to sound or what he wanted to say. He wanted to plead with Emily to come home, tell her that the kids needed her and that he'd like to try again, but he choked on the words.

"Are you trying to make me feel guilty? Trying to punish me? It won't work, Russell. We made a deal, and I expect you to hold up your part of the bargain." Her tone was that of a lawyer about to cross-examine a witness.

What had become of the woman he had married?

Her voice softened. "I called to ask about the kids, and to tell you that I'm working at a social service agency defending abused women. It's very satisfying, with none of the stress of running my own office. Maybe that's been the problem all along."

He hesitated to reply. What could he say? If he asked, she might inform him that she had decided to stay in Ocala, and Russell wasn't quite ready to hear that. But he wasn't sure he wanted her back, either. Or she might decide he didn't know how to handle Melissa, was spoiling her excessively, and say that she wanted Melissa with her.

"Well," he said, "it was good of you to call. Tyler's doing well at school and Melissa loves prekindergarten. We're all fine. Grace especially asked me to give you her love."

"I'm very fond of Grace," Emily said. "Do give her my love. Tell her I'll be in touch with her soon. I'll phone her some evening and thank her for taking Melissa to the therapist. Got to run now, Russell. Bye." And the phone went dead.

Russell continued to hold the receiver, feeling utterly alone and uncertain what to do. Finally he hung up. The next morning, Russell called a therapist a client of his had recommended and made an appointment for himself.

Bill Gearhart did not sit behind a desk as Russell expected. He joined Russell in the parlorlike setting of his office and took the leather wing chair across from him. "It's good to meet you, Russell."

Did this guy know what he was doing? He didn't look like a psychiatrist, although his diploma said he was a medical doctor and had graduated from the University of North Carolina at Chapel Hill. A second framed document informed him that Dr. William C. Gearhart had completed a residency in psychiatry. Russell wondered why he had opened a practice in Weaverville instead of Asheville or some larger city.

"Wondering why I opened shop in Weaverville?" Dr. Gearhart asked.

Was he a mind reader? "Why, yes, frankly, I am. Why did you?"

"I'm from a small town out west, but I went to college in the south. If it's cold in North Carolina, it's freezing in Montana. I looked for a town in the mountains, and I found Weaverville. It's ten minutes from Asheville, about a half hour from Johnson City in Tennessee. I like storytelling festivals and there's a great one over in Jonesboro, Tennessee. This seemed like the ideal place. Where do you live?"

And so the ice was broken and a relaxed rapport established. Russell began to look forward to his visits with Dr. Gearhart, who insisted that he call him Bill, and Russell grew to trust the man and to unburden his heart. The pain of his lonely childhood came pouring out, and his repressed anger toward his father as well as his guilt about his feelings, considering all that Bob had done for him since Amy's death. When he spoke of Amy and about his disappointing marriage to Emily, he wept.

Russell began to understand the dynamics of grief, and how he had never really grieved Amy's death, had never really said good-bye to her. He also came to see that he had expected Emily to be like Amy, which she assuredly was not. He spoke of Grace, his surrogate mother and grandmother to his children. He cried when he related Grace's role in helping Tyler cope with the loss of his mother, and how Grace's angel story had set Tyler drawing and broken through the frozen tundra of his son's pain.

Russell shared his fears: dealing with the pressure of having to make good in the world and his lack of what Emily called ambition. He confessed his insecurities, his sense of being out of place in a large corporation, and Russell reaffirmed his decision to leave that rat race for a simpler, if not as prosperous, life working from his home.

Because he trusted Bill Gearhart, Russell did not resist the probing questions the therapist asked about his life, about Emily and him, and about his son and his little daughter. The doctor was pleased that Melissa was seeing Dr. Wilson.

"I'd have recommended her myself," he told Russell. Then he said, "You need to consider what you'll do if your wife decides she doesn't want the marriage and wants the child. Are you prepared to fight for Melissa?"

Russell struggled with the question. "Would it be right for me to try to take Melissa from her mother?"

"Perhaps it would be. I've seen girls left with most unsuitable mothers to their detriment."

"I just don't know."

Didn't a girl need a mother as she grew up, more than she needed a father? One afternoon Russell sat at his desk staring out at the backyard, watching an avaricious blue jay establish dominance at the birdfeeder. He opened a lined yellow pad, drew a line down the center, and made lists. On the left he itemized the positive things about Emily and their marriage, and to the right the negatives, which lengthened and filled the page. At the top of the positive section he wrote, "Melissa needs a mother." That seemed to be the sticking point, the counterbalance that held him fast and hindered his making decisions about his marriage and Melissa.

Grace had told him, in the strictest confidence, about Tyler's role in caring for Melissa when she was an infant, and about Emily's apparent indifference toward her child. Emily's attitude seemed unnatural to him.

Amy had doted on their son. Suddenly Russell wondered if maybe Amy had gone overboard with their son. He doubted if she slept through a single night for a year just anticipating that Tyler might need her. Maybe that wasn't so normal or wise, either. Clearly, no one was perfect. But overall, wouldn't Melissa be better off with a loving, extended family, which they had?

As the weeks passed and Emily's communications with her family diminished, his anger toward Emily, the longing he felt for her at moments when he was lonely, and the pain at the failure of their marriage, moderated. Dr. Gearhart helped him accept the fact that he could not remake Emily or fix her restlessness, but he wasn't ready to initiate a conversation about divorce. Always, he worried about losing Melissa.

"I don't want to force the issue," he told Dr. Gearhart. "Maybe it's cowardly of me, but something's telling me to give it time, that Emily'll make a life in Ocala, and that life won't have room in it for Melissa. Maybe the situation will resolve itself."

"We'll have to wait and see, then," Dr. Gearhart said.

A few days later, Emily phoned Grace. "I'm going to make a trip up there," she said. "Russell and I have to talk."

"Six months aren't up yet, are they?" Grace glanced at the calendar on the kitchen wall. Talk about what? she wondered.

"No, it's not six months yet, but—well, I need to talk to Russell."

She hasn't even mentioned Melissa and Tyler. "We'll be happy to see you. Where will you stay, at the house with your family?"

"To tell you the truth, I'd rather not do that. I don't want to get things stirred up. May I stay with you ladies? It won't be more than a day or two at the most."

"Of course you can. I'll tell Amelia and Hannah."

"And Grace, please don't fuss. Don't make a special dinner for everyone or anything like that, promise me."

"I won't. You just come along. We'll all be glad to see you." *Liar. Liar.*

"What could I say?" Grace said to Bob later. "I hate the idea that she's coming, but it's better to have the fox where you can keep an eye on it, rather than worry about it creeping up behind your back and getting into the chicken coop."

"Where in heaven's name did you get that from, Grace?" Bob asked.

"Get what?"

"The business about a fox and a chicken coop?"

She shrugged and smiled. "I haven't a clue. Lurina, maybe. Maybe I made it up. But you know what I mean, don't you?"

He scratched his head. "I guess I do."

Amelia pouted. "I wish Emily wasn't staying with us."

"I didn't realize you felt that way. I'd never have said yes."

"She can stay of course," Amelia said. "But there's something about that woman I don't like."

"I thought you liked Emily," Hannah said.

"Maybe at first I did. Now I think she's terrible." Amelia tossed her head in the old familiar manner and adjusted the scarf about her neck. "For her to go off and leave that little girl, to not want to treasure her and love her." Tears welled in Amelia's eyes. "I can't bear the thought. But don't you worry, Grace. I'll be so sweet she'll never know how I really feel about her."

Hannah asked, "Could you get any sense of what's going on with her, Grace?"

"Not a clue."

Breathing hard, his face red as if he had been running, Russell rang the bell of the farmhouse. Grace opened the door and stepped onto the porch. "She's coming. Emily's coming. Of course, you know that. She's staying with you ladies." He flopped into a chair and Grace took the chair beside him.

"Would you like something to drink?"

He shook his head. "Why do you think she's staying with you and not at home with me and the kids?"

"What did Emily say, Russell? Why is she coming? The six months aren't up yet."

"I have no idea. She just said she needed to come, and that she had things she wanted to discuss with me. I assumed she was coming home, to our house. I couldn't believe it when she said she wasn't. How can she do that to the kids?"

"I don't know. I figured once she got here, if she changed her mind, she could just go home."

"I'm really upset that she wouldn't want to be at home with us," he said. "I'm hurt, and I'm angry. I'm going to pick her up at the airport tomorrow. That'll give us a chance to talk on the way in. Maybe I can make sense of this whole thing."

"Maybe she's decided to come back," Grace said. "And she wants to break in slowly, see the kids, talk to them before she plops into their lives."

"If she were coming home, she'd come home. It's something else, and it worries me," Russell said.

"Maybe you're right. While she's here with us, I'll do my best to keep your wife calm."

"You're the only one who can, Grace." Tears brimmed in his eyes. "How can I ever thank you for everything you've done for my family, for me?"

"Just go on being my family and my friend." Grace squeezed his hand.

When Emily stepped into the airport lounge looking as fresh-faced as a girl, Russell's heart thudded in his chest, but he took his cue from her and returned her restrained hug and peck on the cheek. *She's not here to tell me she's coming home to stay,* he thought, and wondered at the odd mix of relief and sadness he felt.

"Luggage tag?" He extended his hand.

"Just this backpack, if you'd carry it for me."

He slung her backpack over his shoulder. *An overnight bag. Light.*

"I'm not staying long." She confirmed his suspicion. "I thought we should talk, and not on the phone."

His anxiety level quickened.

They walked through the terminal and were soon out in the parking lot. The quivers in Russell's stomach began to settle as they drove toward Asheville and then Covington, sometimes making small talk, sometimes in silence. He wasn't sure which was better, avoiding the issues or plunging right into them.

Russell was grateful that his work with Dr. Gearhart had resulted in a deeper awareness of his feelings, a greater tolerance for others, and the knowledge that he could control and was responsible for only his own feelings and behavior. What was he feeling right this minute? Keyed up, curious, and yes, nervous not knowing why Emily was here, and concerned that she would insist on Melissa returning with her to Florida. His distrust of her, which he had never acknowledged before seeing Dr. Gearhart, was palpable now, and he hesitated to speak about himself or the children. So anxious was he to bring the trip to an end, that Russell accelerated beyond the speed limit.

"Why are you going so fast, Russell? You're making me nervous."

Emily's admonishment irritated him, though he slowed the car.

"Things look pretty much the same," she said. "Everything's green, too much green actually. That always bothered me. Don't you get bored with all the green in the summertime? I used to feel claustrophobic, especially on the parkway. That's like driving through a green tunnel. It's so much brighter, and the sky's much bluer in Florida. Why do you think the sky's such a pale blue up here?"

Russell did not reply.

"I wondered how I'd feel when I got here. Well, at least the mountains are beautiful. I never really liked living out in the country, you know. Did I ever tell you that, Russell?"

"Not directly. Maybe you should have." *Don't let her goad you,* he told himself. *You can stay calm and detached.*

"I hated not seeing lights at night. When I first married you I'd lie in bed and worry that someone would drive up that long driveway and rob or kill us. You were never afraid, were you?"

"No." Russell's throat tightened. He reached for a bottle of water he kept in the car and took several long swallows. "I always felt safe, until recently, with the threats we had." *And I was happy. Happy to wake up each day to birds singing, happy to see the way the sunshine slanted through the woods. I shared that house we lived in initially with Amy, and we were happy.* "I was happy living out there," he said.

"And I came along and ruined it for you, didn't I?" Her voice sounded pained. "I'm sorry you gave up your home for me, and that I wasn't the wife you needed or wanted, Russell." She shrugged her shoulders. "That's life, I guess. Marriage is such a crapshoot."

"Marriage means compromise, and many people find a way to do that." *Our life together, our marriage, is over, and I feel amazingly light—indifferent and relieved. But will she fight me for custody?* His chest tightened. *I'll fight her with everything I have, with all my money and my strength.*

Emily reached over and patted his knee. "I'm sorry. You're a good man, Russell, and a kind man." She did not speak again for a long time. "We'll have dinner alone tonight, okay?"

"I guess so." *Still no mention of the children.*

"I'm much happier with my work than I ever was when I had my own practice," she said. "I have a real sense of purpose." She grew more animated, tucked one leg up under her and turned toward him. "The women I work with have absolutely nothing, Russell, and they've been badly treated—sometimes physically, sometimes emotionally—and nearly all of them have been cheated monetarily. There are so many bastards out there. Mean, controlling men who cheat and lie, who abuse women. It gives me pleasure to put them behind bars and to help these women get on their feet."

"It sounds challenging." *Why is she telling me all this? What does she want?* "It sounds like you've found your forte at last."

"Indeed I have." Emily fell silent. After a time, she said, "Russell, I want you to know that I did love you, and I don't regret our time together or having Melissa."

Russell jerked the car to the right, barely missing the side of another car. He was shaking.

Emily braced against the dashboard. "Be careful. Russell, you've driven right past the exit to Mars Hill."

He hadn't seen the sign, the motel that was clearly

visible on the hill above the road, or the gas station. "I'm sorry. I'll turn at the next exit and come back."

At the farmhouse Emily hugged Grace, then excused herself and went into the guest bedroom, calling over her shoulder, "Be right out, Russell, Wait a bit, will you?"

Grace noted the pallor on Russell's face, saw the slight shaking of his hands. Whatever had happened on their ride home had upset him terribly. "Come sit. Let me get you some tea or coffee."

"No. I really need to get out of here. I agreed to have dinner with Emily. I need to shave and change. Tell her I'll be back at seven." He glanced in the direction of the bedroom. "It's over, Grace. Just loose ends left to tie up—I feel it. We haven't said a word to one each other about any of it or about Melissa."

Grace hugged him gently. "I'm sorry. You bring the kids back with you. Bob and I will take them to the Athens Restaurant for dinner."

"I don't know. We'll see," he muttered, and left the house.

From the doorway, Grace watched his car drive away. Pastor Johnson and Denny stood in the middle of Cove Road looking up at the church roof. They turned and watched Russell drive away, then waved at her. She waved back and closed the door. Emily's cheery voice startled her.

"Is Russell gone?" In complete antithesis to Russell's agitation, Emily appeared cool and calm, her eyes untroubled. "It's good to see you, Grace. You've been well, and Bob?"

"Fine. We're all fine." Grace thought about the laundry waiting to be folded, the potatoes waiting to be peeled for dinner, and regretted she had said yes to Emily staying with them.

Emily bit her lower lip. "I've been trying to decide what would be easiest for everyone—seeing the kids tonight or tomorrow, after Russell and I settle our business."

Her voice grated on Grace's nerves.

"May I have a cup of tea, Grace? I'd like to tell you about my new work, which I just love." Without so much as a by-your-leave, she slipped her arm through Grace's and guided the older woman into the kitchen. Once seated, Emily asked, "Grace, do the kids know I'm here?"

"I don't believe Russell told them."

"I hope he doesn't until tomorrow." She accepted the teacup Grace handed her. "I've always trusted you, Grace."

Grace, who never cursed, thought, *Selfish, cold-hearted bitch.* Again she regretted saying yes to Emily staying at the farmhouse.

"It's over, Grace. For me at least, and I hope Russell realizes it's for the best."

"You're sure about this?"

"I'm sure. I'd never come back to live here."

Grace breathed a sigh of relief when the front door opened and Amelia and Mike entered, their arms filled with grocery bags. Grace retreated into silence, grateful that Amelia would make small talk and defuse what might have become a tense situation.

Russell looked at his watch. Two hours had passed since he'd picked Emily up at the farmhouse and headed for the restaurant. They had talked and acted as if they were old acquaintances having a meal, catching up on news. Emily's questions, irrelevant to their predicament, came one after the other: How did Bob like his cottage? How was Roger doing in South Carolina? Was Andy walking yet? Was he talking? What was new at Bella's Park? Perhaps hoping to defer the inevitable, he had gone along with her.

"Would you signal the waiter, Russell? I'd like some more coffee."

He did, and while she waited, Emily's fingers tapped on the table.

She's nervous, too, he thought.

The coffee arrived. Emily sugared it and added cream. She sighed deeply and sat back in her chair. Her eyes met his. "Russell, I've decided to stay in Ocala."

He'd expected that. Next she'd say that she wanted Melissa. Well, he'd find the best lawyer and fight to keep his daughter. "And?" Russell's hands gripped the edges of his chair.

"And, well . . ." Her mouth quivered and her eyes misted. "Russell, I'm so sorry. I was a lousy wife and mother. I've always been a loner and self-centered, I know that. You put up with so much from me."

"But you weren't happy?"

She shook her head. "And you couldn't have been, either. I want you to know it wasn't your fault. Some deep-seated restless dissatisfaction within myself made me unhappy." She drew a long breath. "I've been seeing a therapist. I realize that I should never have married or had a child. I neglected Melissa and I regret that. She didn't deserve that. She never felt secure about me, her own mother."

Russell agreed. And he had loved her and had been happy with her for a time. Now he wanted to hurl invectives at her, to tell her she'd been a lousy mother, a lousy wife, to get back at her for goading him about his lack of ambition. But what would that accomplish? None of it mattered now, and he suddenly felt exhausted.

"My life is incredibly busy," she was saying. "Sometimes I get called out at night. I'd have to hire someone to take care of Melissa, and I'd hardly see her. She'd be worse and it would be my fault, and she'd grow up hating me. I can't do that to her or to myself. If she stays with you, continues seeing the counselor . . ." Reaching over, Emily clutched Russell's arm with both of her hands.

"If she stays with you, I know you won't poison her against me. You'd say kind things about me because you love her so much, and you'd never want to hurt her. Promise me that, Russell, that you'll explain about me, and she won't hate me."

Was he hearing right? She didn't *want* Melissa? The

muscles in his neck and in his stomach began to relax. He wanted to laugh, even to hug her.

"I could visit sometime when she's older, and she could visit me in Florida. You'd let her come, wouldn't you, when she's maybe fourteen or so?"

Russell gripped the edge of the chair for fear he'd float away. "I would never denigrate you in any way or poison Melissa's mind against you. You're her mother. I want her to love you. Of course she'll visit you." He pitied Emily, pitied the loss he knew was hers. Silently, he rejoiced. His heart softened, and for a brief moment, he still loved her.

Emily leaned toward him. "Another thing. I don't want to see the children tomorrow. They don't need to know that I was here."

The warmth in his gut began to recede. "What do you mean, not see them?"

"They're adjusting to the situation as it is, and why upset the applecart?"

"I'm not sure I understand your thinking on this. They could easily find out. Grace, Dad, or one of the others might inadvertently let it slip. Don't you think it would be worse if they knew you were here and didn't see them?"

She shrugged. "I don't know."

"Who are you trying to spare, Emily—the kids or yourself?"

She lowered her head, and whispered, "Myself."

"It's your decision, of course, but I think you'd be doing yourself and the kids, particularly Melissa, a disservice if you left without seeing them."

"If you insist, I'll see them."

When has she ever deferred to my judgment? He sensed her frailty, her fear. "It'll be fine, Emily. I'll bring them to Grace's place in the morning. When do you leave?"

"I'm having lunch with my father, then he'll drive me to the airport."

Damn her. He wanted to discuss divorce and custody right now, not wait for her to send a proposed settlement. "I'll bring them early, then." Russell took a deep breath and reminded himself that he was getting what he wanted: his daughter. He paid the bill, tipped the waiter, and they left the restaurant.

The next morning, Russell arrived at the farmhouse with Melissa and Tyler.

Emily did not rush to embrace her daughter. "You look so pretty," she said, holding her child at arm's length.

Melissa hung back at first, and stared at her with huge, uncomprehending eyes; then she fell into her mother's arms. She clung to her with such ferocity that Russell had to pry her away.

Arms wrapped tightly about her father's neck, Melissa looked from her mother to the bag waiting by the door. "Are you going away again, Mommie?"

"I have to go, Melissa. When you grow up, you'll understand." She came closer and touched Melissa's hair. "You're so pretty, Melissa. Mommie loves you, but I have to go. You'll come see me in Florida."

"When, Mommie? When?"

"Soon." Emily turned to Russell. Her eyes pleaded, "Help me."

But it was Tyler who intervened, taking his sister from their father and crushing her against his chest, kissing her cheeks, turning from the door that Russell was closing behind himself and his wife, and whispering, "It's all right, Melissa. I'm here, and I love you. Daddy and Granny Grace and Grandpa are here, and we all love you very much."

Melissa sobbed, and when her little chest stopped heaving and her tears dried up, Tyler laid her on the couch in the living room, where she fell into an exhausted sleep. Grace and Tyler stepped into the kitchen, and he exploded.

"I *hate* her. I hope she never shows her face around here again! Look what she's done to Melissa."

Grace put her arms about him, and Tyler leaned into her and cried. Then he pushed away and dried his eyes. "I'm acting like a baby. I'm sorry, Granny Grace."

"Don't apologize. Some situations call for tears, Tyler, and this is one of those times. I understand how angry you are. I feel the same. What Emily did was unconscionable. It would have been better had she not seen Melissa."

Tyler slumped in a chair at the kitchen table. "What's going to happen to Melissa? Is she going to come out of this okay?"

"Yes, I think she will, in time. We can give her lots of

love and reassurance. You've always done that, Tyler. She likes Dr. Wilson, and if anyone can help her sort things out, it's that woman."

"My mother died, but I knew she loved me," Tyler said. "But Emily's alive, and she obviously doesn't love Melissa. I thought a mother always loved her children."

Grace felt as if she were turning on a spit. She hated to bad-mouth Emily to Tyler. "We don't know that she doesn't love Melissa. Maybe she knows it's not good for Melissa to be in Florida, in day care while she works. She knows the child is well cared for and well loved here."

"I don't believe she cares about Melissa. You saw how she acted with her?"

Grace ran her fingers through her hair. "I don't know, Tyler. I just don't know." She opened the oven, pulled out a casserole dish she had prepared earlier, and set it on a rack next to the stove to cool. "We'll have lunch when your father returns." She drew a chair alongside his.

"Tyler, my love, Emily's as much an enigma to me as she is to you. It's our job now to love Melissa and get her the help she needs, and be here for her." She smoothed his tousled hair. "We'll do whatever we can."

A whimper issued from the living room, and they quickly went in to the child. "Hi, Granny Grace," Melissa said, rubbing her eyes. "Tyler, did you eat the cookies all up while I was sleeping?"

A few minutes later Melissa sat at the kitchen table

with cookies and milk before her. "Mommie's gone?"

Tyler squared his shoulders. "Yes, she had to go back to Florida. She had an emergency at her work."

Melissa drank her milk and wiped her mouth with the napkin that Grace handed her. "I love Mommie," she said. "She came all the way here on the plane just to see us. But then she had to go away again." Reaching over, the child patted her brother's arm. "Don't be sad, Tyler. Mommie's sick and she has to live where it's always warm."

Grace was astonished that someone so young could rationalize like an adult. This wasn't the end of it, but she would deal with the rest in therapy, please God, and she would know that they all loved her. In time, she would heal.

41
FINISHING TOUCHES

"I'm happy." Grace set a tray of finger sandwiches on the coffee table in the living room. It was one of those rare times lately when the ladies were at home without obligations to anyone else or to be anywhere else.

Amelia looked up from browsing through a book of Impressionist painters and reached for a cucumber sandwich. "I love cucumber sandwiches. Especially when you make them, Grace." She helped herself to another.

Hannah set down her knitting. She had not knitted in years, and now she held up the wobbly blue potential sweater for Andy. "I have to make it bigger than he is. He's growing so fast."

Amelia closed her book and looked at Grace. "What are you so happy about?"

Grace clasped her hands together. "That Russell has full custody of Melissa, and Emily will have visitation rights. That we're all together, that the men are happy. That *we're* happy and we're all in good health."

"Russell seems happier than I've seen him in years," Hannah said. "A miserable marriage makes for miserable people."

"And Melissa has fewer nightmares and throws fewer temper tantrums," Grace said. "It's just amazing what therapy can do. Dr. Wilson suggested I watch a session through a one-way mirror at her office. Melissa played with a family of dolls, and she acted out that day when her mother said good-bye. The boy doll, Tyler, I guess, hit the mother and said he was punishing her for treating the girl doll that way, and he sent her to her room. After a while he said the mother doll could come back, and Melissa actually spoke to her through the girl doll and told her how angry she was at her for leaving. I was absolutely astonished at her ability to work out her feelings, even crying, like that."

"That's amazing and so interesting," Amelia said.

"What a blessing for Melissa, that such tools are available to help her. She has a good chance to grow up and be a normal, happy child," Hannah said.

"Indeed she does," Grace replied.

Words then seemed superfluous. Amelia turned the

pages of the book, Hannah's needles clicked, and Grace fussed with the sandwiches, rearranging them on the plate, filling the gaps left by those already eaten.

Then Grace said, "Imagine: Tyler told me the other day that he's got a girlfriend. At fourteen! They do everything so fast, these young people."

"Too fast," Amelia said.

Hannah lifted her head and, for a moment, the needles lay idle in her lap. "The world has changed so much since I was a girl."

"I like many of the changes. There are more opportunities for women now than when I married Thomas. Think of the things I could have done and been." Amelia leaned forward over the closed book in her lap. "Sometimes I feel my life had so many wasted years."

"Nothing is ever wasted," Hannah said with finality. "You did a fine job as Thomas's wife, didn't you? That was the role you chose then, and you did it well. Life's too short to spend time regretting any of it. I could bemoan the years with Bill Parrish, but they made me strong. I learned to stand on my own two feet. And look at what we've done with our lives these last few years. I think we're remarkable women."

"I agree," Grace said, then she changed the subject. "Going back to things that make me happy, Jerry McCorkle's in jail for life without parole."

"He should have gotten the death penalty," Hannah said. Picking up the blue yarn, she unwound a long strand, and they fell silent again. Then Hannah stopped and looked from Grace to Amelia. "There's something so very special about you both."

Grace tilted her head to one side. "I agree. It's good to be here with you ladies."

Silence filled the room once more, a good and peaceful silence.

Then Amelia spoke. "I'm glad that you've both worked out your arrangements with Max and Bob. It made me so nervous at night to sleep in the house alone. I should have outgrown that fear long ago, but I haven't. What a relief is it that Bob's not pressuring you to live with him, Grace, and Max seems to have adjusted to Hannah living here and visiting over there. How'd you ever work that out, Hannah?"

"It just happened." The knitting needles clicked and Hannah's lips moved as she counted stitches, and she did not look up.

Grace leaned forward and clasped her knees. "I believe the men got used to living alone. They seem to enjoy their privacy. Bob said I was driving him nuts, fussing over him."

"He told you that you were making him nuts?" Amelia stared at Grace.

"He was afraid he'd hurt my feelings when he suggested that I stop looking out of my window at night, and stop running over every time his lights stayed on late. Then he got that medical alert system and that relieved my mind, so it's worked out well."

Amelia took another cucumber sandwich from the plate. "I'm addicted to these."

"What did you decide to do about the new book and the Inmans?" Grace asked.

"It's coming together beautifully. After all the fuss I made, I'm satisfied with the pictures and the family members are also, except for Leeanne, who's never happy about anything. I took copies of the photos to them yesterday. I think it was therapeutic for them to see the 'after the flood' pictures. They talked a lot about what had happened. Even the kids joined in, and they rarely talk when adults are present. All in all, they seemed excited about being in a book."

Their conversation drifted from topic to topic, as it had in the days when they'd sat on the porch every afternoon, before their lives became so busy.

"Good heavens, it's raining again," Grace said. She rose and went to the window. They could hear the patter of rain on the tin roof of the porch.

Grace whirled around. "Let's do something really silly. Let's put on our raincoats and go out in the rain."

"Like children," Hannah said. "Yes." She set aside her knitting.

Amelia sprang from her seat and whirled about the room. "For the fun of it."

Grace headed for the foyer closet. "Come on. Let's wear our new raincoats." The bright yellow raincoats were gifts from Max, Bob, and Mike.

"You always joke about being the Three Musketeers," Max had said when the men presented their gifts. "Put these on and you'll be properly outfitted."

They donned their outfits and headed outside. The

rain fell with a steady beat, dripping from the edges of the porch roof, pooling on the steps and digging a groove in the flower bed below.

"Come on, ladies. Shoes off," Amelia said.

Off came their shoes. Out onto the grass they ran, water squishing between their toes. Throwing back their heads, they laughed and laughed into the sky, then joined hands and danced about the yard as the rain ran down their faces.

"What a perfect afternoon of a perfect day!" Grace called.

And the others nodded agreement as they threw back their faces to greet the rain.

Recipes for *Two Days After the Wedding*

A MEDLEY OF CHICKEN SALADS

CHICKEN APPLE SALAD

4 boneless chicken breasts
2 Delicious or Gala apples
2 celery stalks, chopped into small pieces
Mayonnaise to taste
Salt and/or pepper to taste
½ cup almonds, sliced

Cook the chicken breasts. Cool. Cut or tear into small pieces. In a medium-size bowl, mix the chicken with chopped apple, almonds, and celery. Add mayonnaise and salt/pepper to taste and refrigerate. Serve on lettuce with tomato and olives or other garnish.

CHICKEN PINEAPPLE DELIGHT

4 boneless chicken breasts
1 small can of crushed pineapple, drained
Salted cashews—$\frac{1}{2}$ to $\frac{3}{4}$ of a small can
Mayonnaise to taste

Cook the chicken breasts, cool, and cut or tear into small pieces. In a medium-size bowl, mix the chicken, pineapple, and mayonnaise. Refrigerate. When ready to serve, add the salted cashews. Salt and/or pepper to taste. Serve on bed of lettuce, garnish with tomatoes and olives optional.

CHICKEN SALAD TARRAGON

4 boneless chicken breasts
3 celery stalks, chopped into small pieces
About fifteen green seedless grapes, cut into halves
A tablespoon of dried tarragon
Mayonnaise to taste
Salt and/or pepper to taste
½ cup chopped pecans

Cook the chicken breasts. Cool. Cut or tear into small pieces.

Place in a medium-size bowl and add celery, green grapes, pecans, mayonnaise, and salt to taste. Sprinkle tarragon across the top and toss well. Refrigerate until ready to use. Serve on bed of lettuce with tomato or other garnish.

Serve all three salads buffet style, or with a scoop of each on the plates for a fun luncheon.

APPLE, ORANGE, AND PASTA SALAD

1 large orange
⅓ cup plain low-fat yogurt
1 teaspoon of sugar or one packet of Splenda
Salt to taste
¼ cup dry whole wheat bow tie pasta, cooked and drained (this will expand considerably when cooked)
2 medium apples—Fuji, Delicious, or Gala, chopped into small pieces
2 tablespoons chopped green onions
⅓ cup chopped pecans, or a small package of pine nuts

Peel oranges and cut into sections over a bowl. Save the juice. Stir together 2 tablespoons of the juice, yogurt, sugar or Splenda and mix well. (You may add orange juice if you don't have 2 tablespoons.) Add the cooked pasta, chopped apples, and green onions. Gently mix in the orange sections. Sprinkle pecans or pine nuts on top. Cover and chill for 2 to 3 hours.

CHEESE AND SPINACH NIBLETS

6 tablespoons of whole wheat flour
2 large or 3 small eggs
1½ packages of frozen spinach, defrosted and drained well
2 cups of 2% or fat-free cottage cheese
2 cups grated cheddar cheese (low-fat)
⅛ of a teaspoon of nutmeg
Black pepper to taste
Wheat germ or fine whole wheat bread crumbs

In bowl, beat flour and eggs until smooth. Add cottage cheese, spinach, nutmeg, and pepper to taste and mix well. Heat oven to 350 degrees. Grease a 13 x 9 x 2 baking dish and spread the mixture in it. Sprinkle top with wheat germ or whole wheat bread crumbs and bake for about 45 minutes. Let the mixture cool for 15 minutes before cutting into 1- to 2-inch squares. These can be frozen or refrigerated and reheated.

Helpful Hints from Grace's Kitchen

1. Making beef stroganoff? Partly freeze the meat before you slice it thin.

2. Eggs that float when placed in a pan of cold water should be discarded.

3. Hate that greenish edge you can get around the yolks of hardboiled eggs? To avoid overcooking eggs, place the eggs side by side in a pan of cold water. The water should just cover the eggs. Cook gently until they boil, then shut off the heat and allow to sit for fifteen minutes.

4. The spice caraway is great in vegetable soups (about a tablespoon). Stir well.

5. To enhance the flavor of fish, squeeze fresh lemon or lime juice on it before you cook it.

6. The oil in your pan too hot? Sprinkle a bit of salt or flour in the pan to prevent splattering.

7. When cooking white rice, add a few drops of olive or other cooking oil to the water to keep the grains from sticking.

8. For a quick, delicious fruit frosty: cut a variety of fruit into small pieces. (Grace suggests apples, bananas, strawberries, raspberries, ripe pears, and melons of all kinds.) Place in freezer bags separately and freeze. Place 6 ounces of orange or apple juice (preferably apple) in blender. Add 3–4 pieces of the fruit to the juice and blend well. No ice will be needed; the frozen fruit make a nice, thick frosty. Got a sweet tooth? Add a packet of sweetener while blending.